Acclaim for Felice Picano

"Felice Picano is a premier voice in gay letters."—Malcolm Boyd, *Contemporary Authors*

Felice Picano is "…a leading light in the gay literary world… his glints of flashing wit and subtle hints of dark decadence transcend clichés."—Richard Violette, *Library Journal*

"Felice Picano is one hell of a writer!"—Stephen King

"Picano's destiny has been to lead the way for a generation of gay writers."—Robert L. Pela, *The Advocate*

"These stories [*The New York Years: Stories by Felice Picano*] are as well written and immediate as any contemporary gay fiction."—Regina Marler

"With *True Stories*, Felice Picano enhances his status as one of the great literary figures in recent gay history and does so with wit, verve and as much panache as we've come to expect."
—Jerry Wheeler, *Out in Print*

Also available from Bold Strokes

The Lure

Late in the Season

Looking Glass Lives

Contemporary Gay Romances

Tragic, Mystic, Comic & Horrific

by

Felice Picano

A Division of Bold Strokes Books

2011

CONTEMPORARY GAY ROMANCES:
TRAGIC, MYSTIC, COMIC & HORRIFIC

ISBN 13: 978-1-60282-639-7

This Trade Paperback Original Is Published By
Bold Strokes Books, Inc.
P.O. Box 249
Valley Falls, NY 12185

First Edition: October 2011

Credits
Editor: Stacia Seaman
Production Design: Stacia Seaman
Cover Design by Sheri (graphicartist2020@hotmail.com)

Acknowledgments

Many thanks to Donna Lieberman, Susan Moldow, and Rob Arnold for their support when I was writing certain stories in this collection.

For Tom Libby

Contents

Preface

For people who keep track of things, *Contemporary Gay Romances* is my third collection of short stories, following *Slashed To Ribbons in Defense of Love* in 1983 (reprinted as *The New York Years* in 2003) and *Tales From a Distant Planet* in 2005. The latter was published by French Connection Press, in Paris, France and had a very limited distribution, although the book is still available for sale in the U.S.

The truth is, although I am primarily known as a novelist (and lately also as a memoirist), stories are my favorite way of writing fiction: whether it is a 1,750-word "amusement in prose" or a 30,000-word novella, or anything in between.

When I can know, sense, or even merely get a hint about an ending while I'm writing, I think I'm simply a better writer. Doing that with a novel usually means a five- to ten-year period of gestation before I even begin. With stories, I can start and end in a few sessions, or in the case of longer works, a month.

My first story was written when I was twelve, and my first published story (collected in *Slashed to Ribbons*) was written as far back as 1972. I've now written close to fifty shorter stories, of which over thirty have been published in one form, format, place or another, from magazines and newspapers to anthologies to online magazines. So far, no story I wrote ever became a novel. And only a few stories ever reached the popularity of my novels, although a few of my longer ones—novellas—did.

Among the shorter stories, only one included here was as popular: "Hunter" has been published many times in other people's collections, and it's amazing that readers find it as fresh and relevant now as when I first wrote it thirty-five years ago.

The stories in this volume are—with the exception of "Hunter"—twenty-first century creations. Which makes them unique in my catalogue: they were all written recently, from 2003 to 2010.

They are also "new" in another way, and thus different from my other stories: while two of them are undeniably autobiographical, the others are all stories that "came" to me as "gifts," and one of them even is titled "Gift."

Let me explain, if I can.

Being a lazy person (if efficient), I daydream as much as possible, and it is during these daydreams that ideas for books, plays, and stories first come to me and are developed.

That daydreaming, we now know, is a kind of Alpha-wave thinking. This has been measured by scientists. In the past, writers and musicians often sought it out, calling it their "muse"—i.e., Miss Alpha-Wave—and as often they used artificial means to woo Her, including alcohol, hashish, cocaine, hypnosis, post-hypnotic suggestion, and a bevy of other illegal substances. Unlike these forebears, I was already happily using illegal substances when I began writing. The only question was, could I write without them? Short answer: yes.

However, it was only in the past few years that my

daydreams reached a level where "voices" other than my own began to intrude—distinctive voices that came along with fully formed stories, settings, other characters, etc.

Now, were I not the distinguished, award-winning author that I am, one could easily think, he hears voices. Hmmmm, that sounds a lot like schizo…

Let's not go there. I've already accepted that something like that must already be part of my mental makeup. I mean, in 2008–2011 I was writing three separate books all at the same time: 1) a memoir set in the 1970s in Manhattan, 2) an epistolary novel set in Victorian England, and 3) a novel set in pre-Homeric Greece. And I would stop writing one, and move to the other with utter ease. So schizo…? Yeah, thanks, but I believe I've got a handle on it.

Back to the short story "voices":

For these I believe I should thank or blame my uncle Vincenzo Picano, a person I never met. In fact, a person who died at the age of nine and a half in 1923, brutally murdered by unknown assailant(s), his body thrown into a rural pond in Rhode Island.

I discovered very late in life all about poor Vincenzo, and I began investigating his death. I have written a little and I've spoken and lectured a lot more about this unfortunate lad and his story, and I think somewhere in the great ether, Vincenzo was (is) pleased that the secret of his life and death was finally being made known. I've yet to solve it, it was so long ago and information is so scarce, but I'm getting a grip on the basic situation, and I'm developing a theory and I may still some day publish my findings to date. Partly because it caused so many revelations about my parents, my father's family in America and back centuries earlier in central Italy.

After all that with my uncle, the "voices" began: as though I'd opened up some kind of gate to the "other side."

Each one of the voices was so perfectly and fully formed that when I decided not to ignore them any longer, and allowed myself to become the vessel through which they might tell their story, well, they did exactly that.

Usually the story was written fast—I mean fast: two or three days, with very little backtracking, no need to check facts, and of course their narrative voices were, well, unique and indelible and individual and…perfectly formed. Did I mention that these "voices" were a little annoying until I did decide to tell their stories? Not debilitating. At best a little irksome. And that once the stories were written, I never heard the voices again?

Some of the stories were sad: one was almost heartbreaking, a few were comical, several odd, others rather sinister, and they came from different places—panhandle Florida, somewhere in the Midwest—where is Meriwether Lewis High School? Does it exist? If so, where is it? I'd appreciate knowing, as it is the only clue to the location of one story. Other places include London, England; Italy; New England; and New York City. One is set in a futuristic and pretty much sunken-by-climate-change East Bay Area, California, and another is set on a planet with no name given, circling a binary star.

In time they range from the here and now—i.e., most of them—back to 1890 or so, and ahead to about 2250 A.D.—thus they are contemporary stories.

As to "romances"—well, they aren't your standard gay romances consisting of hot surfer guy Trey having the itch for even hotter garage mechanic Kyle, but they can't get together for some stupid reason or another until they finally do in spastic gushes of sweat and sperm and questionable prose on page 240.

No, these are romances that can and do happen in the real world. In some cases they are "fine romances" like the song, with no kissing; in others, with plenty of kissing and other stuff too. And in other cases, they are—since my "voices" told me the stories, actual stories that happened to actual people, although who these people are (or *were* in some cases), I don't know. None of them told me their real names.

So, yes, most of the stories in this book, including "The Acolyte," "Gift," "True Love...True Love," "Gratitude," "Imago Blue," and "In the Fen Country," are such "voice" stories, stories that came to me as gifts fully formed: for the most part I felt like a stenographer, merely copying them down and then cleaning them up a lot.

Unfazed by all this, my intrepid publisher, Bold Strokes Books, has planned a second volume of stories in six months or so, and most of those are also "voice" stories. They're even stranger than these, and not really romances, some not even gay in any way. They're titled *Twelve O'Clock Tales*, because around midnight is when I sat down to write most of them, and it's a good time for you to read them too....Boo!

Felice Picano

GRATITUDE

Both women had stepped away from the table. Lizabeth, his agent, to the restroom, Andrea Kelton, the editor who'd just said the words to make him float on air while seated still on the big *moderne* banquette, had received a phone call from her office and had wandered off somewhere at the far end of the restaurant trying to get better wireless reception. Leaving Niels Llewellyn alone to sit and gloat. Around him: the delicate tinkle of crystal and silver against porcelain in the overpriced eatery, and its otherwise artful sonic decor of swirling waters covering the multimillion-dollar deals being proposed and sealed by the industrial and media movers and shakers about the big, posh, water-hushed room.

It was something to savor, as had been Kelton's words, "this is unquestionably your breakthrough book. We're so proud to be involved!" Followed rapidly by further indications of how proud they actually were, including the stunning figures of the enormous first printing the company had settled upon, the pre-publication acceptance as a "main selection" by the book club, with its own concomitant huge printing, and even—he was to expect it as soon as this week—an unprecedented further advance upon his advance of a year past, actual cash more than double what he'd received, as though confirming the success of a novel not yet in print, never mind one liable to ever succumb to the vagaries of the marketplace.

Lizabeth returned first, and confirmed the second advance

and pre-sale and huge printing all meant there were to be no vagaries of the marketplace at all now. They—she and he, together for twenty-six long years, through wheat and chaff—had been elevated, as though on an enormous dose of morphine, a good half foot so far above the buy-and-sell mentality that had so enclosed them all of their professional and personal relationship. Niels was now about to become a "personage," and she too, at least in the "industry" a correlative mini-personage. They toasted each other's good sense and tenacity and lifted a glass edge toward whatever literary gods there still might be in this ghastly age, to help them ever onward.

Then Kelton was back, closing the phone and saying, "The advertisements are set now for a national vend. Six major newspapers and three magazines," and Niels sank back into the banquette and listened almost as though he were not the major reason, but instead some hanger-on, or better yet and ironically, given his age, a child, as the glories of his immediate future were trotted out in all the brightest colors with metaphorical pennants excitedly set to fly in front of him.

He was hardly a child. Closer to sixty than fifty. No friend to the reflections of windowpanes and looking glasses that had a startling way of creeping up and suddenly presenting him to his nowadays always unsuspecting and usually horrified self.

"About time," some would say. His previous agent, gone into real estate in Gulfstream St. Pete; his sister, an aged thing upon a stick who lived in Middleton, New Jersey, on a government pension and who he still held responsible for his mother's death: responsible by means of her unbending maternal neglect; was it half a lifetime ago? "About time," a few dusty professors would utter, those not yet retired, who'd gone to college with him, saying it with a bit more fire, a smidgen more respect. "About damned time!" his few pupils over the years would celebrate, wherever they celebrated these days; he expected in their overpriced apartments in the wilds of Queens or Staten Island, after all, who could afford to live in Manhattan except the wealthy and the few like him who actually were more or less rent-controlled unto death?

The celebration soon over, the women once more drawn to the cell phones, someone—he didn't know, he didn't care, which—paid for the, of course, overpriced lunch, and they all stood, made kissing-like gestures in each other's direction and slowly slid out of the water-tumbled dining chamber and into a corridor, into a bar, toward a coat check room, into another corridor, and out onto the front foyer where men with suits even he knew were ridiculously expensive—suits he soon could buy should he care to change his look ("Post-Graduate" one magazine had written of his habitual costume)—were entering.

In the spring afternoon sunshine, Lizabeth spotted a taxi, and Andrea mentioned they were going the same way. Touchy kisses this time from the two of them, as the middle-aged women skipped chattering like preteen girls through the Mid-Fifties street traffic and into the cab door, "No-No"ing another matron foolish enough to try to beat them to it. Then the taxi slid forward, they were gone, and Niels was alone.

"It's April ninth!" Niels found himself saying to three other women, stepping around him without even a look back headed into the restaurant's foyer, then he moved out of their way, forward into the 2:06 p.m. noise and grime of a midtown sidewalk.

"About time!" he repeated to himself with secret joy, wondering with a start how life would be different now. "You're lucky, N.," Scott Fortismann had said to him only a few nights ago, "fate is saving you for last, for when you're ready for it. Unlike poor schmuck me, you'll be able to handle and thus enjoy your fame when it comes." To which Niels had answered, "*If* it comes!" and been clapped on the shoulder and assured all across Riverside Drive and into Scott's hundred-thousand-dollar Merce coupe that it would, it would, Scott Fortismann knew for sure.

Scott of course had become famous early, twenty-eight, world-famous at thirty-four with *Nets*, and so had been famous seemingly forever and it had ruined him. Scott would reiterate that to Niels during their long (and on Scott's part—increasingly booze-tinged) meals. And Niels could see for himself: the lengthy, expensive, disgraceful, emotional, first divorce. The seemingly abandoned children who'd come to hate Scott. Nicky nearly murdering his father that insane afternoon on the yacht in Antigua. Brenda in and out of jail or Payne Whitney or more lately caught up in the bust of the latest escort service to take her in. Scott himself going from wife to wife, girlfriend to girlfriend, even drifting into Niels's territory awhile, with that much younger and somewhat questionable African American minimalist, what was his name, Nigeria Sands? More disrepute at their very public breakup at the Venice Biennale. Providing ignominious material for half a week of say-anything-just-so-long-as-you-show-everything (and they did!) European scandal sheets. Their few remaining friends, their colleagues certainly, and much of the reading public had come to expect Scott Fortismann's very public romances and breakups so they could afterward savor them, endlessly rehashing them, appreciating them, a great deal more than his dwindling output of serious plays.

Scott Fortismann would probably be the only one of what was left of Niels's so-called "circle" (long *perdu* thanks to car accidents, air accidents, overdoses, suicide, cancer, and AIDS) who'd be truly happy for Niels now. The others, well, what had Samantha W. mouthed off last week? "For every artist who makes it in this damned country, fifty others have to fall down in front of a bus." No, they wouldn't so much like it, would they? No matter what they would actually say to his face—and who could blame them?

He'd reached the corner of Fifth Avenue, where a complete tangle of traffic appeared to come from two directions. A crowd of pedestrians was gathered under the construction scaffolding, barring Niels from even seeing what was going on in the middle of the intersection—if not from hearing shouted drivers' curses and the incessant honking of car horns.

When he'd passed here earlier on his way to lunch, three construction workers had been sitting just over there, somewhat elevated, chowing down on hero sandwiches and messily drinking out of big thermoses as he'd stepped around the corner. One of them, maybe twenty-six, slab-sided big, with a mess of thick, bark-colored hair and post-twilight blue eyes, had suddenly stood up and stretched himself to his full six feet and two inches, and Niels had stopped short on the sidewalk and just gawped at the big child-god as the fellow's eyes closed and his mouth smiled and his muscles played along his arms and over his chest, obvious through his thin "Metallica Rocks!" T-shirt, in sheer animal pleasure at such a simple activity as yawning and stretching. Cupid's dart had stung Niels so suddenly then, so utterly, he'd become nauseated. He'd felt such complete astonished unmitigated desire and such an opposing instant equal realization of the impossibility of its ever being fulfilled that he had actually had to turn away and retch.

Andrea and Lizabeth had noticed how pale he was when he'd arrived at their table not long after. They plied him with brandy and fabulous news until he'd forgotten the godling, and his own embarrassment, doubled of course when said deity had noticed Niels about to pitch forward over the two-by-four temporary wooden railing onto the filthy curb. Said deity had rushed forward and grabbed Niels, shouting, "Eeth! Give me a hand! This old guy's goin' under."

He'd been freshly mortified by the shout, and of course, they'd easily grasped him and pulled him over to where they sat, where the third one had plied him with tepid coffee from a thermos, the three of them clucking over him: "Jeez, we thought you was a goner!" "Is it your ticker?" and worst of all, Apollo-in-construction-boots demanding, "Look me in the eye, so I can see you're all right. C'mon, right in the eye! Udderwize we're calling E. Em. Ess. C'mon, fella!"

And so he'd been forced to actually look close-up at those eyes and so be able to determine their exact shade of semiconductor cobalt, which he now knew so very well he could mix it at any paint store, not to mention the naturally frosted three different tones of browns of his leonine mane, or his complexion like that satin found on century-old Valentines, or the exact cut of his Medici upper lip, the slightly fuzzed depth of his matching dimples. Niels had almost lost it again. He'd gaped again, until they declared, "Yawl right, now!" and "Want help inna taxi?" all of which he fended off, with many mumbled thanks and gratefully downcast eyes, getting as far away as fast as he could and then once past the construction site looking back once, only to be startled by his Adonis's head thrust out over the sidewalk and his somewhat worried face, his big right hand stuck out in a peace sign vee, to which Niels at last responded with one of his own, before somehow managing to actually stumble the twenty yards or so to the nearby restaurant.

Niels didn't see any of the three now. Could they have already left for the day? Then he heard one: Apollo himself shouting and then there he was, in a sort of setback where the boarding had been nicked three feet into the building dig to allow for a temporary enclosed chute, probably for rubble to be dropped from the top of the construction to its collection site far down below. Hidden within the crowd, Niels felt safe in turning and gawking at the perfection of the creature as he waved his hands and shouted up some obscure lingo, possibly to one of his colleagues from before. It was almost amazing watching him.

Niels became aware of the crowd thinning, his cover lessening, and was about to persuade himself that he'd soon be spotted again—but would that be so very bad? he might even go over and thank him for his trouble earlier?—when his peripheral vision caught something else.

The enclosed chute next to the construction worker had been shaking from side to side, perhaps as a result of larger pieces tumbling down through it, and at an upper section he could see a piece of something seemingly caught fast. It bulged suddenly, maybe two feet above the construction god's head, then more rubble came down into it, finer stuff, then it moved horizontally maybe four inches on either side. Suddenly it half detached from its lower portion, which swung around a hundred and eighty degrees, revealing, as he'd feared, a good-sized chunk of concrete wedged in tight.

It was the workman's absolute total failure to see any of it taking place at all that impelled Niels forward, through thinning pedestrians, shouting and knowing he couldn't possibly be heard over the noise of the chute, over the traffic, but that he had to do something, or it would disgorge directly over, on top of, right *onto* the fellow's head.

Not even realizing what he was doing, keeping his eyes all the time on the broken shaft, Niels dove across the sidewalk. Panicked even further as the construction worker headed directly under its opening, directly under where more rubble had been dropped down and where the structure now swung side to side. Niels was yelling, "Get away! Get away!" Yelling loud enough it turned out for the worker to turn to the sound of his voice, a split second of surprised but pleased recognition on his handsome lips, his mouth opening to say something back, as the concrete wedge began to give way, and Niels threw himself directly at the worker's midsection the way he'd seen defensive lineman tackle a quarterback on televised football games, with utter disregard for gravity, himself, where he might land even, and he felt the young fellow's complete astonishment as he caught the blow and tumbled sideways virtually head over heels, Niels all the while thinking, "God! Have I done enough!" just as the noise above him reached a thunderous boom and Niels looked up and his vision seemed closed down to an overhead tunnel of unstoppably charging black rubble, and he understood that he'd succeeded in saving Apollo but that now the ton of concrete was for him alone, and there wasn't even time for the next thought, before it all went quite dark.

❖

"...so I told him, Tyrone, 'No! I am not going to that restaurant with you! I don't care how many of your friends are waiting there!' Can you believe that? Him telling me that—just to get me to go? What an idiot...Hold on! I think this patient is conscious. Hello, sir? *Sir*? Better get that intern at the desk. *Sir? Hello. Can you hear me?* Can you recognize. I'm Tyesha Melton, your nurse? How many fingers am I hold...? There you are, Doctor, I was just...Yes, sir, we were about to turn him over like we usually do at this time and he just now opened..."

Niels registered it all, and with a sigh of relief he thought, oh, good! Here I am. It worked. I saved the lovely boy, and suffered some little concussion, and all will be well. The intern, who seemed to be of Middle-Asian origin with untypically bad facial skin but lovely brown eyes simply drenched in several rows of eyelashes, said, "Please, sir. I'm Dr. Kawalor Dohendry, and you have had a serious accident and have been out of commission for four days and three nights."

Niels began to say something but nothing came out—he only could croak.

The nurse lifted a little pink cup of water to his mouth, and he sipped while the doctor looked on benignly, and Niels tried to say something and still nothing came out but frog talk.

"Not to worry, sir," the doctor said, "These things happen. Maybe later we shall speak. Can you nod your head?"

Niels nodded his head and even he could tell that the motion he made, if it existed at all, was very, very minor.

"Good, sir. Good progress, I think. We will now be able to communicate," the doctor said, smiling fatuously.

Communicate? Niels wondered. I, who could write a page-long sentence without the need of more than a single semicolon! You call *this* communicating?

"Your son is waiting in the other room. Nurse, get him," Dohendry said.

Son? I have no son.

"He slept over all three nights in this very room, upon a narrow cot we brought in. He insisted. What a good son! In my homeland, of course, this would be unextraordinary, even expected. But in the U.S. (he pronounced it You-Ass) it is very uncommon for such devotion from a family member. Ah, there you are, sir."

Niels looked up and it was the Apollo from the construction site. Unharmed. Dressed in different clothing, clean pants and shirt, but the same fellow, more gorgeous than ever. He had his hands together, as though he'd been wringing them, and he looked so sad and yet hopeful too now.

"Yes," Dohendry went on to the Apollo, "as I told you would happen, he is fully conscious now." The doctor did something, tucked in a blanket or something, Niels couldn't make out the darting little movement indicative of care. "But as I also told you, he is unable to speak. The crushed trachea, you understand. It is temporary," turning to Niels, "only temporary. It is a like a rubber tube that has been given a blow," he illustrated in the air with a karate chop to one forearm, "and it needs now come back to normal." Turning now to the Apollo, "He is fully conscious and understands. But only in nods can he communicate."

Niels looked with astonishment at the construction worker, who suddenly pushed the little doctor aside, fell upon Niels, and hugged him, sobbing loudly.

"Oh, look, nurse," Dohendry was saying beyond the big clasping body. "Such a lovely reconciliation. I take back all the bad things I have said about American fathers and sons. Every word of it." He then turned to the other nurse and said something rapidly in a foreign language Niels had never heard before. She responded and it necessitated them going to some machine at the end of the room, while Niels remained unable to do anything but bear the big young lovely clean-smelling head and torso and arms of the Apollo thrown about him, still sobbing, until finally the big tanned face pulled back, streaked with tears, cobalt eyes brimming over with tears, and the quivering Michelangelo lips whispered, "Why'dya do it? Why'dya save my life like that?" before he resumed hugging him and sobbing.

It was during these moments that Niels had the most bifurcated emotions he could have possibly imagined. First, of course, and obvious, the pleasure of the big delicious fellow all over him, grateful, delighted, his warmth, his sheer presence; next to that, opposite it, the absolutely below zero chilling recognition that Niels's action had not at all resulted in some little concussion and all would be well, because he was more or less paralyzed, wasn't he? Paralyzed, unable to speak, unable to move anything but he imagined his head a quarter of an inch, side to side.

Niels Llewellyn died then as he had lived in his previous life, realizing what his impetuous and altruistic act had cost him, he felt his spirit leave him and he died. Once again all went black.

But not for long, since he was now in intensive care in a large Manhattan hospital. And so he came to again a few minutes later, only to see Dohendry and hear him saying, doubtless to the Apollo, "We must expect these little setbacks for the next few days. The shock. The shock of it all, and the happiness your father must now feel is naturally the cause of it. He will survive, believe me. A good son's affection..."

❖

He did survive. With all the complications that ensued. Apollo's name turned out to be Danny Masini, twenty-nine, of Center Moriches, Long Island. There was a wife, Sylvia Masini, pretty, demure, sweet, and a little Danny, aged twenty months, a Cupid, a putti, an angel. The other workers from that day came in too: Ethan Skavenger and Anastas Doremates. They visited less often, but often enough, and sometimes with girlfriends. They lived in Merrick, Long Island. They visited him twice a day and every visit went on for hours and was filled with food and balloons, huge pop-up get well cards, and flowers, music playing and people talking, and in short a little get well party. Soon, the nurses hung around more, to flirt with Anastas and Ethan and their friends, and so Niels got constant, adoring attention from them all. Doubled by Dohendry, who had appointed himself the little group's guardian, and who got Niels into total physical and voice rehab, pulling strings for medicines not yet fully approved by the F.D.A. and who visited him daily with new methods, ideas, and potions, even when he was moved to a room down the hall and Dohendry was no longer assigned.

Niels made progress. He seemed to have no choice but to make progress. Soon his croaking was more nuanced, comprehensible to the beautiful Danny Masini, who insisted, despite the difference of their names—for they'd gotten his wallet, his I.D., his card for the paltry catastrophic insurance—to anyone who asked that they were related. How could anyone doubt it? Soon Niels was moving his fingers on his left hand, and with little Danny playing with him, his toes on his right hand, and Dohendry was there saying, "What did I predict? Not of course, with the spinal damage you sustained in the accident that you should expect anything like a full recovery, but with such loving friends, such a family, such a son, why, I think you should expect a wonderful life."

One day, perhaps five weeks later, his agent Lizabeth arrived. She was horrified to see him but hid it quickly. Niels got everyone else out of the room—there always seemed to be at least one of the workers' *cumadre*s sitting with him every day, or someone's teenage brother helping him do rehab. It was understood by all, and totally approved by all, that he would be living with the Masinis from now on, once he got out. On the weekends, various male family members and pals were helping to close in and insulate the sun room that faced west over the estuary down to the Great South Bay. Danny showed him photos and videos with construction progress reports and it would all be very beautiful. It was understood by all that Niels was "theirs" now, and they would take care of him and do whatever was needed, from now on, no matter what it took.

He knew they thought he was a bum, without two nickels to rub together, and he was waiting for the appropriate moment, once they were all settled, and "at home" to tell Danny the truth: that such virtue had a monetary reward too. He knew what Danny would say. "Who needs your money? We've got enough! We're family. Family!"

"Who are these people?" Lizabeth asked.

"What's happening with the novel?" he asked carefully and watched her slowly figure out what he was uttering.

"Everything we spoke of, except," here she almost broke down, "the press we've gotten is astonishing. You saved this man's life. You're a hero. You're a public relations windfall. There's so much demand for your book, Andrea's executives decided to print and ship six months early."

Niels smiled.

She then went on to explain her absence in Europe, at some European book fair or other, and then on vacation after, which was why it took her so long to find out about him.

"Andrea says photographers from *People* magazine want you," she said, awed. "That's a few hundred thousand copies, right there."

"Good," he croaked.

"Good? Look at you, Niels! What happened? Oh, God, it's all my fault. I should have put you into a taxi that day. Just look at you!"

She must have become very loud and sounded upset because suddenly the door opened and two people came in, Tania Skavenger, Ethan's sister, and Danny himself, the look on his face saying leave him alone or by God, I'll…

"What's happened," Niels croaked out the words carefully, quietly, grasping the edge of Liz's sleeve with his crooked (but growing stronger every day) two fingers, "is that I'm happy, Liz."

Lizabeth backed off, all but thrust aside by Danny, who sat down and said, "Look at you, grabbing at ladies! You're something else!" He kissed Niels's mouth and said to Tania. "Get me some of the green jello." Then to Niels, "How you doing? Danny's here and all is well. Ready for some?"

"Really, really happy for the very first time in my life," Niels muttered, as Danny readied the spoon of jello and made airplane buzzing noises, "Okay, sweetheart! Open up wide! Here it comes."

"True Love...True Love..."

When Mike Strong came up to where she was just leaving the lunch tables outside the big cafeteria and asked her to the Fleetwood Mac concert for the coming Friday night, she knew it had to be a mistake. He was so out of her league. But there he was, tall, incredibly handsome with his pale gray eyes and his butterscotch hair, and he was saying that he and Gabe Dell and Shaun Hunt had gotten the three tickets together. Only Gabe's oldest sister was getting married in Cincinnati and he couldn't go. Would she like to join them?

She almost died on the spot right then. It must be a mistake. He looked at her, quizzically, and then Shaun, Mike's best friend since the second grade, with his corn silk hair and his blue, blue eyes and also incredibly handsome, came up kind of behind Mike but to one side and asked, "So is it okay? Is she coming with us? Are you coming with us, Cara?"

So even though she knew that both of them were really far out of her league she said yes and waited until Friday for it to all be a mistake. But instead, Shaun drove up in his brother's pale green Buick sedan and Mike got out and said she looked really pretty and she got in the middle and he said, "Gosh, but you're small," and they went to the concert and had a great time together.

The lead-in act was a trio of girls who sang a combo of country and pop, which was okay, but not earth shattering. They did one old song called "True Love" Cara had never heard before. It went, "And I give to you and you give to me… True love…True love." And when they were done, she said something to Mike like "Wasn't that wonderful? Wonderful?" He smiled and said it was wonderful. She thought, well, so now we have a theme song too.

It was the girl Shaun was seeing, Debbie Josephs, who came up to her the next Monday outside her locker and said they all hoped she would join them that coming Friday night, after school at the burger shop then the movie, and she seemed so nice that Cara said, "Sure. Okay," although Debbie was so very cool—and a senior!—it had to be a big mistake. Had to.

That was how Cara began dating Mike Strong, even though all the other junior girls at Meriwether Lewis High looked at her strangely thereafter, since all of them wanted either Mike or Shaun or Gabe Dell, the three biggest, fastest, handsomest, best football players in the school.

A couple of times when she was getting ready to go out with them—it was usually four of them, double-dating, and sometimes six, tripling—there were times when she was waiting for Shaun's car to pull up to the house in the evening, she'd look at her mom and ask her why, why her? With all those girls, why had Mike Strong chosen her?

"Come on, Cara! You're pretty," her mother always said. "Some big guys like petite girls, you know. You've got a perfect little body. You're smart. You're sensible."

She still wondered if it wasn't all a big mistake.

A couple of times she thought her mother would ask her if

she and Mike were making it, if they'd "gone all the way," and she would of course say no.

But she knew that's what some girls at Meriwether Lewis thought. That she was "putting out" for Mike. Once, coming into Phys. Ed. class late in the gym, she overheard two girls talking behind the bleachers. She was about to go up to them when one of them said, "She's gotta be doing it! Like that Debbie!"

"You don't *mean*?" the other one, who Cara thought was her friend, asked, scandalized.

"Sucks like a Hoover. Blows like the wind. All those football players like that, you know. Since they're not supposed to be wearing themselves out too much before the game."

Their peals of delightedly outraged laughter followed.

How unfair, she thought.

The following weekend, while they were necking in the car, Shaun and Debbie in the front and her and Mike in the back, he bared both her and his own genitals and played with them both until she started making the strangest noises, totally uncontrollably, and having the weirdest sensations down there, over and over again, kind of like burning and being cooled off by ice at the same time. She managed to pull away before she thought she'd faint, just as he made a mess of himself against the backseat. As he was rapidly cleaning it up with a hanky, she pulled up between the two front seats and she saw Debbie was bent over almost double in the front seat. For a second she was going to ask was she sick? Was that why she had her face in Shaun's lap? Did she need a hanky? Then she saw Debbie's head moving up and down and she realized, those girls were right about what Debbie was doing to Shaun.

Shaun saw her looking, and turned and looked right at her, then at Mike, who was trying to pull Cara back from being so close to them in the front seat, and she thought that Shaun had the loveliest and most innocent look on his face as he…well, as he came, she guessed.

A few weeks later she tried to do the same thing Debbie had done to Shaun to Mike. It didn't work. He was just too big. Her mouth was too small. They couldn't find the right angle. Oh, everything went wrong and he had to finish himself by hand. She apologized and all, and Mike kept saying, "Don't worry. I'm okay. Don't worry about it." But she felt she was failing him and because she was still so insecure—it must all be a *big* mistake—he'll find someone like Debbie who *could* do it, she thought. There goes True love…True love.

Some weeks went by and as it was fall semester, finals week, with the team playing two games every weekend one game after another, Cara began to worry about Mike and her. One day she went to his house. Mrs. Strong was waxing the kitchen floor and said, "I think the boys are outside, practicing moves or whatever they call 'em."

They weren't in the big backyard. She thought they might be in the screened-in summer bedroom way out of sight behind the garage where she'd gone a few times with Mike.

Mike was there, stretched out on the day bed with his shorts off and the lower part of his body bent off the edge of the bed. He had his arm thrown over his face. First she thought he was asleep. Shorts and undershorts off too, she noticed, second. And third, that Shaun Hunt was crouched over Mike's lower body, doing what Debbie had done to him, and what Cara just couldn't do to Mike. And Mike was probably thinking of her all the while.

She walked away without bothering them, thinking, it was her fault. He had to ask his best friend to do it. And because Shaun and Mike were best friends and knew each other since second grade and were inseparable, Shaun did what Mike asked. Because she couldn't.

Well, if she and Mike Strong had True love, True love, then it was time for her to prove it. She made a decision: even though she'd earlier promised just the opposite to her mom, and herself—she would lose her virginity to Mike. The very next time she saw him.

They were alone together in her house making out and she was going nuts because of his hand down there, she grabbed his thing, his boner, they called it, and handed him a condom.

"Really?" he asked.

"I can't do the other thing. Might as well do this. But go easy. Okay?"

Well, she had no idea what it would be like, did she? He'd covered her body, he was almost twice as big, with his own sweet-smelling, warm, nicely muscled body, and he cradled her and he invaded her, but he kept asking if it was okay what he was doing and he did everything, just as she'd wanted, and when they were done, she knew why Mike Strong had chosen her, and that it wasn't a mistake after all 'cause he was so happy.

"You are…you are…" he panted afterward, "great!"

And she'd liked it okay and she thought she would come to like it even more.

True love…True love.

And so they got married.

❖

She awakened in the middle of the night, suddenly freed of all pain.

The digital clock read 3:30 a.m. Cara suddenly felt very

light, very free. She didn't understand why, perhaps it was the end coming sooner than anyone had predicted. But she felt she ought to enjoy the freedom while it lasted. She got out of bed, feeling light as a feather—she weighed so much less now than anytime since she was a teenager—put on her robe and slippers, and quietly left the room.

Her daughter Amanda was asleep, clutching the pillow, having kicked off the blankets. Let them stay off. Poor thing must be warm.

Downstairs was dark, and she kept it so until she reached the kitchen. It was amazing how light and free she felt. The refrigerator was well stocked. Shaun and Amanda would see to that: the two of them seemed to always be hungry, and she'd awaken and hear them coming in from the market after he'd picked her up from school, with cartons of groceries and produce.

Mike was so impossibly helpless at things by himself that when her cancer returned and then got worse, Shaun had agreed to move in. He'd broken up with his second wife anyway and was living in some apartment near the business he and Mike owned together for the past ten years. Their son, Neil, hadn't liked the idea of Shaun moving in, but then Neil didn't like anything at age thirteen, except smoking marijuana and playing with small pistols. "They're collector's items," he'd insisted, while she screamed, "Get these guns out of my house!" And so Mike sent their son off to military school, and Amanda, who was seven, loved Shaun, who was her godfather anyway, and so after Cara's third recurrence, with the chemo and the radiation and the exhaustion and all, Shaun just moved in for good and pretty much took over the house.

Thankfully. Because of Shaun being there, taking care of things, there were these cute little caramel puddings in plastic containers in the fridge: not too much for her like most things nowadays, just enough, so she sat at the kitchen in the dim bulbglow with more light from outdoors beaming in through the door window and she scooped a pudding into her mouth. It tasted sweetish, and rich, and she looked outside at the street light flickering and the Werners' garage-hung night light, and she thought, I'm almost in another dimension now, aren't I? I'm in the world of the very, very ill. I have different needs and responses. I'm awake at different times. I'm like one of those men who guard big office buildings all night long. I've become guardian of the neighborhood, protector of the house.

The elation she felt continued even when the fatigue made its appearance, not long after she'd finished eating and washing the spoon. She continued to wander the house checking everything, guarding, protecting. Upstairs she used the loo though very little came out anymore, and her once-beautiful lower torso looked so thin, the hair down there so enormous now that she wasn't taking the chemo—she would cut it back in the daytime, she decided, just like trimming a hedge.

On the way to her bedroom, she stopped at the other bedroom door and pushed it open. This is where they'd placed the queen-sized master bed when her room was filled up with that metal hospital contraption. Mike would sleep there and Shaun would sleep in Neil's bedroom or on the den couch. But Neil had complained bitterly about Shaun in his bed and the den couch was too short for Shaun's long frame and so here they were, the two guys, in the big bed and see, there was plenty of room for two, just like she had told them.

Shaun was on the left, lying on his right side, in almost a straight line, his hands in front of him, faced away from Mike. While several feet away, hogging the space as usual, Mike was on his back, his hands out on either side straight out, so one hung off the bed, while the other just brushed Shaun's back.

She was about to withdraw when Mike became turbulent in his sleep, moving about and mumbling something, becoming more and more agitated. Certain he would wake Shaun, who seemed to be sleeping so soundly, she almost interfered.

Before she could, though, Mike rolled over to Shaun's half of the bed, and after a few minutes he fitted himself closely into Shaun's body, chest to back, torso to rear, legs to legs. She was certain Shaun never really woke up, but he somehow got hold of Mike's still mobile hands and trapped them in his own hands, and held them in front of himself. Mike continued to move about and mumble, then Shaun raised Mike's hands to his mouth, Mike's big hands, and held them there and Mike settled in, nuzzled against Shaun's neck, and was inert.

They lay like that until their snoring began to synchronize. They slept deeply.

Looking at them, she was filled with the greatest peace.

She had worried so much about Mike, how he'd react when she was gone, what he'd do, if he'd act crazy and go off the deep end, and drink and whatnot. She feared that the most, since theirs had been—unexpectedly and so long—such a True Love.

Now she knew she didn't have to worry anymore. Shaun was here and Mike would let Shaun take care of him, as he had let him take his hands and calm him while they slept.

❖

Although she woke up late in the morning after they were all gone, and she felt terrible again—that pain throbbed no matter how she lay—she got up, nuked the remaining coffee, and called their attorney, chewing on the vicodin and morphine pills together. "What's the worst it can do?" she'd asked Shaun. "Kill me?"

She had to explain to Samantha that a decade before, when Mike's hardware and garden center was faltering, he'd signed over all of the house into her name to protect it, in case the business went belly-up. The business had survived, once Shaun joined as partner and began to manage, and in fact it had even flourished, but they'd never changed the deed back to the two of their names. Besides a few pieces of jewelry, the house was really all Cara possessed: she wanted to make sure it was disposed of properly.

"Does your husband know you want the house shared equally between him and Mr. Hunt?" Samantha asked.

"Mr. Hunt is my husband's best friend since second grade. He's responsible for us keeping our business and for me being able to stay in the house while I've been sick. I want him to have half."

"Okay, as long as you know what you're doing! I'll draw this up and be over when? Tomorrow afternoon? I'll need to bring two witnesses for the signing."

That night she woke up again in the middle of the night, painless, and enjoyed a few hours of wandering about. Once she thought, I'm already kind of a ghost, aren't I? This amused her more than she could say.

She looked in on Amanda and of course looked in on the men before she went to bed again. The guys slept together, on different ends of the bed, facing away from each other. Even so, one of each of their legs crossed the other's at the ankles. Seeing that she began to giggle and pulled out of the room so as to not wake them.

That afternoon, she dressed for the attorney. She put on a little makeup. Samantha hadn't seen her in a year and was terribly shocked, even though she tried to cover it up by coughing and pretending she had a cold. The witnesses waited in another room, watching daytime TV while Samantha went over all the terms of the will. Both witnesses were elderly, and the man touched her on her wire-thin upper arm when they left, and said, "Better, this way."

She already knew that.

Three weeks later, her ghost nights ended abruptly when she blacked out during Sunday breakfast. Amanda and Shaun were making pancakes, her daughter counting out the number of blueberries in each one, being precise as only a seven-year-old could be. Mike was setting the table, going back and forth from the kitchen to the breakfast table. Although she pretended to be poring over the newspaper's TV guide, she saw that the two of them managed to brush against each other or physically engage in some way, each time Mike passed Shaun. She suddenly thought, that's what it's like to be in love, isn't it? You can't leave him alone, can you, Mike? I couldn't leave you alone, remember?

They'd finished eating, and she'd declared, argued really, that she'd help with the dishes, when she suddenly saw big, irregularly shaped, cartoon-comic, electric green and yellow stars in front of her face, reached out for them, and went out like a light being shut off.

❖

It was all pretty vague and hazy except a lot better than the throbbing pain, and she had to rally with great effort inside the intensive care unit to tell them, no, she wanted no extra efforts: Hadn't they read her living will? Get her out of here.

In the regular room later—the next day? She wasn't sure—Mike was sitting next to her and talking. She looked at him and thought, you know, he may be thirty-eight, but he still looks great. He probably has another good forty years left in him, doesn't he?

She remembered him and Shaun in that screened-in summer room, and realized: they'd been doing that ever since. Maybe long before he'd met her. But definitely ever since.

Hmmm.

She must have fallen asleep, because now the intern and a nurse were doing something with her body, using tubes and machines and who knew what foolishness, looking pretty frantic and Mike was standing at the back of the room, sobbing, and she thought, Oh Christ I can't let Mike Strong cry like that. That's not manly. I'll have to do something, something, but what?

When behind him, there was Shaun Hunt. Shaun put his hands around Mike's front and held him there, and Mike let him hold him like that, and he stopped sobbing and she thought, you see, God, I've done something good in this life. Maybe only one thing, but it was a good thing.

Because she had to admit she'd never *really* believed what had happened to her at that school dance so many years ago. She'd always known that it had to have been some kind of mistake—she was so out of Mike Strong's league. She was.

Only it hadn't been a bad mistake, but instead a good one.

Without her, they'd never be together, would they? Society wouldn't let them, back then. They wouldn't let themselves be together, back then. But now, now, they could be together, for all kinds of reasons. They *were* together. They were even legally bound together through the house because of her.

Her work was done.

She could go now.

Because Shaun gave to Mike, and Mike gave to Shaun… True love…True love!

An Encounter with the Sibyl

I had become separated from the group of tourists in yet another of those interminable villages in the Tuscan hills when I turned at a sudden vine-clustered wall and happened upon a tiny piazza.

The past frantic twenty minutes I'd been threading my way through a high-walled labyrinth of narrow alleys where every door seemed bolted shut and the lowest windows began some ten feet above my head, shielded from view by fractious-looking bushes. So the little open area I now happened upon was more than a mere opening out—it was a veritable expostulation!

Hardly larger than a tennis court, the little piazza, like the rest of the now-nameless town—for in my panic, I'd forgotten its name—was surrounded by tall, tottering, umber brick walls. But as I stumbled out of deep shadow and into the glare of the late May midafternoon, I saw that one wall was lower than the others, indeed only thigh-high, capped with rough-hewn flower boxes, carnival with bright geraniums. And beyond the little wall and gala crimson blossoms…beyond was an astounding view from a great height: the depths, the widths of an unsuspected valley, traveling ahead so ruler straight, and for so distant a passage, I swore that if I squinted, I'd be able to make out the Tyrrhenian's triple-blue coast waters.

More surprising still, the piazzetta was inhabited and made use of. Since I'd left the others, I'd not seen a soul: not a grandmother lounging upon a towering windowsill, not a mongrel sunning amid the gnarled olives that dominated every tiny plot of garden. Along the view-end of the piazza, a miniature café had been erected: a mere three or four spindly white metal tables with elegant matching chairs, seemingly from some long-shuttered hotel—my only hint in the barbarous town of a more elaborate way of life. A single octagonal fluttering tutti-frutti umbrella had been raised between two tables. Grottoed within its shade sat the oddest beautiful people I'd ever seen.

Either of them would attract notice on the busy modern thoroughfare of any metropolis. Because the young woman was in profile to me, I suppose I noticed her first: her long neck, her honey skin, her heavily lidded sloe-eyes, her nose which, while not quite aquiline, suggested Senecan tragedies, her full, unparted lips, the tiny brushes of golden hair scalloped around her ear, the close fit of her oversized bone-colored raffia sun hat. She was sensual and chaste; all flesh yet as though carved of alabaster: such a curious melange I'm afraid I stared, rudely, astonished that she could also possess mobility. She stretched a long, fine-fingered hand before herself as though in benediction, or admiring her fingernails, and as she did, she caught not only my eye but that of her companion opposite, and her lips moved.

She'd addressed a young man whose smashed gray fedora had been tilted askew, framing in a nimbus of ash felt a richly colored chiseled perfection. True, his nose was slightly snub for so refined a harmony, his lips fuller if possible than the woman's, his eyes more deeply set, the shallow triangle of teeth open to view excessively white against his tanned skin. Even within the shade of his hat brim, his eyes flickered darkly as he unconsciously lifted a hand in gesture to me, as though encompassing the vista, reminding me of one of those burghers of old Flanders painted as an afterthought at the extremities of a vast triptych, some merchant who sponsored the artist, and was thus allowed to eternally present his city—minuscule in the background of some stupendously dramatic, infinitesimally detailed *Deposition from the Cross*.

The slightly over-elegant gestures of the two as well as the evidence of napery, china, and glassware suggested a meal consummated, and dawdling, as though neither wished to make a decision to move. At first I thought them siblings because of their strong resemblance in beauty, then lovers from their languorous and wordless communication. Until I noticed the third member of their party.

No wonder I had missed this figure, so ensconced was it in the shell of a high, hooded, wicker-work chair. At first, all I could discern of a personage was cloth, as though linens and pillows had been enthusiastically plumped and allowed to softly deflate.

In that moment of trying to make out the figure inside the hooded chair (for I'd convinced myself that it was a person), a very small peasant woman came into view on the piazza. She was quite round and wide-faced, with ebony hair pulled back into a doubly braided bun, mounted upon the back of her head like a spare tire upon the side fender of a Rolls-Royce Phantom. Even more amazing was her costume, one almost parodistic in color and cut, it made her so much the tour guide's *contadina*. She'd stepped out of a double door from which she must have seen me stagger into the piazza and addressed me.

"'Giorno, Signor. Voi rifrescarlei!"

Her plump hand swept toward the tables, offering me a seat. Her words of welcome drew forth slow turns from the Etruscan couple.

When I didn't immediately answer her offer to refresh

myself, she added brightly, *"Noi siamo molto gentile,"* attempting I guess to reassure me. Instead, she confused me further. Who of us I wondered, were very civilized? She and I? Or the other three?

I took a seat at the only other already-set table, sharing the umbrella a bit, and the taverna owner—for that was who I supposed the plump woman to be—nodded in approval and after asking if I was hungry, and not waiting for a response, obliged me with an oral menu: pasta and risotto of the day, coffee, *gelati di noce*, and *delice*.

Thinking I would rest here a minute before venturing down into the contentious little town again and attempt to locate the others, I ordered coffee—with milk, so I wouldn't receive the standard bitter, dark double sip of *espresso*.

"Niente di mangiar?" she asked appalled, as if I'd asked to drink blood.

I wasn't hungry. Couldn't eat a thing. Then, fatigue taking over, my little bit of Italian by now spent, I added in English, "Just something to drink."

The woman with the exquisite profile moved an inch to look at me better.

"She asks what food you will take," her companion said, turning in his chair just enough that I knew I was being addressed. He concluded by favoring me with the slightest hint of smile: it devastated me.

"Is it required?" I fumbled back at him.

The peasant woman waited, her apron edge twisting in her fingers.

"Not required," he allowed, and I couldn't for the life of me place his accent, which didn't match any I'd heard so far in this country. "Yet," he went on, and seemed at a loss.

"Yet preferred?" I tried.

He bowed almost imperceptibly in my direction, then

smiled more fully. The pearly gates opened, irradiating the piazza, dazzling me.

"If I must eat...then...anything!" I said, casting my gustatory destiny to the winds that played with the stranger's lapels. To the woman waiting, I said, "Anything sweet. Anything but chocolate," I tacked on, as an afterthought.

A soft sputter of what I assumed to be a dialect of Italian between the man and the peasant woman conveyed the information. The *contadina* curtseyed in our general direction and flounced off, like a dismissed *comprimario*.

"May I ask," his ravishing companion suddenly spoke up, "why *not* chocolate? Have we not heard it scientifically proven that chocolate is the food of love?"

Her accent was identical to his, and perfectly inscrutable, her voice as dusky in contralto as his had been burnished in baritone.

Under differing circumstances I might have disputed her statement, but I was weary and unwilling to extend myself. "I'm allergic to chocolate."

In truth, I liked chocolate as much as the next person, but the Italians' use of it so far in my trip had sated my limited palate for the stuff. I'd not eaten a chocolate I was comfortable with since I'd crossed the Grand Corniche into the country.

"Allergic? Exactly how allergic?" I heard twitter from the depth of the hooded wicker chair in a thin, high voice with a pure American accent, startling in its directness.

"I get fevers," I fibbed.

"Hives too?" she asked primly.

"Not for years, no."

"Red streaks on your arms? Rashes on your abdomen? Blotches on your bottom?"

"Sometimes."

"*High* fevers?" she probed.

"Low but insistent."

"A dry mouth?"

"It's been so long since I…"

She ignored the attempt at qualification. "You see, Ercole. All the symptoms," and she seemed to subside back into the pillows of the wicker-work in what I was forced to assume was hypoallergenic musing. In the enfolding silence—striking by the absence of birdsong—I thought of the rising pitch of her interrogation, and the name by which she had called him. Something classical, no? Hercules? Yes. And the young woman then would be whom? Dejaneira? Diana? Aphrodite?

I must have muttered the last name aloud, in Italian.

"No, no!" the young woman laughed.

Ercole now motioned to me, clearly asking me to join them.

"American?" the still nameless lovely young woman said rather than asked when I took the fourth seat at their table. She swanned a long, tanned wrist at me, and I took her hand, unsure whether to kiss it. The air around us smelled of almonds—almonds, spun sugar, something vaguely metallic. I took the soft hand and she looked at me from within the striated illumination of her sun hat.

This close, her eyes were rounder, hazel, green, golden: no, the same cream color of those long bars of *ciocolata Jesu* sold on the Via Urbana in Rome.

"The Grandmama believes it is a sign of old nobility to be allergic to chocolate," she now said, amused. "Having blue-blood. We—Ercole and myself—we eat liters of it." She laughed, sharing the secret with him and I would have given her the keys to my house to hear that laugh again.

So charmed by her, and by the fact of the heap of white skin, white hair, and bones I could make out among the purple material of the wicker chair, that I missed their names in the long liquidity of Ercole's "Pardon me to introduce ourselves, etc." I did regain presence of mind just long enough to register that he called the old woman Principessa Someone or other.

Our waitress returned carrying a tray of milky looking drinks in tall mauve coolers, each glass set within a chased silver holder sculpted in relief, so that frolicking Nereids barely fended off the advance of amorous Tritons, all of them about to be swallowed by wide-mouthed, rather jovial-looking sea serpents. They looked old and valuable. Where was my coffee?

I turned to ask if one of these was it, and was interrupted by Ercole, smooth as glass, saying, "Better than the coffee you ordered, signor. A dessert and drink in one."

I sipped at it with a Bronzino-thin merman of a spoon. "Amaretto?"

"Amaretto, yes," a touch of eagerness in his voice, "something else too."

"Brandy? *Eau de vie de Poire*, perhaps?" I hadn't a clue.

"It is quite special," the young woman said, pointing to the Principessa's nearly non-existent lap where I now made out a mauve glass flask, the same tint as the coolers, and like them encased in a chased silver carrier with nautical allegories.

"Absinthe?" I tried, half-joking.

They laughed and shook their heads no, and I laughed, a bit bleakly, I admit, wondering if I were being slipped a mickey, or if Ercole had mentioned among that long list of surnames I'd scarcely listened to, the name Borgia.

"This is your first time here?" the young woman asked, changing the subject. "You are here on vacation as a tourist? Or to study?"

"A little of both."

"You pardon my curiosity?"

She might have asked me the number of my bank account,

and although it was so depleted now it would hardly matter, I still would have gladly given it.

"And you adore the country?" she enthused softly.

Well…" I began, and stopped.

Manners decreed that I ought to say yes, certainly, I adored their country. But the truth was a bit more complex. Not that it wasn't altogether lovely to look at, so many beautiful places and things to see. But I was more or less alone in Italy—and that seemed to make all the difference, didn't it? Unable to see Italy with Sarah, I was somewhat lost, even forlorn.

I ought to note here immediately that we'd had no falling out and that Sarah had abandoned me suddenly, without warning, two weeks before, outside of Monaco. She'd simply asked me to stop the Renault and she'd stepped out, grabbed her two pieces of luggage out of the backseat where she'd placed them that morning at our *pensione* in Nice, and she'd walked into the little train station and onto the steps of a waiting train taking her back to Paris. All without a word or a hint of explanation.

I'd still not gotten over her doing it, nor even worse, her utter calm in doing it. How she'd met the train precisely on time, how she'd known precisely where I had to stop for her to catch it. (Had she planned in the *pensione* the night before, as I'd written out postcards, as I'd slept? She must have!) How she left me without a hint of complaint, or kiss, or word of goodbye. I'd thought our trip together, our being together, heaven. How could she have thought differently? What could I have done to so alienate her? To not even deserve an explanation?

Once Sarah and the train were gone in the other direction, I sat in the rented car until the train barrier was lifted from the road in front of me. The cars behind me honked for me to move on and so I did. I drove to Florence, just as we'd planned, Sarah and I, in our carefully-mapped-out itinerary made months ago on the front lawn of her father's bayfront summer house.

I'd then continued to travel through Italy, following that itinerary. Not as though Sarah were still with me, naturally, but as though I couldn't admit that she was gone. I suppose in some way I expected to be stopped at another crossroads or train trestle and have Sarah as suddenly step out of a car with her two pieces of luggage and hop right into the Renault again, to continue our journey, without a hint of explanation. That would be unlike her, of course. But what she'd already done was so utterly unlike her, what difference would that make? And should that occur, I'd never ask for an explanation either.

I kept to our plan. I stayed at our decided-upon *pensiones*, I walked the foreplanned narrow alleys of Florence, purchased silver stuffs and tooled leather book jackets on the *Ponte Vecchio* exactly as we said we would, and I mailed them home from the American Express office near the Spanish Steps, a week later, to announce my arrival in Rome. No letter, not a hint of a note to our parents about what had happened.

Once, only once in those weeks did the full realization of Sarah's deed impinge upon me fully—sickeningly. I was sipping Pernod and water and picking at some local variation of Nesselrode pie in an outdoor café on the Via Veneto. It was sunset, and all Rome appeared bathed in the final hot flush of twilight. Up the via, the Borghese Gardens had already flamed up and dimmed into moody shadows. But a small street perfectly perpendicular to where I sat was an eye-hurting red-orange, as though that half of the city was engulfed in fire.

The café was sparsely peopled, as most Romans were returned to work or home after their midafternoon siestas. But a lovely young Scandinavian woman swerved off the via into the café and sat opposite me. She spoke in what I took to be Norwegian.

When I tried to tell her I didn't understand a word, she reached into a colorful woven carryall and pulled out a dozen or so frothy looking cookies, each wrapped in tissue paper. She unwrapped each sweet, popped it into her mouth, and offered me a few too, which I enjoyed. When we'd eaten them all, she lined up the parti-colored tissues on the edge of the table, crushed each in such a way it stood up, struck a match, and set fire to its upper tip. First one, then all the other papers lifted up off the table as they burned, flaming as they fluttered, rising a foot or more perfectly vertical in the air, and evaporating into lilac-colored smoke; not a jot of ash descended. Then she stood up and without a word walked off.

I was so delighted by the little performance, and the mystery of the papers rising as they burned, that I turned to my left and said, "Wasn't that strange and wonderful and exactly what you would have wanted to happen at dusk on the Via Veneto?"...And Sarah wasn't there.

Of course not. She hadn't been there in some time.

I remember seeing a documentary film about the Eichmann trial in Jerusalem, some years before. At one point, an accuser suddenly stops testifying. Holding on to the edge of the podium, the witness looks around the courtroom, then slides off, crumpling onto the floor, as men rush to his side. Explaining the incident to the camera later on in the film, the man—who'd suffered everything short of death in one of the Nazi camps—explained, "I realized all of a sudden that Eichmann was just a man. Only a man. But if one man could do that, well, then *any man* could. I could too. You too."

Something on the order of his sudden realization leading to an instant and overpowering emotion happened to me at that café table. William James called it a "vastation," a lovely turn-of-the-century word, don't you think? I stood up to leave the table and I realized not only that Sarah was not with me, hadn't been with me, and would probably never again be with me, but that I was alone: in Rome, in the world, in the universe, and I would probably always be alone. I reacted as that Polish Jew at the trial had, as William James said that he and his father before him had done: I fainted back into my chair.

Amazingly, I didn't hurt myself, and I came to soon after, thanks to the ministrations of the waiters.

That night, I didn't follow the itinerary Sarah and I had planned for our third night in the city—the Coliseum by moonlight (we'd even checked to be certain it would be a full moon) followed by dancing in one of the ancient Roman baths converted into a discotheque. Instead I remained in the room of my *pensione* and I pondered. I slept poorly. The morning following that, I checked out, obtained a road map, and left Rome for the hills, deliberately headed north and east, when our plan had meant for us to go south, to Naples and Capri.

From then on I would follow no itinerary. I would wander. I'd drive around at large, waste time, try to discover what I had done so wrong that Sarah had walked away from me without a word. Failing that, I would be miserable.

I'd left Rome two days before and I still remained haunted by questions. Earlier this morning, I'd awakened in a hotel in Lucca, walked out onto the terrace where a half dozen other Americans happened to be breakfasting, and I'd allowed myself to be talked into being part of their group on their visit to this particular town—Spiegato, was it? No, that meant mirror, didn't it?

Whatever its name, the town was completely off the beaten track for tourists and contained, they assured me, but a single attraction, an underground chapel dating from early

Christian times. The Americans weren't a church group, so I never discovered why exactly they'd hit on this specific village and its single feature. But so they had. I'd followed their van for a few kilometers, then lost them. Once arrived, I'd circumnavigated the lower part of the little place in fruitless search of the tour group, their ecru van, the ruins, or anything at all interesting. One time, I'd thought I'd seen two from the group strolling high up a road too narrow for the Renault to traverse, so I'd parked and followed them on foot, and eventually arrived here.

"No?" the beautiful woman questioned me. "You don't at all adore our country. Not even a little?"

"Right now I do," I allowed. "Here. Now."

"Ah!" Relief flooded her face, sending her from a momentary anxiety, leaning forward across the table toward me, back into her chair back smiling.

"He likes the place fine. He has a dilemma."

The accent of the sentences was American. Rather specifically New England American. And the voice had issued from the depths of the hooded chair.

"Grandmama hears great sadness in your voice," the young woman said. I wondered if the old Principessa was blind, but didn't dare look closely at her to check.

"Hesitations," Ercole added. "A tragedy, perhaps!" He said it not to me, but to the air.

"No. No tragedy," the prim old voice declared with utter certainty.

If this was the family's idea of social chatter, I found it peculiar indeed. Even more peculiar when the old woman spoke again:

"She's gone back to Paris. To the man who seduced her."

I sputtered into my drink.

"You didn't know?" she went on. "It happened in an

elevator. One of those large, over-elaborate pneumatic lifts. But he'll soon throw her over, of course. Her name begins with an S. Sandra. Susan…"

"Sarah!" I said, despite myself.

"Sarah, yes. Forget Sarah. You never belonged with Sarah. It was not a mistake, but mere propinquity. You'll do far better in life without her. Far better in all ways."

"That's hardly possible. Her family's terribly affluent. Whereas I…"

"Please." Ercole softly tapped my fingers still. "Do not contradict." He put a finger to his lips. When I looked at his female companion, she too had a finger to her lips, and she even winked at me. Meaning what? That I was to humor the old woman?

"Your fortune, when it comes," the old Principessa went on, "will be far more considerable than poor Sarah's. It is linked to a man. A man you haven't yet met. You'll encounter him in the corridor of a railroad sleeper."

She paused, or fell silent.

As though she hadn't spoken at all, the others smiled, sipped their drinks. When the young woman spoke again, it was to say, "Tourists seldom find their way to our charming little piazza," which, following what the old woman had uttered, was a trifle banal.

She looked to me for response, as did Ercole. Unnerved by the sham conversation, I still managed to get out: "Too bad, as it's a spectacular lookout."

"Ercole said before he thought that he heard others also coming." She pointed to the steeply sloping road I'd clambered.

"A tour group. Searching for some ancient chapel," I explained. "You know it?"

They didn't seem to. "Few find their way here," Ercole

said, I thought almost sadly. "Were you looking for the chapel yourself? Or for the others?"

"I'm not really sure what I was looking for," I admitted. "You live here?"

"Oh, no," the young woman answered with a laugh, as though a spectacular view, like too many sweets, simply wouldn't do. "Nearby."

"In a *palazzo*?" I wondered. I'd look it up later in the guidebook.

"A very small *palazzo*," she admitted, playfully stroking my fingers. Meaning I'd be unlikely to find it listed, nor discover thereby the ancient Principessa's name.

I was about to ask where the little palazzo was located, not that I was trying to inveigle an invitation, when the old woman began speaking again.

"The man in the sleeping car will be immensely wealthy, extraordinarily powerful, and vastly influential. He will take an immediate and consuming interest in you. You will rebuff him, but he will persist. Finally, you will agree to dine with him."

What she said seemed so unlikely, so absurd even, that I let her words wash over me, uncontested. After all, I had this lovely company, this view, this marvelous drink—whatever it might be.

The old woman seemed to chuckle. "Just at the moment that you do decide to throw your lot in with his, the man will make certain demands of you." She laughed in a particularly smarmy manner, all the more lubricious coming from someone so proper. "Ah, how shame will blossom on your young cheeks as you perform what he requires of you. First shame. Then acquiescence. And finally, delight in your sordidness."

Well, really!

"I don't quite see the point in—" I tried.

Ercole and his companion hushed me.

"*You'll* think it sordid," the old woman said. "I, of course, make no such moral judgments. You, however, will think it very low. And you will then enjoy it all the more for how low you think it."

Her voice had grown weaker, her words softer.

"He will transform your life..." she added, by now in a whisper. "And eventually...you'll come to...thank him.... to thank...this...Sandra...Sarah...even...more..." Her words trailed off.

I was suddenly aware of the sound of my breathing. I suppose I was waiting—dreading was more like it—for her to start up again.

When Ercole began to speak, I was almost rude in hushing him.

"No, my friend," he insisted gently. "There is no more she will speak. Now, the Grandmama sleeps."

Indeed, her light, irregular snoring could soon be heard, made the more resonant by her hooded chair. I was both relieved and I admit now, disappointed. I'd wanted her to go on, to say more, balderdash though it seemed.

After several minutes more of silence, Ercole rose like a column of smoke and appeared to float to the flower boxes atop the low wall that overlooked the valley.

As though she'd been watching from indoors, awaiting this very move, the peasant woman who served us appeared again and began to clear the table. As she worked, she sang a lilting, wordless little tune.

Ercole's companion arose as liquidly as he had, and also, from awkwardness I guess, so did I. She strode over to where he stood and slid a tanned arm over his shoulder. Brother and sister—or were they cousins? lovers?—remained still and silent, out of reach of my many questions, looking over the valley. When they turned and separated, Ercole went directly to the wicker-work chair, which I only then noticed was mounted upon wheels. He tilted the chair gently, waiting. His companion came to where I stood.

I have to admit I was still so perplexed by the old woman, and even more by the suddenness of their departure, I thought I must ask at least one more question: any one would do, as long as it were answered.

"In the flask?" I asked. "What was it we drank?"

"Water. From a spring near our little *palazzo*." She laughed and moved away from me in a flutter of soft clothing across the piazza, toward a large, pre-war limousine I'd not noticed until that moment. Its huge back door was open, its darkly clad driver stood against the sweeping side fender, his hat brim shadowing his face.

Ciaos were tossed at me, and answered by the peasant woman, busily folding up the big umbrella and wiping off the table.

The driver, Ercole, his companion, the wicker wheelchair and its occupant were all inside the car before I could move. The car doors were closed and the limo seemed to glide down the narrow hilltop street, vanishing in a silken putter.

"Fortunato lei," said the peasant woman: Lucky me.

When I asked her why, she pulled down the lid of one eye with a finger—a gesture I thought astonishingly odd—and replied, *"Parla La Cumaia."*

"La Cumadre?" I asked back, not certain I'd heard her correctly, wondering if she meant that I was lucky to have spoken to the Principessa, who was her *cumadre*, some sort of honored relation of hers.

"No, no," she corrected me, and repeated, *"La Cumaia,"* syllable by syllable. As I was still baffled, she shrugged and still humming that careless tune, she went back inside.

I remained at the parapet, looking over the magnificent view another five minutes or so, embarrassment rising inside me. That *Commedia dell'Arte* gesture of the peasant woman, the absurd questions about chocolate, and finally the old woman's obvious delectation in spelling out in some detail an unsavory future for her own countryman—it all seemed some elaborate and tasteless joke, with myself the unwitting victim.

To hell with her! With all of them! Beautiful or not!

I traipsed angrily out of the piazza and stumbled back down through the town. I didn't encounter the tour group again, and didn't see another human being. When I located my Renault again, I drove out of the mountains and west toward the sea coast, headed for Genoa. I don't know why exactly. I guess I just felt like getting away from these damned hills and their bizarre denizens.

Later that night, I arrived at the *pensione* where I'd planned to be with Sarah. Although I was five days earlier than my reservation, they took me in. They also handed me a letter from Paris. Sarah had to leave me, she wrote, and she had to live her own life at last. She couldn't continue living a lie. She adored Eugen. She liked me as a friend. She hoped she hadn't ruined Italy for me. She would try to explain it all to me more fully someday.

After dinner, I went to an American movie playing nearby. It was subtitled in English, which I thought odd, but that dose of pure, unaccented English made me feel considerably better somehow. It also convinced me that I'd had enough of Europe for a while. It was time to go home.

On my way out of the cinema, I passed, then walked back to and into, a bookstore. To my surprise, I found some not-too-dated American newspapers and even a magazine. I scooped them up greedily, feeling a bit less homesick. I was now certain everything would be better when I left Italy. Sarah could do whatever she wanted, with Eugen or with whomever. I no longer cared.

About that, at least, the old woman had been right: Sarah and I didn't really belong together. We'd simply been thrown together early on in our lives and had hit it off and little by little we'd been persuaded by others that we were a couple, eventually persuading ourselves and each other that we belonged together and ought to be married. Why? We'd never been madly—not even tepidly—in love. Merely comfortable together. That might be fine if we were forty-five years old, or seventy-five. We were still young. There was nothing to stop either of us from having a perfectly marvelous life apart. And if I had been betrayed by her, well, better now than after we married. I would return home a "wronged man"—never a bad position to be in. And, after all, it was a new experience being dumped. One of many experiences I hoped to now acquire.

I'd paid for the magazine and papers and almost stepped out of the bookstore when I recalled the word the peasant woman had used to refer to the Principessa. My Italian had never been more than barely utile, but I was curious. I asked a clerk for and was shown to a large Italian-English dictionary.

"La Cumaia," it read. "Cumaean. Also prophetress. Female seer. Specifically, the Cumaean Sibyl of Ancient times." Still wondering, I asked the clerk in Italian how commonly used that word was in his language.

Not common at all, he replied. *"Strega"* was usually used, and sometimes, the higher toned *"Sibylla"*; the latter now considered antiquated, heard only in Donizetti operas. My word, he pedantically informed me, was rare. A particular seer so ancient, he assured me, that in Virgil's epic, she had prophesied to Aeneas—fleeing the destruction of Troy—that his descendants would go on to found the city of Rome.

That was all I needed to hear. The old Principessa might be a hair sensitive, I'd even allow her to be slightly psychic—she was not over three thousand years old.

Edified, if unsatisfied, I left the bookstore planning to spend the night in my *pensione*, reading American periodicals. Passing a kiosk just closing for the night, I made an impulsive purchase of a bar of Cadbury's. I'd already eaten it when I got to my room. I crumpled the foil wrapper as I entered, tossing it in a high arc into a distant wastebasket. This first return of high spirits cheered me, and I fell asleep an hour later, newspapers splayed over my blankets.

I awakened about four in the morning with the strangest sensations: my mouth was parched. I had a slight headache. My forehead was beaded in sweat from what seemed to be a low-grade fever. I itched in various places on my body—my forearms, around my breastbone, across my backside. No nausea: nothing remotely severe enough to be called food poisoning, never mind enough to dream of awakening the staff and trying to find a doctor at that hour of the night. But I was terrifically thirsty and I felt distinctly weird. When I got up to drink water, I noticed in the light above the antique washstand that I had red welts on my chest, rashes on both arms, and yes, when I checked, blotches on my bottom.

But I'd been lying. I *wasn't* allergic to chocolate. At least, I *hadn't been.*

I tried to recall that inane, provocative conversation: the old woman's exact words in her sharp New Hampshire accent. Could she have somehow wished the allergy upon me? Inflicted it in some way, perhaps through the enigmatic drink her grandchildren—if that's what they really were, and not instead her confederates!—had given me?

Then I had an appalling thought: what if that about the allergy to chocolate had come true, because *everything* we'd said—all of us—in that magnificent spot, *had* to be true. And did that mean…What exactly *did* it mean?

I took a tranquilizer and finally managed to get a few more hours sleep. The following morning I felt better: the symptoms were gone. I had to find out if what had happened was merely a hallucination of the night, so I ordered hot chocolate with my breakfast. Its fumes were enough to make of my mouth a miniature Sahara, to cause my arms to prickle, to cause me to begin to squirm in my seat. A sip would not be needed: Damn if I wasn't suddenly allergic to chocolate!

Great, I thought: I meet an antediluvian prophetress, the very one who foretold for old Aeneas, and what do I get? A new allergy!

I began to worry. Still, there are ways around predictions, aren't there? You can't, for example, meet someone in a train corridor if you aren't *in* a train, can you?

I was driving a car. Yet, somehow at the customs shed in Ventimiglia, at the French border, the next morning as I was leaving Italy, I looked in the glove compartment for my international driver's license, green card for European insurance, and rental car registration, and they were gone. The customs authorities impounded the Renault and phoned the rental agency in Calais who told them yes, I'd rented it, but for two weeks, not three, and they needed it back immediately. The Italians held on to the keys.

I tried hitchhiking. Dangerous on that stretch of road where cars zoom out of long waits at customs. And also, as I quickly discovered, illegal. I barely escaped arrest.

Right near the customs shed was a train stop. Okay, I decided, taking the train would be all right. Only being in a sleeping car would fulfill her prophecy. This was a regular train. Seven cars consisting of seats only. I'd buy a cheap ticket to Paris.

Outside of Lyons, however, we stopped awhile for several cars from another train, including a dining car, to be added on. As I'd missed lunch and it was approaching twilight, I decided to get something to eat. A conductor pointed the way, five cars straight ahead. It was only when I had opened the door and walked a half dozen steps inside that I realized that the third car, which must have been added on along with the dining car, was a sleeper. Panicked, I turned and began to rush back out of it. I ran right into the arms of Achille l'Extringnon, the Belgian electronics billionaire, who almost fell over.

We went to Paris. We dined together, as the Principessa said we would. And Achille offered me a position as his right-hand man in Brussels at an outrageously high salary, and I said I would think about it. I mean, after all, without Sarah, there was no real reason to return to the States immediately, was there? And I'd always been intrigued by electronics.

Naturally, I've done some serious thinking about this. Who wouldn't? And I've come to the conclusion that the old woman was only partly right. True, Achille may be unmarried, unattached, but he seems an honorable enough fellow and he doesn't seem to have the least...how can I put it...insalubrious intentions regarding me. Or if he does, he's so far kept them to himself. At any rate, at dinner—and what a dinner!—I made my position clear. Or at least I think I did. Yes, I must have, and Achille seemed to accept it. Of course, he's insistent in some ways. The hotel suite, for example: as I had nowhere to stay in Paris, he insisted on that, and it was quite nice, as I suppose all the suites at the Crillon are. And since he owns it—he seems to own a great many things—he wouldn't dream of letting me pay for the week we stayed. You know, things like that.

Otherwise it's great. Of course two little subjects still pestered me. Try as I might, I could no longer recall the old woman's precise wording—and I was sure that remembering her exact words contained the key to how I must handle myself with Achille.

Second, of course, was that damned business about the chocolate. Some of the finest in the world are made in Belgium, and from the first Achille sent boxes of the most scrumptious-looking delicacies: white and milk and bittersweet, with hazelnut and raspberry cream and champagne-flavored fillings: simply irresistible. I finally told him to take them back, I'm allergic. But Achille had a solution to that little problem and after the briefest of medical tests by one of his doctor friends, I received antihistamines. At least I think he said they're antihistamines. Whatever they are, the pills work wonderfully well and now that I've moved into Achille's *palais* in Belgium, I can eat all the chocolate truffles I want. In fact, the pills make me feel so generally good all the time that I take four a day, as prescribed, whether I plan to eat chocolate or not.

There he is at the door, now. I should go. He's got wonderful plans for us for tonight. Every night, if you must know. It's beyond my dreams. Simply magical…

Oh, by the way, did I mention that I'm absolutely certain that once I've fully settled in here, I plan to meet some nice girl and fall in love?

Gift

This is what I know about drowning: some persons can hold their breath longer than others. No one can hold it longer than five minutes seventeen seconds underwater without a special apparatus. Of course there may be someone in the Guinness Book of Records. But I've not met him.

This is what I know about Kevin Mark Orange, age seven and three-quarters. He vanished at 2:15 p.m., a Thursday afternoon. As it was late April, it rained twice that evening, obliterating any footprints or tire marks.

That, at least, is what anyone knows who listened to the 6:30 p.m. local ("K-RUF—We're soft on you!") television news that also showed two photos of Kevin, one taken a month ago, with his chocolate Labrador, named Bre'r Bear, and one taken over a year ago with his little sister Jean-Eartha Orange, no age given.

This is what I called and told to Sheriff Harold ("Hal") B. Longish, one hour after that broadcast. "I know where Kevin Mark Orange is. I don't know the name of the place exactly. I can't take you there, because I'm only a kid and can't drive. I never met that boy in my life. I don't know anyone who does know him. I can't tell you how I know. I just *do*!…*But* I can draw you a map."

So, of course, after wasting another hour, the sheriff and his deputy arrived. They were naturally doubtful. So I said immediately, "Sheriff Longish, your deputy had a left-hand upper molar pulled this morning. And also your mother's cat named Harlequin ran away for the sixth time yesterday night and she called and begged you to look for it."

"How in tarnation!" his deputy, a woman named Sheryl Jamison, asked.

Sheriff Longish looked at me and said, "Sher, this lil' critter may actually be the real thing."

I laughed and said, "I *am* the real thing."

"How old are you?" the deputy asked.

"Nine years, four months, and two days yesterday," I replied. "I learned everything I know outta that series of books," pointing to the encyclopedia that Granny-Mama had left to her by a cousin twice removed. "And online my I.Q. is one hundred and fifty-three."

They looked at each other awhile and at that moment I realized she had aborted his male fetus in the second trimester, one year and six months and fourteen days ago up at a clinic up outside Tallahassee, even though they never were married and in fact were supposedly happily married to other people.

He sat down, she stood behind him, and he said, "Boy, draw me that map."

So I did, with magic markers on the plastic board hanging at my side.

"That wide oval," I explained, "is Lake Pishimere, that lil' pond-like mostly dried-up thing about four miles down the route 208 from where Kevin lives."

"We've got people looking not far from there," Sheryl Jamison said, and picked up her cell phone and speed dialed.

"What are those three exes in a row?" Sheriff Longish asked me.

"Those are beached and wrecked flat boats from ten-odd years ago."

"Hugh?" Sheryl spoke into the phone. "You at the dried-up lake, right? You see any wrecked boats there?"

"He took Kevin on a path between the last boat and the blackberry bush in full bloom," I said, drawing a line to show it.

"Go as far as the blackberry bush," Sheryl directed into the phone, "then turn north."

"He was assaulted on the flat rock there." I drew it kind of smushed in. "He pulled down Kevin's pants and did it to him three times."

"Oh, Jesus! Be my Savior now," Sheriff Longish said in a plummy kind of praying voice, and Sheryl added, "Amen, Lord."

"He dragged him a little further up and strangled him there," I said, dotting the line now, "using the elastic from the underwear he took off Kevin. He left him there, where the two old cypress trees are rotting away in still water."

"Lord, hear my prayer," Sheriff Longish chanted.

Sheryl Jamison amened that, then repeated my directions into the phone.

Eight minutes and thirteen seconds later, she got a report that they had found the boy—just like I'd said.

Granny-Mama brought the two of them beers from the icebox and they all gathered around me and kneeled for a prayer, holding hands all around and stuff.

"He just knows things!" Granny-Mama explained to Sheryl Jamison over a piece of that morning's fresh-baked cheddar corn bread. "You know. Where things is gone missing to. Who's going to ring on the telephone. He predicts all the elections on the TV. He's got A Gift, you see."

"It's the Lord's compensation," Sheriff Longish said, still

using his holy voice. That way he didn't have to say anything pitying about my physical condition, all twisted up as I am, and in a wheelchair and barely able to do the normal stuff for myself that most anyone can do.

It wasn't until three days later that the sheriff came to visit again. This time he was alone. He asked, "You see it happen? That kid Kevin being…you know, and all? In your mind's eye, I mean?"

"I sorta did. Yes sir. And by the way, sir, as we are speaking, I'm seeing in my mind's eye your eldest boy, Drew Longish, age sixteen years, four months, and twelve days," I added, "at home, right now, smoking maryjane and sucking his best friend, Tommy Thorn's, dick."

I thought Sheriff Longish was going to smack me hard, he got so red in the face, almost purple, and his fist just got all stony. But he just stormed off and tore hell out of the dirt in front of our house driving away—I guess in a hurry to get home and catch a look.

Granny-Mama had been listening behind the door and she came out and we laughed at what I'd told him. We agree, Granny-Mama and me, on most things. All kinds of things we hear, and things I see. We don't care what those folks are doing. But them others do care a lot, don't they?

"Be a while before that sheriff comes by again," I said.

"I thought you kinda liked him?" Granny-Mama said.

"I did. Kinda." Nice-looking man. Big hands. "But he'll be back. Know why?"

"Because he never axed you who simonized and kilt that lil' boy," she answered.

Granny-Mama may not know her words right—she can barely read—but she can be smart.

❖

He did come by again, that Sheriff Longish, two weeks later, with this pretty little blondie woman all dressed up tight as she could be in a gray suit for men, except it was specially tailored for her. Right off I knew she was going to be trouble for me. You see, they carry dark spots on them, all those who are going to be trouble. It sorta stains their clothing like moss or something, alive and growing, nasty. Hey, I thought. This is interesting. No's one been trouble for me in a long time. Not since Granny-Mama took me outta that hospital ward in that awful place near Stark. I was kind of excited, you see. It gets kind of boring around here. And she was something new.

"So! You're a Fed-er-al-ay!" I said to the blondie woman. "F.B.I.?"

She looked at the sheriff and he looked at her. On the drive over here, he'd wondered if his stick is too fat to fit into her pussy thing. He don't much like her attitude toward him and he hoped it would hurt like hell should he ever get the opportunity.

"That's right," she said to me. "So you must know why I'm here."

"You're here onaconna the serial killer...Underwear Man," I added, giving the secret name her unit up in Birmingham, Alabama, called him, because of how after he's done sexually molesting his children of both gender victims he always strangles them with the elastic of their unmentionables, just like he did with Kevin Mark Orange.

"Now, this is a top secret operation," Sheriff Longish said to me. "So everything you hear and say is among only us three. Understand?"

I said I understood. Anyway, he was okay today. He'd calmed himself down before he got home that other day and he'd stopped "to think." Which meant he'd allowed Tommy Thorn some time to get the hell out of the Longish house before he went in himself. The weed smoke was covered over with "Summer Rain" air freshener and Drew Longish was extremely occupied at that time doing his trigonometry homework, for which he only got a C+ and that only because he cheated from Suzanne Hillyer on the last pop exam. His father didn't even notice the dried jizz on his son's hairless chest, visible if he'd carefully looked through the half-unbuttoned shirt. I guess he was so relieved not to have caught the two of them *in flagrante*, as the newspapers write it.

The blondie lady said there had been five others in her state and one up near Pensacola. The time between the crimes was getting shorter, she said. She knew I wanted to keep some other lil' innocent kid from being done in. Would I help? Would I tell her whatever I saw?

I said I would, though I didn't give half a crap for any of those lil' kids, in Alabama or Florida, for that matter. I did it for Sheriff Longish. Told him what I'd seen was an ordinary feller. Good looking. Very ordinary feller, just like everyone else, except he favored pale blue shirts for everyday use.

I then asked to see blondie's revolver and she showed me as she asked all kinds of questions that I gave her indefinite answers to, whether I knew them or not. Looking at her gun I knew then that a forty-seven-year-old black woman named Mariah Gregg who took in colored's laundry for food money had been caught in a crossfire and had died two years, one month, and nine days ago with this very weapon up in Dunwoody, Mississippi, in an unrelated case.

While she took a call on her cell phone out on the front verandah—as Granny-Mama grandly calls that lil' porch—Sheriff Longish stayed with me and told me, "You're not one hundred percent accurate, you know."

"If that's what makes you feel good to believe, you go on ahead," I told him back.

When blondie stepped back inside the house her suit was even tighter on her than before, and her stains was actually standing up to look at me.

"The Underwear Man has struck again," I told the sheriff, before she could say a word. "This time it's a girl missing."

He looked almost angry. "Why in hell didn't you say something?"

"Just got the message this minute," I lied. "I guess it come in along that cell phone call."

He looked at me funny. But she took control of the situation. "Is she still alive?"

"Yes ma'am."

"Can you tell where they are?" she asked.

"Where's she been snatched from?" Sheriff Longish asked.

"Lake Geneva Village Mall."

"She'd been left inside a 'cerulean' Chevy Cobalt sedan," I added. And rubbing it in, "I told you he favored light blue."

"You got a map in your mind's eye yet?" he asked me, kinda roughly.

I was going to say maybe I do and maybe I don't and what's it to you, when blondie asked, "What else can you tell us?" Being all nice to me.

"He's gonna let her go," I told blondie, ignoring the sheriff.

"What? Why would he do that?"

"Onaconna she's peed herself bad. He hates peeing like that," I said.

"Weren't there urine traces on the others?" Sheriff Longish asked her.

"Nothing substantial or long standing, no. Maybe at the moment of…"

"He hates the smell of it," I repeated.

"You go," Sheriff Longish told blondie. "I'll stay with him. Just in case..."

"Hold on!" She called on the phone: "What make and color is the vehicle?" she asked, and when she was answered, she did something with her lip to show I was right. "Jackson, we think he's ditched the child. Headed south on..."

"Southeast," I corrected.

"Headed southeast on..." She looked at me for confirmation. "Is it 207? The road from the Lake Geneva Village Mall?"

I nodded yes.

Twenty minutes later, they found Liza Beth Morgan, aged six years and four months, sitting on the side of the road, unharmed, hysterical, covered from the neck down in her own urine. They didn't find Underwear Man, as he was long gone.

"You just earned yourself a government commendation," blondie said to me.

"What good is that piece of paper? It ain't money, is it? You can't eat it, can you?" Granny-Mama would wonder aloud later on when she saw it arrive by special delivery mail. But blondie already had something else on her mind involving me. I could tell, because the stains were getting bigger and nastier.

❖

Granny-Mama couldn't understand why I would agree to it.

"They'll give you plenty of money, if'n I do," I explained. "Enough to get that big screen Hi-Def television you been after. And then some."

"The kind they show in the newspaper?" She'd tacked that ad over her bed like it was some movie star.

"I'll make sure they get you that very one," I told her.

She thought a bit and said, "Well, then, all right. What about you?"

"I guess I'll have to take my chances," I told Granny-Mama.

"You're a lucky child. Nothing bad can happen to you, if you will it so," she insisted.

I got doubles of Rocky Road for dessert then, messy as I can be with it, onaconna she was already contemplating watching *Wheel of Fortune* on that big TV.

Next day they came out in three big white vans with turning TV mesh dishes on top and seven other vehicles, KRUF, KTAK, and even the big TV station from Gainesville, this being the biggest story from the area since the student murders a quarter century ago.

I was dressed just like we'd discussed in pale blue shirt, with dark blue pants and even blue running shoes, although I'll never run in them. My hair had been barbered by a pretty woman from the TV station, and blondie and me had rehearsed exactly what I was going to say, like it was a play or something.

"Are you *sure* about this?" Sheriff Longish kept asking me, every chance he could get me alone, which wasn't too often. So I had to reassure him. He didn't like it one bit, and he was right not to. Not with those stains on even her shoes and fingernails now.

After they'd all gone, they left me a videotape so Granny-Mama could watch as much as she liked. She thought I was as good as a TV actor-person.

"Shouldn't he have protection?" Sheriff Longish asked blondie twice, once all the vans and other TV vehicles had gotten their interview and "statement" from me and were tooling off up the road.

"You planning on sleepin' over?" I asked him.

Blondie and me laughed at the look on his face.

Nothing happened for two more days and so we moved into what blondie called "phase two," i.e., getting me out in the public, away from here where Underwear Man would think there were sharpshooters behind every copse of red leaf.

This was exhausting but kinda fun. "Phase two" made me a celebrity—the psychic kid who knew all about the serial killer. It got me out in a local Wal-Mart, at another, this time higher-end, mall outside of Gainesville, and in a county hall meeting in the First Baptist Church on Highway 225 up near Lawley.

It was while driving home from that event that I saw Underwear Man for the first time in person. It was outside Dan Deavens Elementary School, and he was the crossing guard for all the little kids. Wearing a pale blue shirt with the white plastic stripes across his chest and his back and a pale blue cap. And of course his stains were all but three-dimensional, they were so many and so strong. I almost gave him away then, laughing at how much sense it all made. What better place to find kids? To find out which ones to take? What better way to gain their trust than wearing that uniform? He was even younger looking and better looking than I'd seen in my mind's eye. With big blue eyes to match. The kind of boy who'd model underwear for those Sears flyers that Granny-Mama would keep stuffed in her bathroom drawer and think I didn't know about.

He was very careful in holding all the kiddies back safely as we passed them by. They all knew who I was by then because of the TV and newspapers and they yelled and waved. And so did he. Our eyes locked as we slowly drove by. "Hello, Underwear Man." I mouthed the words to him. Then we were gone.

How he finally got me was kind of a surprise. But by

then he'd been on the hunt over a year and seven months, so he'd gotten pretty good at it. I'd been left alone less than a minute in the disabilities restroom the following afternoon, when blondie, who was guarding me, was distracted by what sounded like shots—actually fireworks he'd planned—going off outside the back window, and she stepped away briefly.

"Your face is very nice, but otherwise you ain't very pretty!" he said to me, just before he applied the chloroform hanky. That had been my fear, of course, because all the others had been so very pretty, head to toe pretty, pretty like he was, pretty like he must have been as a lil' child when he was being sexually molested.

Later on, when we was alone, and he was doing it to me, he kept on saying "So soft! So soft!" about my skin and body. "So soft!" Which was a nice compliment.

It hurt at first a lot, but then I thought about Sheriff Longish and that made it better. Of course I could have just peed myself all over to stop it, but I wanted to see what it felt like. Sex, I mean—having heard and read so much about it.

He'd read and heard by then too about the name the F.B.I. had given him and why. So even though he had my underwear ripped apart with his teeth when he began biting me to do his molestation and he was really ready to use it around my neck, he restrained himself. Taking a great deal of effort to do so, so he wouldn't be ever caught that way again.

"You'll have to leave, now they know where you are," I told him.

He was crying by then, the fit having passed. "I know," he said.

"You should go to Mexico," I said. "Unless you don't like dark-haired kids."

He looked up at me and smiled. "That was just what I was thinking."

This is what I know about drowning: some persons can hold their breath longer than others. No one can hold it longer than five minutes seventeen seconds underwater without a special apparatus. With all my conditions, I certainly can't. So when Underwear Man pushes my wheelchair into the pond. I'll just gulp as much water down as I can all at once and hope my body doesn't try to struggle. That'll happen in six minutes. He's cleared the pathway of all debris down to there and is walking back up to come get me. Sheriff Longish will blame himself for a while. But he'll get over it.

They say that drowning is the easiest death. And after all, my work here is done.

Imago Blue

When he opened his eyes upon a seamless, all-enveloping, pale lilac light, he immediately realized that he knew for certain these four things:

He was alive.

His name was Blue Andresson.

His official vocation was Investigator: privately established, financed, and (as a rule) client-paid; specializing in Difficult Interpersonal Relations and Potentially Criminal Conflicts.

And lastly, if he reached his hand out he would encounter—while his elbow was still slightly flexed—the surface of a soft, protective Heal-All within which he had been enclosed, and which had served to return him back to full physiological health over an unknown period of time, while he was seriously injured or chronically ill, and which a thrust-out fingernail would easily rip open.

There was one other thing he wished he knew but did not: What was he doing inside a Heal-All in the first place?

There would be time enough for that. His sense of his body odor was growing stronger by the second from long enclosure and he must get away from it. He reached out his right hand, struck the smooth surface, tore at it, and it collapsed all about him with a soft hiss.

Instantly a soft chiming began somewhere below the plinth upon which he lay.

He tried to sit up and found it difficult: His muscles wouldn't work, not even supported by his hands. He tried again and felt slightly nauseated.

The room around him was an even softer lilac color, nearly pearl; its surfaces were smooth, indistinguishably similar, at least from this level and position.

He tried to sit up again and this time achieved an inch or two of head height. His body was unclothed and the Heal-All's therapeutic dews were quickly drying in the ambient warming air. His chest hair was sparse, golden; his abdomen flat, muscled, his legs were long and also golden haired, his feet were large and personable.

A fourth attempt to sit up got him onto his elbows facing his large perfect toes, and what he now saw, since it slid open with a whoosh, was a door, through which three completely clothed and hooded figures stepped and immediately came to his side.

"You're awake, Mr. Andresson? How do you feel? Not too disoriented, we hope?" said One.

"You must be thirsty. And hungry too, I'm guessing," said Two.

He was. And nodded so.

"Your personal secretary has been notified," said Three. "You're unexpectedly early and she is out of town on her own business and can be here in a few hours. Should we contact her? Or a friend or relative? Your mother is listed as next of kin. There is as well as a relationship that might have been as close as fiancée before your injury."

A slight transparent tube arrived from out of nowhere right at his lips and he received a delicious cold drip of water that he then sucked at greedily. After which he said, "No. Thank you, don't bother anyone," somehow surprised by the deepness of his voice (was it because of this resonant little enclosed chamber?). "In fact, my secretary need not hurry back if she doesn't have to. I'd prefer her to finish her business already begun."

What he wanted more than anything else was time, he'd already decided. Because now there was another unanswered question: "How long have I been here? In the Medical Cocoon?"

"Close to a year": One.

"Don't worry about it, Mr. Andresson, you were very seriously injured": Two.

"You're fine now. Perfect, in fact": Three.

No, I'm not, Blue thought. I don't remember things. Things I believe I ought to remember.

The plinth tilted slowly and a shelf came out at his feet. He realized he was being stood up.

An opposite wall mirrored over and he could see himself in it.

"You see. You're perfect": Three, again?

He was in fact, physically perfect. Medium-height, handsome in a square-jawed, straight-nosed, blue-eyed way, with thin lips and a facial fuzz of light hair. His upper body was strong and muscular, with well-developed arms and legs. No scars apparent anywhere, naturally; the Heal-All would have gotten rid of any. No sign of any kind of deformity. Everything looked size appropriate, except maybe slightly larger than normal genitals. He figured he must be about thirty years old.

Why did all this seem ever so slightly, although by a mere hairsbreadth, off? Blue wished he knew.

There was more chiming now and One said: "Contamination is nonexistent. Quarantine off!"

Their masks melted off the medicals' faces and two were revealed as females, one male.

"We're going to stand here and help if you need help walking. Take one tiny step," Female one said.

She and the male medical held out supportive arms for him to lean upon. Blue did put out his hands and he was able to stand away from the plinth for a few seconds before total exhaustion set back in.

"Excellent start. Your physical rehabilitation will set in later today," Female one assured him. "It will be constant, and, I'm afraid, rather annoying at first."

"But it's necessary," the male said. "If you're to get on your feet and be a full member of our community again."

"We think you can do it in a few days. Less than a week," she added.

He lay back on the plinth and it slowly angled back so he was in a partially sitting position again.

They left and Medical Number Three arrived again with a tray in which he could smell simple food. Eggs, toast. He was ravenous.

The tray attached easily to the extensor sides that he just now noticed were part of his plinth-bed, and he could reach out for the transparent bulbs of food.

"We'll begin therapy with you reaching," Three said. She was the least attractive of the three medicals and the nicest.

"We'll also be exposing you to visual, audio, and then intellectual stimuli," she said.

A Vid-set suddenly turned itself on where the mirror had just been, with soft-focus moving pictures of the outer world: a countryside, a pond, an ocean, along with music he almost recognized.

"All you say is 'more' and it will provide you with stories, newscasts, weather, sports, specific information, whatever you ask," she added. "You can also ask it to repeat. Or to be only music, or only voice."

"I understand," Blue said. "I can control it by my voice."

"There is an important intercontinental air-race final taking place," she suggested.

His hands could barely grasp and hold the bulbs containing 1) a poached egg 2) a fruit juice concoction 3) a weak herbal tea. When he dropped the last one it bobbed right up and floated toward his hand again as though somehow attached.

He could do this, Blue decided.

Three fussed about him, covering his body with a light sheet, tucking it in, beneath. As she was leaving he asked:

"What was it?"

"What was what, Mr. Andresson?"

"My serious injury?—I can't seem to recall it."

"You really can't?"

"Not at all. No."

"That's probably because you were shot in the brain."

"I was shot in the brain?"

"Yes. Twice. Once in each lobe. In the brain twice and once each in the kidneys, the liver, and the heart."

With that, she sailed out of the room, humming to herself.

❖

Andresson Investigations inhabited a stylish three-room suite on the ninety-eighth floor of an upscale bronzed glass building at the northwestern transportation-hub edge of the city. The rooms were spacious, comfortably lighted with diffused and slightly dimmed afternoon sunlight, and with built-in storage areas. His own office appeared to be the most functional and most characterless of the rooms.

Another, slightly smaller office, had been converted by his secretary for use in her new part-time business, which as far as he could figure out involved stock option bids on speculative off-world futures. It was filled with computers and printer-scanners, all merrily chugging away by themselves, accessible to his secretary he assumed through the Vid-net. The third room, the outer waiting area, had received the most attention of the three in terms of design and expense—fine carpets, posh furniture, gleaming coffee tables, sculptures of lighting, individual framed artwork, etc. It all showed Andresson Investigations to be a successful business—to have been once successful.

It was six days after he'd awakened and Blue was just too bored and itching to do something, anything, to remain in the Heal-All Center. When he'd checked out, he'd been warned by Medicals One and Two there that he was still only at about seventy-four percent of his required physical capacity to continue his vocation as usual and that he would have to continue therapy for weeks more.

He'd noted with satisfaction in the downstairs lobby of this edifice that a new health club had opened twenty-six stories below. He'd sign up later today.

His secretary, a woman approximately forty-five years old, had not yet appeared except by Vid-screen phone. When she did, she remarked that although his vocational insurance had covered all the expenses included in keeping the agency afloat for six months, that she had become quickly immersed in her own sideline, and that she'd begun showing profits early enough in that sideline that she took over the suite's lease, utilities, and other incidentals for the following five and three-quarter month period.

She told Blue she was prepared to share the quarters with him for as long as he wished. She had no interest at all in his line, she stated rather bluntly, being a "fearful type, unlike yourself," whom she characterized as "curious and adventurous." She had referred his newer clients to a competitor at the other end of the city who was prepared to refer clients back as soon as Andresson was once again in business. She doubted that he would need a secretary for another few months yet, and she agreed to hire one for Blue when he did.

I'm an investigator," Blue had thought, the first time he'd clearly been able to think about his past and future in the Heal-All Center. "I'm privately established, financed, and client-paid. So I must have been pretty good. And I specialize in 'Difficult Interpersonal Relations' and 'Potentially Criminal Conflicts.' So I must have been very good."

It wasn't lost on him also that he couldn't have been all that good, or at least all that lucky, since he'd ended up so seriously wounded that it had required almost a year to return to health. Surely something or someone he'd been investigating had been responsible for putting those five bullets into fatally strategic spots of his body.

As an investigator it was his job to find out how that had happened—and why.

But right now it was his job to find out who he was, since that also remained alarmingly unfilled and in fact mostly blank.

His desk had six drawers. Two locked, one with a touch-print, the other with a key and vocal recognition. He had the key, and while the drawer's primitive system hesitated at first, it must have been voice-keyed because it did open upon the second utterance of a simple sentence, "Open up for me. Go on, open!"

In the first were leather billfolds filled with cheques and cash cards. Confirming that he was quite well off in business.

The other drawer held six files that had still been "open" at the time that he was so seriously injured.

He began reading them.

Looking for a stylus to take notes with, he rummaged in a bottom drawer and there Blue came upon a small leather woman's purse. Inside it, no ID but the expected articles: lipstick, compact and powder, breath mints, eye shadow, etc. Presumably, he thought, it belonged to the fiancée who had been mentioned in the Heal-All Center twice, but who had made no attempt to see Blue while he'd been there.

No surprise. He probably wouldn't have seen her if she had tried to contact him. The reason being, he didn't remember her at all. Didn't remember any kind of close sexual or affectionate relationship with a woman. He could bring up no face, voice, nor perfume that was at all familiar.

Some other faces did come up as he remained awake and pensive, if very slowly: his mother's (after four days) and just barely, and actually just before he accepted a Vid-screen phone call from her, confirming that's who she was. She rather looked like a much more refined version of himself, at least from the neck up, with a porcelain complexion and a darker version of his light hair. She also had a familiar-sounding voice, but Blue didn't truly recognize her, and he didn't hide that fact, and she was sweet and accepting about that fact, saying twice how she'd been certain he'd never awaken and certainly not with a full memory, not after what the medicals had told her when he'd first entered the Heal-All Center.

Once Blue had seen some Vids of her, his former secretary also seemed somewhat if again not deeply familiar. She'd been fairly new anyway, he'd been told, having only worked for him for four months before his shooting, so there was no big surprise there.

In what little there was of Blue's memory beyond the

cognitive, the practical—i.e., what the brain surgeon-bots had hurriedly worked on getting reconnected before sticking him into the Heal-All cocoon a year before, there had been traces of memory of a male his own age, or thereabouts, nice-looking, darker-haired, slender, named Bern or Burn, something like that.

A relatively strong trace memory of affection was connected with him. Perhaps they had been boyhood pals who'd remained friendly after they'd grown up. That would be okay. He would probably be trustworthy—if anyone could be considered so in a life that had nearly ended, violently, explosively, like his almost had. No word from this friend, of course, and frankly Blue hadn't trusted his "mother" or his own memory sense of her well enough to ask her who this male friend might be.

But he had no trace memory of any woman. So whom did this purse and this make up belong to?

"Face it, Blue," he said to his bathroom mirror, shaving before leaving the Heal-All Center, "She could be anyone. You're a hot and handsome man." Medical Number Three had slipped in while he was napping on Awake Day number two and made her own investigations of certain lower body areas of his physiological condition. When he'd joked about it to Medical Number One, she'd asked, "Would you like that to stop? Or continue?" He'd said "continue, please" and she had replaced the lower-status doctor with herself. This also had not been surprising. As far as he could figure, his personality structure was undoubtedly that of a person who'd had great looks and who'd used them to get what he wanted and needed. Except…

Odd, this memory business.

Now Blue recognized that he had the most difficult job of all: finding out which case had come so close to doing him in.

He'd need to know that. He hadn't decided whether to avoid anyone and anything connected with it in the future or not. Maybe, some little mental itch suggested somewhere in the periphery of his mind, maybe he might also figure out why he'd been targeted.

❖

It was later that afternoon that the downstairs auto-desk called and told him he had a visitor. A Vid showed her to be a woman in her mid forties, made up rather severely, dressed carefully, and surprisingly ethnic looking, perhaps from off-world? He knew from the Vid-channels he'd been watching that very few people chose to highlight their ethnic origins by retaining inborn characteristics. Especially when it was so easy to lose them. The name given for her was Dusk Martila, with no matronymic or patronymic supplied, and which meant nothing to him.

Naturally Blue asked the auto-desk if she'd been to his office before, and it named the date he'd been told he had been killed. Negative. Several weeks before then and once since, the auto desk said, so Blue let her come up. The auto lift CT scanned her for metal and other types of weapons or powders or explosives. Negative.

"What can I do for you?" he greeted her at the door. Close up, Martila was taller, and more prepossessing. Her voice was somewhat guttural, too, with a slight and difficult to place accent, so she'd not had vocal cord reparation either. On purpose, it must be, as she dressed well-to-do to be able afford the simple operation.

"Blue Andresson?" she asked, slightly surprised.

"We've not met?" he asked. Then added, "You heard of my Heal-All experience?"

"We have met, yes, but you are—changed," she said.

"Only physically," he assured her. "You didn't take Davis's suggestion to go to my colleague, Mr. Chango Blocksson?"

"I did. We met. I didn't trust him. Not like you," Martila said, not looking to be all that trusting in Blue either; at least not at the moment.

They sat and his work screens brought up her case and the work done so far, and in seconds they were discussing the business she'd come for: which had apparently been held in abeyance for almost a year. It was a Missing Person: and both a Difficult Interpersonal Relation with a Potentially Criminal Conflict. Her first husband had vanished three years previously, mysteriously, from his place of business, which he shared with his wife. Through Blue's earlier efforts, she had already received permits to continue operating the family business in full sole authority, and even sell and or lease it out. But now she had met a countryman, she said, and he wanted her to get a more permanent declaration so they could unite their businesses and "other matters," which Blue took to be interpersonal and probably marriage. "Also," she added, "before you ended up in a Heal-All, you left a message saying you thought you had an idea where my husband might have gone to. I took it you were looking into that idea."

Blue didn't recall that at all, of course. And if he had, he had left no clue to himself among these screen files on the case.

Martila renewed the bank number where money could be deposited into his agency's account and left. For the next half hour, Blue listened to his many notes on the case as the auto-Vid played them back to him. To his surprise, he made a mental connection that the pre-Heal-All Blue had never made before, concerning a bank account and an important client.

He caught Martila by pad-phone in her private vehicle,

not very far away from his office, and checked the information. The minute Blue mentioned it, she grew excited.

"Yes," she said, darkly, "this I can well believe of this person," and she used some kind of foreign obscenity. Blue said he would need as much information as she had on the new suspect, and he would delve into it more deeply.

Feeling renewed, and suddenly comfortable in his new skin now that he had proved to himself that he was useful, he strode over to the floor-high windows and stared out through the triple-paned, multiply tinted glass. The blue-white sun was setting, quickly falling behind the artificial-looking skyscraper scrim of the city's far horizon. Only the dull orange sun still hung in the crepuscular sky, casting a warm evening glow.

❖

"It was a lovely funeral, Blue," Andre Clarksdotter gushed. "I spared no expenses. After all, you're my only child. Our life insurance was all paid up and it had accrued so well; it's been decades since anyone has died and I decided to do it up full scale. Everyone came. Family, of course, they flew in from all over. Many of your school friends, and even some of your clients."

She'd pre-fed the Vid-screen before arriving at his flat and it now showed moving Vids of the ceremony—sound turned down—and afterward at the celebratory feast. He could clearly see sitting next to his mother the very same young man who'd popped into his memory upon awakening, and who appeared at least as upset as she was. Then the Med Center people arrived and Blue's inert and by then fully cocooned body was ceremonially placed in the Heal-All, people said their good-byes, and it was floated out.

Andre already knew of Blue's memory loss and couldn't

have been sweeter or more explanatory as he asked who each person shown was. When he reached the bereft, handsome young man with the dark curling hair, she said, "Bruno. Of course."

"Bruno?" He tried it out and it sounded right.

"Bruno Thomasson, your adoring fiancé. He hasn't found anyone else, you know, in all the months since. In fact, Blue, from what he was saying the other day when I called to tell him of you, I do believe he wants to try to see you again."

"Bruno?" Blue now asked, stunned. "Then I was…"

"A woman. Yes, Blue. Didn't anyone explain it to you at the Med Center? We seldom come back the second time as the same gender. Your aunt / uncle Clay Clarkson? the one who died in that fall, climbing the Capsilian Mountains? She once explained all the complex genetics of it to me, but you know how dense I can be about scientific matters."

"So that's Bruno!" Blue now said, not Burn, of course, and looked at the Vid-screen as the compelling figure was highlighted and zoomed in on, the large dark, misty eyes, the downturned full lips and picturesquely sunken cheeks.

"You don't have to see him, you know, if it makes you—nervous," Andre settled on, and changed the subject back to those in the family she would never speak to again because they simply never even acknowledged Blue's death, never mind Andre's grief.

It all began to make sense now: the purses in the office and at Blue's flat with no ID in them. The scarcity of male clothing in the closets: two suits—both new looking. Scarcely anything in the way of male accessories. Only the most basic toiletries in the bath. It also explained the rare photos: all of them of other family members, not one of them showing Blue.

He had to ask, "Mother? What kind of woman was I?"

Andre only wavered a second. "Frankly, Blue, you were

a complete pain in the ass. You were a physically tough, emotionally cold, adventure-loving, overconfident, thoughtless, hard-living, self-absorbed egomaniac to almost everyone but Bruno. You drove me crazy as an adolescent. I needed most of the family and sometimes City Services, too, to help raise you. In truth, you were such a bitch to most of us that it was a constant wonder that someone didn't kill you years ago."

As Blue absorbed that, Andre added, with a nervous little laugh, "We're all hoping that those qualities will fit you better—now that you're a male."

When Blue chuckled, Andre added, "You know, Blue, while it's a difficult adjustment for many, some people only begin to really find themselves when they're second-born."

❖

Chango Blocksson's Vid-screen image was of an older man, but his voice was older than his appearance and Blue was forced to conclude that he'd done at least one expensive voluntarily short period in a Heal-All age-proofing himself. Blue's mother had done two of those herself and looked almost Blue's age.

Two of the cases Blocksson had taken from Blue's six had been solved. Cases closed. Two of the clients, Dusk Martila and another woman, had chosen to not to accept Blocksson's services. And two cases remained in progress: one a long-term private investigation by two wealthy brothers of their industrialist father's concerns: "Very straightforward and utterly paranoid," according to Chango. "They think he's hiding their eventual heritage." Another, an equally long-term search for an amateur pilot, a playboy, lost over Oceania, whom his family needed declared dead—or alive, and non-compos mentis, they almost didn't care which.

"I don't buy anyone involved in these two cases as even possessing a weapon, never mind using one on you," Chango Blocksson declared. "Their motives aren't impelling enough," he added, even before Blue could ask his opinion. But it confirmed Blue's own surprisingly strong investigative intuition.

"This Martila woman, however…well, her I just don't know. They're off-worlders, you know: Albergrivians, and whatever those people do is weird and mixed up with that cockamamie religion they've got."

"The sixth case?" Blue asked. "Did you look at that long enough to see if it was more than a simple potential female infidelity?"

"It looked like a simple female love triangle. By the way, you look terrific," Chango added. "And I've got to thank you. I met my fourth wife at your funeral. A second or third cousin of yours who came along with others. We're married five months: So we're now distantly related. She says you should come to dinner. Bring that guy Bruno, too, if you're still seeing him?"

"Should I be?" Blue asked.

"Everyone at the funeral seemed to think so. He was all busted up. But of course things may be a little iffy between the two of you."

After Chango signed off, Blue made a Vid-call to Bruno. Luckily, he wasn't in and asked for a message to be left. This close up, Bruno's photo made a very strong impression. Shaken, Blue left no message at all, even though he knew the Vid would take a trace of his call.

All the rest of the day, Blue threw himself into the Martila case. Leads had developed in the year since he was gone, and suddenly they began edging out into possibilities.

One lead directly shot into a Albergrivian Benefit Society, and its president, a publicity-shy character named Aptel

Movasa who had moved the organization out of downtown to a local Civic Center hub, only a few streets from Blue's office. Perhaps a drop-in visit was in order?

Blue had used the transportation hub stations there but he didn't recall ever going beyond the little concentration of public buildings another two streets over to the commercial area, which, now as he walked that way, was clearly evident by the increased pedestrian traffic.

The familiar, male-female, two-headed bust stood at one end of a pedestrian-only street, and it was also marked that it tolerated none but ultra-light, public, surface vehicles. The second thing Blue noticed were several storefronts given to inter-world transport, inter-world freight, and inter-world currency conversion. In each window, the strangely square script of the reformed Albergrivian alphabet translated simple phrases.

The north side of the street, for most of the block, was given over to what seemed a modern enough looking hotel named Rha Cantrobergle and described as an "Alberge for Off-Planet Travelers." Sure enough, across the street, the next half dozen shop fronts on the southern side were given over to Albergrivian ethnic food specialties, what appeared to be native clothing and other dry goods, and what might be a combination tea room and Skimko parlor.

His phone-pad went off and he read the tea room's address as the same as last given for Aptel Movassa.

He knew he would look out of place the second he stepped in the door, so he didn't attempt to be anyone but himself.

Through the haze of Spital-Leaf smoke, only one person of the dozen or so elderly Albergrivian gentlemen seated around floor-mounted smokers looked up from the games at their complex Skimko boards.

"Zha Andresson," Blue introduced himself to a clerk. "Seeking Zha-Kas Movasa." The ethnic honorific got a few more heads turned his way.

"Does Zha-Kas know the Zha?" the tea-counter clerk asked. He was young, thin, typically unattractive, and given his awful complexion, unquestionably addicted to carbonated drinks.

"Unfortunately, this Zha has not had the pleasure," Blue said. He knew he was being scanned from another office or at least being checked out by some minion just making a Skimko move at a table nearby.

The clerk caught a nearly invisible signal and brought one refill to a pair of ancient players, and a barrage of Albergrivian chatter ensued. The clerk bowed away, taking the used cartridge with him.

"Zha-Kas Pirto remarked how more lovely than an Albergrivian woman are the young men of this world," the clerk tittered.

Blue turned and bowed to the flatterer, who curlicued an age-spotted hand in response, without looking up from his complex, three-level game.

Behind his counter again, the clerk apparently read off a message, because he said, "Will the Zha follow, please."

Behind the back wall curtain of red-reed, a small elevator slid open and Blue stepped in.

Just as the doors closed on him, Blue heard a baritone shout he was certain was directed at himself; too late for him to worry how hostile it might be.

The lift flew up twenty-five floors and flashed open onto what seemed to be a rooftop garden with a central fountain. Beneath an awning, a standard desk much altered by colorful ethnic throws and runners, and behind it was an elderly Albergrivian, almost hidden within a throne-like chair constructed of the same red-reed, this time twisted into arabesques.

Blue bowed slightly three times approaching and used the correct honorific and Movasa waved him to a seat. A slender youth almost identical to the clerk downstairs immediately brought them wide-mouthed mugs of a fragrant purple-tinged tea, and vanished. Movasa quickly sipped his, to show it was harmless and tasty.

Blue followed and presented his credentials.

"A simple case of a vanished businessman," Blue explained. "It eluded my predecessor. She apparently was unaware of the wide-ranging knowledge of the Zha-Kas."

"To the contrary," the soft-voiced, unattractive old Albergrivian said. "She sat where Zha Andresson now sits, and she lacked all the social graces. How could a person speak to her?"

"How indeed! Apologies."

"She might have been a sibling to yourself, Zha."

"We never met," Blue truthfully said, couching it so that if lie detection were built into the table or chair he would not be suspect.

"She was lovely, like the women of this world. But she could not equal yourself, Zha. Already in the tea parlor below they are replaying the Vid taken during your brief visit and perhaps saying and doing unclean things…in your honor, Zha."

Blue had done enough homework on Albergrive society to believe this might be taken either as a provocation or as a compliment: he decided to take it as a compliment. He smiled.

"Worse than her attitude, Zha," Movasa went on, "Was her ignorance of proper manners."

"The Zha who wishes to"—Blue purposely used an Albergrivian word that could either mean "crucial conversation" or "sexual intercourse," depending solely upon its tonal inflection—"with a Zha-Kas must acquaint himself with proper manners."

Movasa laughed at the double-edged witticism.

"Tell, me Zha Andresson, how may this old Zha-Kas be of help?" Movasa asked.

"An attractive woman client"—and here Blue used the Albergrivian term he'd especially learned to describe one who was both widowed and yet not—"seeks her husband long missing." He produced his phone-pad and flashed the most flattering videos of her he could locate. "This Zha naturally believes the Zha-Kas would be able to assist. Her name is Zhana Martila. She wishes to now be Zhannia Martila," making it clear that she wanted to be single again.

"To remarry a Zha of this world?"

"Indeed not. To marry an Albergrivian. But," Blue quickly added, "I believe one who is mainstreamed into this world's society and work."

"A lad ignorant of the ways of his people," Movasa said.

"Or one who is knowledgeable and…uninterested."

"More and more such Zhaos exist," Movasa sighed, using a term unfamiliar to Blue. "Perhaps seduced by love. And Zhana Martila? What does Zha Andresson think of her?"

"We have only met once, briefly. But she is honest, and she seems without external motive. Three years her husband is gone. The Zhana seems to be beyond anger, reproof, or even revenge."

"On our world, one favor gives birth to another," Movasa said.

"This Zha will of course be in your debt in the future,"

Blue admitted. He suspected this was how the old power-broker worked anyway.

"This Zha will put out a"—here Movasa used a word meant to signify query but also demand—"for this missing Zha Martila. You will hear from me in three double sunsets."

"Whatever future, non-illegal, request you make of this Zha will be yours," Blue assured him.

They sipped their tea and watched the blue sun prepare to drop below the horizon. The sky flashed green several times, then settled into dull orange.

Movasa was called indoors, and Blue stood up and began bowing to leave, but the old man pulled him over and gave him a kiss on his cheek. "So lovely, these males!"

As Blue stepped into the elevator, Movasa looked out of his office and said, "This will take you directly to the street. That way you may avoid disrespectful words."

"You mean like those words I heard as I stepped in before?"

"Those words were not so much disrespectful as they were descriptive—if crude." Movassa smiled.

❖

Bruno Thomasson looked far better in a video than he did even in still photos. Blue found himself reminded of what the Albergrivians had said several times about the "lovely males" of this world. No wonder women like his mother worked so hard to keep up.

When he'd returned to his office after the meeting with Movasa, Blue had immediately taken a "crash-course" in that paired planet's people's interpersonal relations, with an especial look into their sexuality, a topic he'd ignored totally before going to meet Movasa, if not exactly to his peril, at least to his slight discomfiture.

He was surprised to see that same-sexuality was a fairly recent development among those off-worlders, and one that had only taken fire when the two planets had once made contact. Even now, it was not much practiced on their home world, and it seemed to be chiefly a cross-cultural phenomenon, actually more spoken of than acted upon, even here in the City, among those who visited or had immigrated. Among Albergrivian women it was all but unknown at home, and it was rare here; however, it seemed widespread among Albergrivian men who had relocated. But even among those newcomers, the author of the short documentary Blue watched believed, it was more spoken of and written about than actually practiced. Acceptable mostly because of some ancient Albergrivian texts and poems that everyone learned at school in their early years, detailing the legendary loves of great warriors and their teen male lovers.

Blue's world's athletes and male celebrities were the main fantasy choices of both younger and older Albegrivian men, who filled out their fan clubs and paid astronomical sums for porn-Vids of their idols (a few of whom seemingly and quite callously produced them specifically to cash in, ruthlessly locating and exploiting the very few existing Albergrivian beauties for their videos).

Blue wondered if he might bring this topic up later on at dinner, because at long last Bruno Thomasson had called back and left a message asking if they might meet for dinner.

Blue would have to see. He tried to recall what his mother had said about Bruno, besides the fact that he'd been smitten with Blue as a woman enough to propose marriage. Given the vast Thomas family holdings, its long and colorful history, and its political and financial status in the City, Bruno must have been crazy about such an unlikely mate for him as a tough woman investigator. So Blue was gracious as he could be on the Vid-screen responding and said he was "looking forward" to "seeing Bruno again"…

The restaurant Bruno chose was an expensive one, so he wasn't hiding this meeting from his clan. In honor of such a classy date, Blue dressed as well as possible.

All the more of a surprise then when the maitre d' showed him to a private table set apart from the rest of the diners by floor-high mirrors and metal panels.

However, at it sat not Bruno Thomasson but two strangers. They introduced themselves to Blue as Thomas family attorneys, and immediately asked if Blue would sign a quitclaim on the family.

"That's not legally needed," he said, only half surprised by this tactic. "As a Bi-Vivid I have no claim whatsoever upon Bruno Thomasson no matter what prearrangements were made."

"Agreed. This quitclaim, however, provides you with the following sum"—the female of the two pointed to the line and the large amount—"but only if Bruno Thomasson also signs it."

Meaning that if Bruno wanted out after this date, buying Blue off would be more or less legal.

"I'll sign. But I may not ever claim the money. Wealth is so…boring! Don't you think?" Blue asked, sipping his cocktail. He scrawled a signature almost as an afterthought.

Evidently they didn't agree it was boring, because they got up and left without another word.

"That's *not* something the old Blue would have done," Bruno said. He'd been behind a panel or mirror observing and stepped forward now. His voice was velvety and higher than

Blue would have expected. He was taller, too. Beautifully dressed, of course. "Or something *she* would have said," Bruno added.

Blue smiled politely and held out a hand, saying "Blue Andresson. The Second." He offered the cocktail already delivered to the table.

Bruno gestured, and Blue invited him to sit.

"Also, Blue the First would have phoned me immediately upon awakening from the Heal-All," Bruno said.

"A year in a Heal-All does not, despite the popular myths, provide full memory retention," Blue said. "And then there is the natural awkwardness of the situation."

"You mean with the attorneys. Not my idea at all. I assure you, Blue."

"I believe you, Bruno. But no, the awkwardness I meant was that both of us now use the same restroom facilities. My predecessor's very flimsy personal file on Bruno Thomasson did not include or highlight...personal flexibility," he ended up saying.

"Very flimsy file?" Bruno asked.

"Extremely flimsy...for such a professional investigator," he admitted.

"Maybe she kept it all in her head?" Bruno suggested.

"Unquestionably."

"Whereas she was herself quite flexible," Bruno said, and smiled a bit.

"Your eyes are pale green," Blue said. "That doesn't show in photos or videos. There they look gray or blue. Is that color natural?"

"Completely," Bruno said. "Do you like green eyes?"

"On you, yes."

"You are the same size and general muscular build as the First."

"Does that satisfy you?" Blue asked.

"Yes."

"Let's order," Blue said. "I'm hungry."

Again Bruno's smile. Blue's predecessor had been as frank.

The dinner proceeded with discreet little references back and forth. Before dessert, Blue said, "I meant it before. I have no claim on you or your family at all. I died. And the fact that I'm alive again is merely a product of our inborn physiology, and has nothing to do with your previous engagement."

"So you believe that theory that existence under double suns provides for double lives," Bruno asked. "Bi-Vividism, you called it."

"It seems irrefutable, at least among the higher vertebrates. And it seems to apply both to us and to the Albergrivians."

"How scientific and how philosophical of you."

"Isn't it? So if you leave after dinner and I never hear from you again…well, that's fine with me."

"Is it, truly?" Bruno asked.

"I said it was."

"Except, my dear Second, the spy camera my attorneys had placed under the table to ensure that you carried no hidden weapons also reveals something else." Bruno froze the picture and passed the phone-pad to Blue.

"Oh that! Well, I've got an excuse. This body is new, and I never exactly know how it will respond to *any* specific stimulus."

Bruno did something with a foot under the table and then froze that and passed the phone photo to Blue.

"I, on the other hand, have been in this body for many years. And I'm even more surprised to see *this* reaction."

The photo he showed now was of his own lap.

Their desserts arrived: tottering cream and cake towers of deliciousness threaded with platinum candy.

"As my predecessor might say," Blue looked at Bruno closely, searching for anything resembling an imperfection, "I'm pretty much ready for anything. Lead the way."

"You see, Second. *That's* new," Bruno said. He picked up Blue's hand and brought it to his mouth, where he nibbled on the edge of Blue's palm before saying, "Your predecessor would have *led* the way…I think I'm going to like this change."

❖

The address Aptel Movasa had sent over was in the River Heights section of the City, and quite upscale. The Lanscro Vidis Air-Skimmer Showroom was a sixtieth-floor penthouse, all the better for off-the-roof test-drives, Blue assumed. It was quietly posh, with the fountain and gardens he'd come to expect with well-to-do Albergrivian business offices. A dozen of the luxurious Black Hawk and Silver Hawk models were strewn about the lawns and flower beds: ranging from the sportier four-seaters to the deluxe seven-door, fifteen-window limos with separated brougham-style driver pods, only available in muted colors. Blue's eye, however, was immediately drawn to a tiny, quietly glowing, low-cut, cobalt blue two-seater, identified as a Thunder Hawk.

"The upholstery matches your eyes," he heard behind him and turned to the voice belonging to a middle aged Albergrivian gentleman who was taller, stouter, and better looking than any off-worlder he'd ever seen.

"Zha-Kas Lascro Vidis?" Blue asked.

"None of that is needed. It's *Mr.* Vidis to you. What do you think? Stunning, isn't it? Brand new. We have the first three Thunder Hawks off the robo-assembly line in the entire City." He continued on with specifications, speeds, handling and maneuverability reports. "Mr…?"

Of course the Vidis dealership would have the first three of the model. This was probably the highest-end and most successful air-skimmer dealer in town.

"Andresson."

"Mr. Andresson. Well, should we wrap it up for you, Mr. Andresson?"

"Let me think about it. Meanwhile, I have come on a slightly less mercantile matter."

"Ah."

He immediately turned Blue away, heading him toward a two-story high, glassed-in office area.

"Zha-Kas Aptel Movasa believes you might be able to help me in locating…someone."

"Aha. You see, my dear." He turned to a woman in her late thirties, less slender than most of her race, with bright eyes and the typical straight black hair. She was dressed well, if very quietly. "I was telling my wife, Mr. Andresson, the minute we noticed you arrive, that you would be someone special. You know Movasa?"

Blue reached to take her hand but she bowed slightly and moved backward out of reach. He noticed she wore dark laced gloves. "Pleased to make your acquaintance," Blue said.

She immediately and wordlessly withdrew as the two men sat on facing if not matching love seats, but she seemed to Blue to hover, and even listen in on their conversation. For all he knew she might even be recording it.

Blue explained his purpose and said that Movasa had somehow or other gotten word that Zha Martila might have worked in some capacity for Vidis.

The Albergrivian denied it, politely enough, and turned to just behind Blue to ask his wife if she remembered any such named worker either here or at their other showroom. Evidently not. She then said something and Vidis told Blue she had another appointment.

Blue then explained why he needed to find Zha Martila for his client. Vidis sympathized and assured him he would put out the word among those who worked for and with him for this fellow off-worlder.

They drank more of the purple tea, iced this time, with little pale yellow flowers crushed over the surface for a slightly spicy flavor. It was a pleasant, if inutile half hour, and Blue left relaxed but frustrated. Of course Movasa had promised, but then perhaps that promise was less substance than off-world formality.

Even so, as he stood in the lift dropping through the open courtyard of the center of the building, Blue felt odd, as though something were not quite right.

He'd come to realize in this short period since his renewal that his intuition was actually quite useful. It had worked with the meeting with Bruno last night; it had worked with Movasa, and now he explored it a bit more.

The problem wasn't Vidis, who seemed about as straightforward an Albergrivian as any he'd encountered—one reason, Blue guessed, for his success in the City. The problem was Mrs. Vidis. She looked slightly off; she acted oddly, and those black laced gloves…Definitely something wrong.

He'd begun going to the exercise club in his office building, so he was both confident and ready for most anything when he stepped out of the lift and into what he only now saw with one step out was not the glittering lobby he'd entered from before, but instead a lower floor, possibly a basement.

One glance at the lift's inner panel showed him he was two floors below the street. Not where he had signaled: so someone had brought him here.

Blue immediately flattened himself to a side wall, and thus missed the thrown kris that embedded itself into the lift's back wall, as the doors closed. He dropped down and tumbled to the other side of the little corridor while a second kris embedded in the wall he'd just been at, and he rolled forward in a zigzag pattern hearing two blades more whizz by him.

He was inside a shallow doorway when he saw a figure in his peripheral vision and dropped down to miss the fifth and he thought last blade, then he exploded out and into the corridor, where he used his martial arts knowledge to jump atop the figure, wrapping his legs around its midsection, pummeling it with the sides of his hands as the figure fell down sideways and tried to escape.

It was Mrs. Vidis, as he'd suspected, And as she lay upon the corridor floor, he held down first one hand, then the other, and tore off the lace gloves.

Each thumb was deformed, thinner than normal, and artificially padded: often the sign of a recent, voluntary, Heal-All experience.

She turned to him, her eyes blazing with fury. "How could you possibly know?"

Blue wrapped her hands in a silk handkerchief and knotted it twice, then stood up and pulled her to her feet.

"Know what, Zha Martila?" Blue asked. "That you were my murderer? Or that you had undergone a gender transformation in a Heal-All?"

"Either," she said, softly. "Both?"

"Surely you've already learned what an advantage it is being both genders? Take you, for example, ruthless as a man to hide your secret, and yet in the end with inefficient upper body strength to throw me off just now. Your trade-off worked against you, Zha. And mine worked for me."

"Stop calling me Zha!" she pouted, not prettily at all, then said, "So now what? You turn me in?"

"Not necessarily. After all, I'm coming to like this body. Like your own new body, it feels a lot more natural to me than the other one ever did. I take it Zha Vidis knows nothing of this?"

"Nothing at all. He only knew that I needed an operation before we could marry. I paid for it myself."

"I have recorded this entire encounter, Martila. This is what I'll need, to keep your secret." Blue outlined it: 1) a death notice for Dusk Martila. 2) a signed confession for the murder of Blue Andresson, the First, and 3) "appropriate compensation."

"The confession is so that I won't ever try this solution again?" she asked. "Yes. Yes. Of course, yes to all three of terms."

❖

He'd heard about and once, too (in another life, he believed), had even seen videos of the Bruno's family's in-City estate. It covered the rooftops of three buildings, in a giant L, those connected by various hundred-story-high transparent, enclosed galleries.

He'd driven into a large lift and had been lifted to a valet at a parking area, one floor beneath the penthouse itself opening to a large open to the sky garden. A young usher checked his face against the list, seemed impressed, and handed him off to an usherette, all of them clad in the bronze and teal family colors. She brought him to a raised deck opening onto several four-story-high, half-open rooms: scene of Bruno's birthday party. People he assumed were family members were streaming across the galleries from other buildings onto the deck. Blue immediately spotted the two attorneys from last week, both of whom smiled, and one of whom even raised a glass in a toast.

As he stepped onto the top step of the deck and stood looking over the hundred or more guests, he heard a voice speak out, "Blue Andresson. Fiancé to Bruno Thomasson." All heads turned to him, and a stylishly slender young woman with dark hair, closely encased in a platinum-threaded gown, sprang to take Blue's hand, saying, "I'm Claudia, Bruno's younger sister."

When the meetings and greetings died down, Bruno appeared, casually dressed, unlike the others, in an iridium-threaded open-necked blouson and slate gray slacks. He was barefoot and bareheaded and he cut through the crowd to kiss first his sister and then Blue. Applause greeted him and even greater applause greeted these gestures.

An hour later, Blue had met most of the immediate family as well as a score of nephews and cousins and great aunts. He felt enveloped by all but perhaps Bruno's mother, the family matriarch and current CEO of most of its holdings. She'd been polite but cool, and Blue thought he could live with that.

They had come to the toasts and well-wishings and the gifts, when they were all startled to see a Thunder-Hawk air skimmer approach and settle upon the roof, just beyond the deck. Its large, multicolored ribbons signified that it, too, was a gift.

Partygoers dropped down to look it over, and it was wonderful to see.

Blue heard the matriarch, Marcella Thomasdotter, saying

to someone, "It's not from me! I *wish* I'd thought of it as a gift for him."

Bruno pulled Blue along and over to the skimmer, where someone had found a tiny gift card. He immediately turned and threw his arms around Blue, kissing him again and again. The applause rose and died down.

Sometime later on, Blue was just coming back to the party after a visit to freshen up when an usher intercepted him and led him to one edge of a large chamber where Marcella was seated. She swanned out a hand, which he took and kissed and then sat down across from her.

"I didn't like you the *first time* I met you," she said.

"I'm afraid I can't remember that meeting, although I've tried," he honestly told her.

"His adjustment is a wonderful proof of his continued commitment," Marcella said.

Bruno, she meant.

"Yes, it is. And I'm grateful."

That somewhat mollified her.

"And the bauble?" she waved in the direction of the air-skimmer. "I hope it didn't set you back too much? That would be imprudent."

"No. Not at all. It turned out that someone owed me," he said with a casual shrug. "It was merely a piece of business."

"He looks good in it," she said; Bruno was in the driver's seat and waving to them indoors.

"Diamonds always shine brighter for their setting," Blue said. "That was one thing I learned—the first time around."

"Live and learn. Then live again and learn even more," Marcella quipped. She stood, and when he did, too, she took his arm and began to lead him out to the party. "Of course you'll both live here in one of the residences when you're in-

City. But we really must find something unique for you in the countryside. Do you like the beach?"

"Does Bruno?"

"I think we're going to get along, just fine, Blue. Just fine."

Hunter

It was sunset when Ben Après drove up to the hanging shingle that read "Sagoponauk Rock Writers Colony," and on a smaller, added-on shingle, "Visitors see Dr. Ormond." An oddly autumnal sunset despite the early summer date and no hint of dropping temperature, as Ben stepped out of the ten-year-old Volvo that hadn't given him a bit of its usual temperament on the long trip, as he urinated on a clump of poison ivy until it was shiny wet, as he surveyed what appeared to be yet another rolling succession of green-humped New England hills.

The muted colors of the sunset fitted Ben's own fatigued calm following a week of torment, his final uncertain decision to come, and his more recent anxieties since the turn off the main road that he'd never find the place, that he'd driven past it several times already, the directions had seemed so sketchy.

He found himself gaping at the sky as though it would tell him something essential, or as though he'd never see one like it again. Then he made out some houses nestled in a ravine: the colony. He'd made it!

❖

Dr. Ormond was easy to find. The paved road that dipped down into the colony ended at his front door in a shallow oval parking lot radiating dirt roads in several directions. Two cars with out-of-state plates were parked next to a locally licensed beat-up baby-blue pickup.

The active, middle-aged man who stepped out of the house chomping an apple introduced himself, then looked vaguely upset when Ben introduced himself and asked where he would be staying.

There appeared to be a mix-up, Dr. Ormond said. Another guest—and here Ormond threw the apple down and went on to mention a woman writer of some repute—had unexpectedly accepted the colony's earlier invitation, thought by them to have been forgotten. She'd taken the last available studio. They hadn't been certain Ben was coming this season either. Victor Giove hadn't heard from Ben in weeks. Of course, Victor hadn't heard from Joan Sampson either, and she'd come too, though naturally they were all delighted she was here.

Ormond motioned behind himself sketchily. Ben saw a white clapboard, pitched-roof house standing alone on a patch of grassy land. He supposed that was her studio: the one he was to have lived in.

Before he could ask, a plump, middle-aged woman—her apron fluttering, her hair in disarray—was waving to them from the doorway. She'd already telephoned Victor, she called out. He was on his way. Mrs. Ormond, Ben supposed.

He leaned against the Volvo. Darkness was quietly dropping into the ravine. One or two lights were turned on in the Ormonds' house, other lights appeared suddenly in more distant studios. Ben wanted to wake up tomorrow morning in this enchanted little glen, to spend sunny and rainy days here, long afternoons, crisp mornings, steamy nights. He would not allow the mix-up to affect his decision. After all the inner turmoil, he was glad he'd come. He wasn't leaving.

Above all, he was grateful to Victor Giove, who was

jogging toward them now, accompanied by a large, taffy-colored Irish hound, the two racing, skirting the big oak, circling Ben and Dr. Ormond, the dog barking, then nuzzling Ben's hand for a caress; Giove hardly out of breath, glad to see Ben. He took Ben's hand, clasped his shoulder, smiled, and was as openly welcoming as Ormond hadn't been.

Victor was tan already. His curly, dark head already sparkled with sun-reddened hair. He looked healthier and more virile than he'd ever looked in the city: an advertisement for country living with his handsome, open-featured face, his generous, beautifully muscled body that loose clothing like the old T-shirt and corduroys he was wearing could never disguise. Ben felt Victor's warmth charge into his own body as they touched, and he knew that all things were possible this summer: even the impossible: even Victor Giove.

"There's no place here for Ben to stay," Dr. Ormond protested, once they'd gotten inside the Ormonds' living room.

"What about the little cottage?' Victor asked. "That's empty."

"What little cottage?"

"Out by the pond. I passed it today. It's all closed up. You don't need a full studio, do you, Ben? Of course he doesn't. He'd love the little cottage."

"It's a half-hour walk from here to there," Ormond said, unpersuaded.

Ben suspected he'd be crazy about the little cottage.

"He's young," Victor argued. "It's not far for him."

"But it isn't ready."

"Sure it is. You helped clean it up yourself. Remember? It can't have gotten more than a little cobwebby in the meanwhile. Besides, he can't go all the way back now, can he?"

Ben told them he'd already sublet his apartment in the city. He had nowhere else to go.

"You see!" Victor was triumphant. "We've got no alternative. Come on, Ben. Dinner's ready. Afterward, I'll take you to the little cottage."

"Victor," Ormond said, his voice unexpectedly throaty, "That cottage belonged to Hunter."

"It belongs to the *colony*."

"You know what I mean."

"Ben's here," Giove said firmly. "Hunter isn't."

"That's true enough."

"Then it's settled."

❖

Four of them ate dinner. Joan Sampson was to have joined them but she called to cancel, saying she had work to do.

Ben did know they had no such thing as community dining at the colony, didn't he, Frances Ormond asked. Everyone took care of themselves. Except, of course, everyone dined with whomever they wanted to. She hoped that Ben would feel as welcome at her table as Dr. Giove was. It was impossible for Ben to not like the transplanted urban woman who'd evidently found peace in Sagoponauk Rock. Like Victor, she radiated health and happiness. Ben would later discover that as a rare enough quality at the colony. Others had brought their sufferings and neuroses, unable or unwilling to let them go. They argued around kitchen tables just as badly as they had in Manhattan bars. They outraged and scandalized each other in country bedrooms with infidelities and treacheries as though they still lived in West Side apartment complexes. Over the following week, Ben sized up the colony members quickly. Only Mrs. Ormond was judged to be sound.

And Victor, of course. Victor who was the reason Ben had come to Sagoponauk Rock, and the reason he had almost not come. Even after Ben had sublet his apartment. Even after Ben had turned off the exit from the New England Thruway and had driven north for what seemed hours more.

After dinner, Victor got into the Volvo's driver's seat and drove through the dark, rutted road to the little cottage. Ben held an extra kerosene can Frances Ormond had provided, unsure whether or not the electricity was turned on.

It was, they discovered, after a longish, silent ride through the deep darkness of the country, passing what would later become landmarks to Ben on his night walks and night drives: the community house, the first two studios, then Victor's, the apple orchard, then the fork past the pond.

The cottage was L-shaped: a large, bare bedroom separated by a small bathroom and cavernous storage closet from a good-sized study area that opened onto a small, single-wall kitchen with a long dining counter.

Victor built a fire to help clear out the mustiness and the unseasonable chill. Ben went through the kitchen cabinets and found a bottle half full of Fundador. They sipped the brandy, talking about the program they'd tentatively set up the past April at school, which Ben as an apprentice writer would follow at the colony. He was only to show Victor a piece of writing when he was satisfied with it, or unable to find satisfaction in it. Some of the others at the colony never shared their work with each other. Victor and Joan had agreed to meet regularly to read to each other. If he wanted, Ben could join them.

Although it was only a three-and-a-half-month stay, Ben had decided he would write day and night. Not only the few short stories Victor asked for, but a novel too: the novel, the one he'd planned, the one he believed he'd been born to write. Free here of most distractions, he felt certain he'd get much of it done before the last school year rolled around again. He already loved the cottage.

Only the bedroom—after a second look—didn't seem as cozy as the rest of the house. Ben thought the bedroom's coldness was due to its appearance: low ceilings, uncarpeted dull wood floor, only a few pieces of furniture—hardly inviting. Perhaps a single night's sleep would warm it up. The double bed—higher and wider than the one he was used to—was firm yet comfortable when he tried it out.

Victor had gone into the bathroom. He found Ben stretched out on the long wide bed and he stopped, lingering on the threshold.

For a long minute, they looked at each other. Ben—his hands under his head for a pillow—felt suddenly exposed, then seductively positioned, inviting. Giove seemed suddenly bereft of his usual composure; uncertain, fragile, even frightened. Neither of them moved. Ben could feel the tension of the possible and the impossible filling the room like a thick mist.

"It's getting late," Victor said, his voice subdued, his hands suddenly gesturing as though controlled by someone else. "I'll come by in the morning to show you around the colony."

Ben was embarrassed now too and quickly sat up, then got off the bed to see the older man out. In an attempt to cover over the shame he'd unexpectedly felt, he asked, "Who had this cottage before me?"

"Stephen Hunter, the poet," Giove said, looking out into darkness.

"You're kidding! I didn't know he stayed here at the colony."

"Oh, everyone important comes to Sagoponauk sooner or later."

Ben was about to say something about how happy he was

that the cottage had such a stellar literary past, but Giove said good-bye and was gone.

Ben settled into the dank chill of the sheets they'd located in the big closet and thought of that moment in the bedroom, of Victor's suddenly coming upon him on the bed, his hesitation, his distracted gestures, the sudden quiet tone of his voice and his sudden decision to leave. If he had remained another minute, come into the bedroom, come closer to Ben, the impossible would have been possible—in this very room.

Ben climaxed with a sharpness he hadn't experienced masturbating in years, not since he was an adolescent. Wiping his abdomen with a hand towel, he wondered whether it was the fresh country air or seeing Victor Giove again after so long.

❖

Victor didn't come by in the morning to show Ben around; Ben didn't see him until dinnertime. But that was only the beginning of Victor's fluctuations of intense consideration and total aloofness that formed itself into an inescapable pattern.

That first morning, Ben didn't much care. The bedroom faced east and he awoke to a sunny splendor of bright clear light through nearby trees flooding every inch of what seemed to be a really handsome, though sparsely furnished room.

After a breakfast of bread and honey provided by Frances Ormond the night before, Ben wandered around the colony. He was still too awed to closely approach any studio, believing the other colony members would be intensely concentrating on their writing, and thus not to be disturbed. But he had enough to look at: the pond, surprisingly large, still and lovely, quite close at one edge to his cottage; the apple orchard stretching for miles; the lively stream that formed a tiny marsh where it entered the pond; the large old trees, many varieties he'd never seen before; the young saplings everywhere; the fruit and berry bushes in demure blossom; the wildflowers surrounding the houses; the cottage itself, beautifully crafted out of fine woods, so that built-in tables, drawers, and cabinetry were perfectly integrated by color and grain, all of a piece.

Following Mrs. Ormond's instructions, he skirted the colony later on, driving up to and along the two-lane highway, locating in one direction a truck-stop all-night diner, a gas station, and after another five or six miles, the tiny hamlet of Sagoponauk—where he purchased a backseat full of groceries and supplies. Driving in the other direction past the colony, Ben found another gas station and an old clapboard roadhouse containing a saloon and an Italian restaurant.

The peace that had settled on him momentarily the dusk before returned when he drove back to the colony and arrived to see the little cottage—highest placed of the houses on the property—aglow with fuchsia and orange, its western window reflecting a brilliant summer sunset.

Victor apologized when he saw Ben. Besides doing some writing that day, he said he'd had to fix a propane gas line to Joan Sampson's oven and hot water heater and then help Mrs. Ormond pick early apples for saucing.

Ben was embarrassed by the apology. He could spend all day with Victor. That was why he had come to the colony. But now that he was here, he could not justify deserving Giove's attention. Victor wasn't merely gorgeously unself-conscious, he was altruistic, giving his time and energy to anyone who needed it. Obviously there were others in the colony who needed it as much as Ben.

So Ben contented himself. Especially after the first few weeks, when he began to realize the impossible love between them could only occur suddenly, impulsively, unforgettably: like any other miracle.

Victor's comings and goings appeared to fit some obscure plan. Ben wouldn't see him for days, only come upon him mowing a shaggy patch of lawn, or wrapping heavy black tape around a split waterpipe of one of the studios. Then Victor would come by the little cottage early one afternoon, spend all day, remain for a hastily concocted dinner, talk about people and writing and books until past midnight. Only to disappear again for days. Only to reappear again as suddenly, stretched out on the yellow plastic lawnchair at midday as Ben returned home from a walk, or suddenly diving past Ben's surprised face into the clear water of the pond and swimming to the other shore. His appearances were unpredictable; the hours he spent with Ben so full of talk, of complete attention that Ben would be charmed into persuading himself that Giove was merely being careful; getting to know Ben better: making sure of him totally, before he would suddenly turn to Ben, put his arms around him, and…

That was when Ben would feel frustrated all over again, full of lust, and he would have to go into the bedroom, to lie down, to picture how it would be, sometimes masturbating two or three times after Victor had been with him, feeling his fantasies becoming so real that the impossible *had* to happen.

Once, Victor came by after dinner when Ben was writing. Giove lay down quietly on the sofa, began to read a magazine and fell asleep. When Ben realized that, he could no longer concentrate. Even sleeping, Victor was too disturbing. Ben wandered around the cottage, trying to wake the older man by the noise he made. He even tried to fall asleep himself. But it was an absurd attempt—the bedroom felt as cold, as uninviting as the first night he'd spent there.

Finally he decided to waken Victor—he was so tall he had

to sleep bent up. He would awaken with cramps, pain. Ben didn't say it to himself, but he suspected that once they were in bed together, Giove would relent.

Victor woke up, stretched, stood up, looked once at the bedroom hallway, as though trying to make up his mind whether or not to stay, then said he wouldn't hear of it.

That night, it was hours before Ben could fall asleep, even after he'd taken a mild sedative.

He had purposely not touched himself during those tormenting hours of unrest. During the night, however, half-awakened, he felt heat emanating from his genitals, couldn't fight it off, and worked groggily if efficiently to bring himself to orgasm. Dazed, exhausted, he sank back into slumber.

The following afternoon, Victor was at the pond again when Ben arrived for his daily swim. With Victor, sitting on the tiny dark sand beach, wearing a huge sun hat, was a chaperone: Joan Sampson. Ben remained with them only long enough to be polite.

After that day, Victor and Joan always seemed to be together. Victor was seldom alone.

Even without her interference, Ben thought she was the least sympathetic person he'd met in the colony. She epitomized all he disliked in the others: their utter sophistication and true provinciality; their brusqueness, their bad manners, their absorption with themselves and lack of interest in anyone else except as reflections of themselves. Joan's frail child's underdeveloped body and the expensively casual clothing she wore, her birdlike unpretty face and unfocused blue eyes that seemed to look only with disdain, her arrogance, her instant judgements and devastating condemnations of matters she couldn't possibly know, her artificial laugh, her arch gestures and awkward mannerisms—she might have been a wind-up toy. Next to her, large, naturally graceful, athletically handsome Victor, his Victor, looked bumbling. Together they were grotesque.

Ben now went out of his way to not see them together. He pleaded work when they asked him to join them for dinner. He didn't show up for readings of their work. He stopped going to where he thought they were likely to be.

The impossible, he began to see, was indeed impossible. He had to forget Victor, to forget him, and above all to stop fantasizing about him.

❖

When the cold showers and manual work he made for himself around the cottage no longer served to keep his mind off Victor Giove, Ben began to run miles every day along the two-lane road, to swim hours at a time, in another, larger, pond he'd discovered a short drive away. When he realized these methods were not working either, Ben got into the Volvo late one night and drove to the all-night truck-stop diner.

Two vehicles—one he recognized as belonging to the owner—and a large red semi were parked in the gravel lot. Ben pulled up close to the truck, hidden from both the diner and the road, and waited. When the truck driver finally came out of the diner, Ben rolled down his window and asked for a light for his cigarette.

The trucker was close to middle age, and heavy set, definitely not Ben's type, but he had kind brown eyes and an engaging grin. He lighted Ben's cigarette. When he asked Ben if he wasn't a little young to be doing this sort of thing, Ben shrugged, then leaned back in the car seat with a loud sigh. A second later, the trucker's lower torso filled the car window frame, the worn denims were unzipped, not another word said. Ben sucked him off and came without touching himself.

The following night, Ben stopped at the roadhouse and struck up a conversation with a traveling salesman who had a suitcase full of encyclopedias. After a few drinks, Ben was able to convince the man he wanted something other than books. The salesman was younger than the trucker, thinner, better-looking, just as obliging. They drove separately away from the roadhouse, met a mile farther at a turn-off, and made love in the backseat of the salesman's car for over an hour.

Ben drove out late every night. One time he picked up a long-haired hitchhiker who offered him grass. They smoked, and Ben drove twenty-five miles before he got up the courage to ask if he could blow the kid. Sure, the hitchhiker said, unzipping. I was wondering when you were going to ask.

Several times, he repeated his first night success at the truck stop. He also discovered the Exxon station outside of Sagoponauk had a removable plank at exactly the right height between the two booths in the men's room. High school boys came there after unsuccessful weekend night petting sessions with their girls, and local older men furtively used his services at various odd hours. Ben became bolder, picking up strangers leaving the roadhouse. He was often misunderstood, at times threatened. The bartender, a married partner in the place, offered to guide likely men Ben's way in return for occasional favors. A week later he took his first payment, sodomizing Ben on a shiny leather sofa in the office after the roadhouse had closed.

During all of these experiences, Ben never felt less frustrated, less craving of sex, or less in love with Victor Giove. But he told himself that whatever else he was doing, at least it was better than fantasizing about Victor and masturbating. That seemed to help.

❖

Although he had gone to sleep very late and was even a little drunk when he'd finally gotten back to the cottage, Ben awakened instantly, fully, as soon as he thought he heard the footpads in the darkened room. Fully alert, tensed, he kept his eyes closed, pretending to be asleep. Whoever had stopped at the foot of the bed was looking down at Ben.

Despite his terror, Ben didn't panic. Then, oddly, he felt a wave of intense lust passing through his body. Odd, since the young man he'd spent two hours with on a blanket inside a clearing they'd driven to had been both passionate and solicitous of Ben's pleasure. Ben had felt both mollified and physically exhausted when they'd parted with a long, lingering kiss. Despite that Ben now felt a biting, itching, erection, a pressing need to masturbate, as though he hadn't had sex in a month.

The fear returned, Ben almost shivered. He pretended to be disturbed in his sleep, mumbling loudly, rolling onto one side before waking up.

During his exertions, whoever had been at the foot of the bed left the room. Ben felt alone again. He listened for noises in the other rooms, waited a long time hearing nothing, then got out of bed and crept first into the corridor, then into the rest of the cottage. The doors were locked, the rooms empty. Puzzled, wondering if it was a dream, Ben went to sleep.

❖

Several nights later, he again wakened, sensing someone at the foot of his bed. Once more he felt a scalding, sweeping lust over his lower limbs, the need to touch himself. Then fear reasserted itself, and he was cold again. While he was sleepily trying to get out of bed, whoever it was got away. He was certain it wasn't a dream this time.

Ben thought about the matter for the next two days and determined to ask Frances Ormond who else had a set of keys to the cottage. Walking to the Ormond house, he came upon Victor Giove, surprisingly alone, sunning on a blanket spread over the grass behind his A-frame studio. Victor's gloriously tanned body was clad only in a pair of worn, red swim trunks.

Ben moved on with a wave, but Giove hailed him over so insistently that Ben reluctantly joined him, and even took off his shirt to get some sun.

He was "pale as February," Victor assured him, and he would burn unless he put on some suntan oil. When Ben began to splash it on, the older man said he was doing it all wrong; he would show him how. As Ben lay on his stomach, he expected to feel the large, strong, applicating hands transformed into messengers of caresses. They weren't. They were brisk, efficient, they spread the lotion evenly, nothing more.

Giove didn't seem to have noticed that Ben had been avoiding him. Their conversation was the usual: what Victor was writing, what Ben was doing, what was happening among the others at the colony,

Ben stayed almost an hour—once his disturbance at their near-nude closeness vanished. When he got up and put on his shirt, Victor said:

"You should get more sun. And rest more. How are you sleeping? You look sort of done in to me."

Ben was so stunned he couldn't answer. Why would Victor say that to him, unless it was Victor himself who was visiting him at night?

When Ben finally did say he was sleeping well, Giove seemed skeptical, then added, "Well, you know best." He rolled on his stomach, and his wide shoulders, his long, muscled back, two solid buttocks stretching the bright red nylon of his swim trunks, his thighs and legs—honey brown and flecked with sunbleached hairs—all jumped out at Ben. He wanted to fall down right there and kiss and lick every inch of that body for hours on end. The black, curly ringlets of Giove's hair shone like white gold in the sun. Shoving his itching hands into his trouser pockets, Ben managed to mumble a supererogatory good-bye before tearing himself away from the spot.

He was imagining things, Ben told himself, walking away. Victor had only asked how he was sleeping because he'd probably heard Ben driving past his studio late every night for the past three weeks and he was concerned.

Frances Ormond confirmed that she herself had heard Ben's Volvo at two and three in the morning at least a dozen times. She was far less subtle about it.

"That's the way Stephen Hunter began his terrible descent," she said, "staying out late, coming home late, getting drunk in roadhouses. Summer after summer. Night after night, toward the end."

Ben thought it was none of her business, but defended himself by pointing out that he had written the two required stories and had already begun his novel. Late hours helped him work, he said.

She pursed her lips as though to counterattack, but changed the subject, feeding him coffee and freshly baked berry pie instead.

She told Ben no one else had keys to the little cottage. None were needed: the locks didn't work; anyone could get in if they wanted. Stephen Hunter had once told her he'd had enough of locks in the city, he wouldn't have any functional locks out here. It was his undoing, she added, because it enabled his murderer to get at him so easily.

Without much prodding, she narrated the grisly tale of

three summers past. The young vagabond had been captured in a saloon a few towns away. He'd confessed and was imprisoned. At first he made some foolish claim about Stephen owing him some money and refusing to pay; about them being friends for years. Under pressure his story changed to one of revenge. Stephen had molested him, he said. It wasn't convincing, even to the unsophisticated local sheriff.

Back at the little cottage, Ben discovered she was right—both doors could be opened, the locks just flapped on their hinges. Should he have them repaired? Yes. But whoever was visiting him at night did nothing to him, did nothing but look at him. Was that reason enough to change something Stephen Hunter had done? Ben would never bring anyone he met back to the colony. He congratulated himself he never had. And he still couldn't get Victor Giove's words of earlier that day out of his mind. He was once more almost certain it was Victor.

So he didn't repair the locks. And the next time he was awakened in the middle of the night and sensed a figure at the foot of the bed, Ben felt only a few seconds of the usual fear. The figure remained motionless. It seemed to be the right size for Victor. Then Ben began to feel the intense warm itch sweeping from the tips of his hair to the soles of his feet.

Slowly pushing back the light blanket, Ben let the dark figure warm him with its gaze, then began touching himself on his legs and groin. He thought he heard a sharpened intake of breath from his visitor, and Ben let go, slowly, luxuriously caressing and stroking himself, thinking of Victor at the foot of the bed watching him, wanting him, not daring to touch him. His climax that night was shared; he was certain of it.

When he opened his eyes, the room was empty.

❖

He was visited every night for several weeks. Every night, Ben awakened, sought out the outline of the figure against the lighter darkness of the room, and succumbed to fantasies and sex.

During the day he often told himself he ought to be sure it was Victor and not someone else. But who else could it be? He searched the eyes of the other colony members he came across, looking for any signs of guiltily secretive interest. He found nothing even close. Then he would come upon Victor Giove, racing around the lawns with the big Irish hound or sitting reading in a hammock strung outside Joan's studio, and though they seldom exchanged more than a few words, every word, every phrase seemed so couched with meanings relevant to their shared nights, Ben was convinced it must be Giove.

Didn't everything point to it? Victor's insistence that Ben remain at the colony that first night? His unceasing friendliness? His increased reticence with Ben since the night visits had begun? He seldom spoke to Ben of Joan, or of her work, as though it were only an excuse. Ben came to believe their new silence—when they met at the local grocery store or out on walks, they now barely spoke—was more eloquent than words. It spelled content.

Ben would have to be a fool to spoil it. The impossible had become the possible. Not in the open way he'd at first, naïvely, imagined it would be, but tacit, secretive, and for that reason somehow more passionate than he'd ever fantasized. Victor must still have hurdles of attitudes, ingrained prejudices to jump, before he could admit what he was wanting, feeling. Ben would give him time. Who knew what the next step would be in their growing closeness—so long as Ben didn't force it.

❖

Ben had been visited that night, as usual, all his lust and wakefulness drawn from him, as it always was, replaced by deep, calm, dreamy sleep.

People were marching down a small-town street. Batons twirled, trumpets blared, signs and crepe-covered floats sailed past. Children bounced eagerly behind. The drums passed by very close, going bam bam BAM! Bam bam BAM! again and again, sounding lovely and rich and mellow at first, then ominous, then emergent.

Ben awakened to someone hammering on his front door. He thrust open the bedroom window to the cool mountain summer morning. It wasn't quite dawn.

"Ben! What do you know about drugs?" It was Eugene Ormond, evidently recently awakened himself. If he hadn't looked so panic-stricken, Ben would have laughed.

"Joan Sampson's taken a pile of them. We're sure they're some kind of sleeping pills."

"What did they look like?" Ben asked.

"We found one that fell on the floor." Dr. Ormond showed Ben the shiny red and blue capsule: a Tuinal.

"She's got to vomit them up," Ben said, and jumped into the car with Dr. Ormond and drove to her studio. "Then black coffee to keep her stimulated."

"Frances thought the same. I hope she's all right."

"Where's Victor?" Ben asked. "He would know, too."

They pulled up alongside the studio. Ormond looked at Ben oddly, then said:

"Didn't you know? He's back in New York, has been for the past three days. That's what all this nonsense is about."

Before Ben could register the news, Dr. Ormond was pulling him out of the passenger's side of the stopped pickup and into the studio.

Joan was audibly vomiting, Frances as audibly cursing

about the stupidity of trying to kill yourself over a man, for Chrissakes, even one like Victor. There was a final spasm of nausea, quiet, then Frances Ormond half dragged the smaller woman out of the bathroom and, spotting Ben, asked him to grab the other side and help her walk Miss Sampson around a bit while Eugene made coffee, "doubly strong, Eugene!"

Their charge was light but weak, her arms useless, her head kept lolling against Ben's shoulder. Words and saliva dribbled out of her mouth. He found himself totally repulsed.

They wheeled her around like that another five minutes. Another fifteen were spent feeding her coffee and ensuring she didn't vomit that up too. Then more walking around.

Joan was visibly recovered by the time the phone rang. She still looked awful and had allowed Ben to bring her into the bedroom, where she was noisily sobbing, but at least she seemed awake, safe.

"Get that, will you, Ben?" Mrs. Ormond asked, looking from where she was cleaning the spattered bathroom floor.

Ben lifted the receiver and said hello. There was a confused mumbling from the other side. Then:

"Joan? Is that you?"

Victor Giove, perplexed.

Ben looked away from the phone, unable to say anything for a minute. Holding his hand over the phone, he barely uttered, "It's Victor." Saying the name was more difficult than almost anything he could remember doing in his life.

"Of course it's Victor!" Frances Ormond declared and took the call.

"You see," Joan sobbed, standing at the threshold of the room. "He's seeing *her* again. He was with *her* all last night. He couldn't stay away from *her*. That's why he went back!"

Frances Ormond hushed her. Ben moved away from them, feeling as though he were on the set of a movie where everyone was playing a role, and only he didn't know the scenario or have a script. He still couldn't believe Victor was in New York. Yet there he was, calling long distance, in response to a call Mrs. Ormond had put through.

Ben left the studio and walked slowly back to the little cottage. He felt dazed by the morning's events, but not so distracted he didn't notice it had rained the night before: the dust around the cottage was still damp enough although drying fast. Two sets of footprints led to the tire tracks where Dr. Ormond had parked the pickup a few hours ago. Although he walked around the cottage twice, Ben could find no other sets of prints or tracks.

That night he drank some brandy, which kept him awake longer and made his sleep lighter than usual. When he awakened later during the night by the urgent panting breath at the foot of the bed, he immediately turned to the bed table and turned on the lamp.

The room was empty.

Energized by the need to know, Ben leapt out of bed and ran out to the other rooms. He even looked outside. When he returned to the bedroom a few minutes later, he thought he made out a wisp of mist curling into the lower edges of the large storage closet. The closet proved to be empty. But the morning chill caught up with him there. He began to shiver so badly he had to get into bed and pull up the covers, awaiting sunlight.

❖

"Stephen Hunter was homosexual, wasn't he?"

Frances Ormond looked across the distressed oak-parquet of the old table at Ben.

"I guess they still don't talk much about those matters in college, do they?" she asked, instead of answering him.

"The vagabond who murdered him was a hustler, wasn't he?"

"You seem to know all the answers. Why ask?"

"In the bedroom?"

"Stephen tried to get away. He hid in the storage closet."

Ben wasn't surprised to hear it: only vaguely chilled to know his line of reasoning had been so on-target.

"And Victor and Stephen were friends, weren't they?"

"Not by then, they weren't. They had been. Close friends. But that summer they had a falling-out."

"Because Victor wouldn't sleep with Stephen."

"You do have all the answers, don't you? Yes, Victor looked up to Stephen as though he were a god. But he couldn't bring himself to love him that way. Generous as Victor is with himself. Sometimes too generous, if you ask me. People want more than Victor can give."

"And that's when Stephen began picking up hustlers."

"No. He'd done that long before he met Victor. You've read the sequence he titled 'Broken Bones,' haven't you?"

"Years ago," Ben admitted. He'd never dreamed it was about hustlers.

Frances got up from the table and went to another room. She returned with a copy of Hunter's *Collected Poems*. Ben found the page and reread the first few poems in the series. He was shaken by the harsh, beautiful images of lust and fear.

"This is why you said I was heading in the same direction?" Ben asked.

"I don't care what you do—just be careful."

"I've never brought anyone back to the cottage," Ben said.

"I never said you did. Borrow the book," she pleaded. "Read him again, Ben. He has a great deal to tell you. All great poets do. But I think Hunter has a special message for you."

❖

Like every literature student of his generation, Ben had read several of Stephen Hunter's poems in college, and had even memorized one, a sonnet: "August and the scent of tragic leafburn." Aside from that one, however, Ben had always thought Hunter overrated. He had preferred the more formal poets—Stevens and Auden and Lowell—to what he termed the "wild men": Dylan Thomas, Allen Ginsburg, and especially Stephen Hunter. Not that his opinion made any difference. Hunter was in every anthology; his work was written about, discussed, interpreted and reinterpreted.

Ben rediscovered him, reading through all the poems in a few days, reading them again, then selecting out single poems and analyzing them for himself.

Hunter's famous *Odes to an Unruined Statue* were suddenly opened to Ben as though they had been written in a language he could never understand until now. Victor Giove was the beautiful man/object—the unattainable; Hunter was the critical observer and adoring fantasist. *The Window Elegies*, those five intensely wrought poems of dense metaphors and precise yet oddly angled images, were illuminated as though a light had been switched on behind them in a basement room. Their visionary style and metaphysical message were all held together by the carefully delineated details of different windows through which the poet had seen a loved one. The description in one of the elegies might well be that of Victor's A-frame studio, here at the colony; the window Hunter had looked through night after night, spying on Victor.

Ben didn't go near the large closet, which he never used anyway.

Nor did he sleep in the bedroom any longer.

He felt safe on the living room sofa, even though it was cramped. And, whether it was because of his deep new fear or whether there was a natural boundary to the presence, Ben was not awakened once by his nocturnal visitor while he slept out in the living room.

The locks had to be repaired, of course, if only as a precaution. Who knew how many other hustlers had come back here with Hunter. And he began to haunt his previous places of fast, usually anonymous, sex again, returning home late at night and sleeping deeply. When he didn't go out, he would stay awake at night, working, and instead sleeping during the day. Everything he now did seemed tinged by an undercurrent of excitement, as though anticipation were slowly building, but toward what he couldn't even begin to say.

Victor Giove returned to Sagoponauk. Ben sometimes came upon him swimming at the pond. Although Joan was no longer with him and the older man waved Ben over to join him, Ben would invariably plead some lame excuse and quickly leave. The one time Ben and Victor were thrown together, right next to each other, at the Ormonds' for dinner, they found they no longer had anything to say to each other.

What Ben had thought to be a mutual secret contentment, he now saw otherwise: Victor was perceptive enough, experienced enough too, to understand what Ben wanted from him. He was trying to avoid having the same kind of problem he'd had with Stephen Hunter, even if it meant having no relationship at all.

Ben knew that evening for sure that he'd fallen out of love with Victor. He'd probably done so a week earlier, with Joan snivelling against his body. The golden aura that used to light the other man's steps through the tall grass, the sparkle that used to dapple his dark curls as he lay in the sun were gone. His eyes seemed tired. His face lined. His laughter constrained.

Ben knew why too. No man he could ever deem desirable would have been fool enough to not give so simple a matter as his body to a once-in-a-lifetime-met genius like Stephen Hunter.

❖

It was August when Ben moved back into the bedroom. "August and the scent of tragic leafburn," he reminded himself, when he awakened once more out of a deep sleep.

He knew instantly that the presence at the foot of his bed was Stephen Hunter.

His body was beginning to tingle warm under the blanket cover he had protectively pulled up in that instant of realization. But Ben still shivered. The air about him stirred in cool eddies unlike any air he'd ever known. He heard what seemed to be fragments of whispered lines from poems, mixed with pleas, demands, obscenities. Stephen knew Ben: knew who he was, what he wanted, what he'd given up. Ben's teeth began to chatter. All he had to do was reach over to the lamp table and put on the light, and he would be alone again, well out of harm's reach. But if he did that, Stephen might never come back to him. Ben wasn't sure he wanted that either.

He suddenly thought of Victor Giove. Large, muscled, beautiful, generous Victor. He thought of Victor's smile, the bulge of his crotch in those tan worn corduroys, the roundness of his buttocks in those scarlet swim trunks, his rippling chest, his furrowed back, those ringlets of black curls, his Florentine profile.

The room became warm and still. So warm. Ben had to push the blanket away from himself, letting the heat seethe around his torso.

Keeping his eyes closed, Ben thought of Victor walking, running, swimming. Then someone else pushed Victor out of the picture and came into focus: a broad-shouldered, tall, thick-bodied man with intelligent deep-set eyes of indeterminate color, a craggy face, long, straight, honey-colored hair, unclipped mustache and full beard: the face, the body, the very photograph from the frontispiece of *The Collected Poems.*

Stephen Hunter was a great poet. A genius. A man who'd felt as deeply, as spontaneously as an oil geyser. He'd flown higher than a parachute jumper on mere thought. He'd filled himself with wisdom and suffering equal to any philosopher, any monarch. Compared to him, Victor was an oversized primate.

Ben relaxed, seeing without sight the figure moving in front of him, as though undressing, feeling the figure reach out and slowly caress him, the multicolored eyes gleaming softly, the mouth working to form wonderfully original phrases of manlove lewdness. The raking gaze swept over Ben's body like electric fire. Only such a genius could provoke, could produce such utter pleasure, Ben thought—as he gave in.

He was only slightly jolted when Stephen Hunter accepted. The sudden touch was of large, warm hands pressing upon Ben's spread thighs, the brush of warm skin on either side of his loins, like a large cat. But the tongue that invisibly licked and then engulfed him was that of a man, the long bony nose and unkempt facial hair, when Ben reached down to gingerly touch them, were those of Hunter's photo image; and Ben knew he had finally found what he had come to Sagoponauk Rock Colony looking for, and why that first sunset had been filled with implications he could not at first decipher.

❖

By the end of the summer, Ben was a complete recluse. He had not been seen by anyone in the colony in weeks when most of the members went back to their teaching posts around the country. Joan Sampson and the Ormonds—the last to leave, in mid-September—tried to find him, but gave up after a series of attempts.

But the Ormonds and Victor Giove used their colony houses on a long late-October weekend. The little cottage was empty, although lived in, increasingly messy, dusty, ill cared for. Victor felt guilty about the boy and walked around calling him for a half hour, waiting another three hours one afternoon for Ben to show up, until it was sunset. Victor left notes that were never answered and were never found on subsequent visits.

On the Thanksgiving break, Victor again drove up to the colony, this time to shut off the waterpipes against the winter and to make certain all of the studios and cottages were locked. He once again drove to the little cottage, hoping to find Ben and to talk him out of his foolish decision to remain isolated. He didn't find the boy, but walking away from the spot, he gasped when he noticed the roof of Ben's Volvo sticking up out of one end of the pond.

Although the pond was dragged by local and state police for two days, no body was ever found.

Victor relayed the sad, ambiguous news to Frances Ormond, who contacted Ben's family in far-eastern Long Island. Neither of them heard back from his relatives.

The last two days of the Christmas holidays, Frances Ormond drove up to the colony by herself. She found several studios broken into, cans of tinned food opened, eaten, discarded. She cleaned up, repaired the windows and doors with local help, gathered all the remaining boxed and canned foods in the studios and her own house and dropped it all off in two large cardboard boxes near the little cottage. She never told anyone else she did this. Secretly, she was proud that Ben had gone and done what she'd always wanted to do, live here in the wild all year. Proud of him, and envious too.

It turned out to be an extremely fierce New England winter. Storms raged weeks at a time. All but main highways were blocked by high snow drifts, and after, by ice layers, most of which lasted until late March. Livestock froze in heated barns. Old people were stranded and died. Children and stragglers from stalled cars were lost in blizzards. Many local farmers closed up their houses and went south. Others remained indoors, barely surviving.

Even though they managed to get into the colony by early March, the snow plows couldn't get anywhere near the little cottage.

Easter brought the first thaw. Victor drove up to the colony, bitterly hoping he would find the boy and that Ben would finally listen to reason.

The door to the little cottage was still iced over and had to be kicked hard to open.

Inside, the main rooms were icily cold. Fires had been built, tins cans charred over the fire. Liters of kerosene and sterno cans littered the living room floor. But Victor couldn't tell how long they'd lain there—a day? or a month? It did seem as though the boy had gotten through the winter. That was a relief. He'd probably suffered so much that he'd return with Victor to the city without much urging. Victor sat down to wait.

Although it was still cold, something seemed to be missing from the cottage that Victor couldn't at first define: a disturbance he'd almost subconsciously sensed every time he had come here or stayed here since the day they'd discovered Stephen Hunter's corpse in the storage closet.

When it finally got too cold to stay seated, Victor got up to leave the cottage. He wrote a note to Ben saying he would be at his studio. Ben could find him there. He was about to walk outside when he realized that the bedroom door was closed.

Could the boy be hiding from him in there?

Victor opened the bedroom door and remained still for a very long time.

The nude, emaciated body of Ben Après was stretched out on the bed as though in utter ecstasy. His skin was ashen, pale blue with frost, perfectly preserved down to the frozen splashes of semen that had splattered his gaunt abdomen and hung off the tip of his erection.

Victor understood why he no longer sensed the supercharged presence he'd felt for so many years in the cottage: the insatiable Stephen Hunter had finally found someone worthy of his love.

The Acolyte

1.

It had come upon Edwin Landsdowne so suddenly, and at first blush, so commingled of what he might have most desired, should he have ever dared express it, along with what he was most desperately anxious that none ever intimate, that he could scarcely credit it, when, in regally passing out of the shower-saturated cemetery, thence into a shuttered brougham, Mrs. Van Pryor, the Widow Van Pryor now and eternally, paused in her courtly, her tragic, her umbrella shielded, her manifoldly supported progress, to single him out, to briefly lay a laced glove so raven's-wing as to gleam purple upon his inky serge-encased forearm and to quietly intone, "Come to me in the morning. I utterly depend on you now." Scarcely were the fingers gone than she was surging forward, enclosed within the obscured depths, and thence completely out of view.

He could do no more than feebly mutter, as though in entreaty, "Was it myself you so noticed? Are you not perhaps if only a little in error?" when that so recently blessed forearm was taken in a more virile clutch, not to be let lightly go, by his associate of the morning's melancholy burden, accompanied by another genial limb clasped about his slender waist.

"What have I been prognosticating, my young princeling?"

Francis DeHaven whispered. "You are already chosen for the distinguished assignment!"

Brooking no possibility of contention, DeHaven all but carried off Landsdowne to his own splendidly more *sportif* conveyance, where his driver, the inaptly named Samson, a groundling of lean figure and low demeanor, immediately flogged the horses into a mad splash toward his master's Leicester Square club. Once settled amid napery, silver service, and the company of gentlemen greater than himself, poor Landsdowne could only submit to his friend's continued blandishments. That he was the inestimable Anthony Van Pryor's publisher, coming along, and into, his patrimony only in the last decade of his remarkable elder's career, and as well as Landsdowne's own editor, learned *cicerone*, and literary savior, could only assist DeHaven in his contentions.

The younger had already been previously apprised by his companion that there were certain uncollected papers of a personal character—journals, letters, incunabula, whatnot—the which Van Pryor had maintained in strictest confidence he'd long pledged to compile, left bereft and rudderless with the great man's sudden leave-taking, papers that would, without question, affix the finest polish to his heretofore altitudinous repute.

"Precisely, she intends your inimitable charm and skill to take the errant pages to hand and ready them as only you could," DeHaven assured his friend, waving two uplifted fingers to summon more French champagne. As precisely, Landsdowne perhaps uncharitably mused, was it that those errant pages' collection and publication under anyone-at-all's hand would permit many further opportunities for champagne luncheons for his debonair publisher and whoever might happen to fall into his company.

"Still, Francis," he countermanded, "you are unable

not to admit that there aren't heaps others more advanced in the art and experience who would fare better with the great man's incunabula. I held him in such estimation, I tremble to impose…my mere person."

"Perhaps so, my uncommon angel of authorial modesty. But it is precisely those heaps of others' art and experience that is most *un*required for this most precarious of assignments. Your trembling estimation," and here DeHaven accentuated his words with an almost amatory look in his olive-green, Italianate eyes and a feather-weight, soigné, yet altogether proprietary contact with Landsdowne's barely bearded chin, "While your consternation at possible over-imposition will exactly qualify you for the enterprise and for my own poor silly requirements."

All further contention was deemed superfluous as the terrapin *consommé a la Madeira* arrived, followed by omelets of pigeon eggs and *Homard Americaine*. He must content himself with lunching sumptuously and allowing DeHaven to show him off to his brother club members, with his customary effusions whenever they happened to be abroad together, embarrassing *mots*: "Isn't he a beauty? With talent to burn! And enough morality to raise a Cathedral. Could a DeHaven possibly be luckier?"

2.

A rustling as of the feathers of a multitude of predatory avian life immediately preceded Henrietta Van Pryor's entry into the dimmed afternoon parlor. Her arrival was rapid and fluttering, yet somehow not exactly equilibrious, as he turned from the shower-speckled glass giving onto the apparently dilapidated garden to salute her with renewed murmurings of regret and sorrow. She was in weeds, as expected of course, profusely so, as though she'd betimes anticipated the mournful state she'd arrived at and had scrupulously yet luxuriantly preselected those ensembles that would best accommodate her face and figure. An ebony exuberance of gauze, crinoline, and organza all but restrained her from settling into a *fauteuil*, and once ensconced she plied a crow's-wing of fan, subtly festive with minuscule diamants, that even when wielded to cover half her face did little to distract one from her colossal, her seemingly lubricated eyes, as she thanked him.

She appeared to take inordinate pleasure in the plural possessive when she began to speak: "Our publisher has assured me of your reluctance, your naturally immense admiration, your temerity in the face of such a labor…" She paused. "Which, rather than discommoding me, all the more reassures me that we both have chosen correctly… Francis has conveyed the 'terms' and you find them adequate?" she then added rather than asked.

"Adequate" rather than generous, Landsdowne might have responded, had the situation been other than this particular one. For herself, he expected, the "terms" were far more beneficent. But as *their* publisher had inebriatedly nuzzled Landsdowne's cheek in parting as he'd mildly nudged him out of the landau following their previous day's club luncheon, he had also bemoaned the unbearable exigencies, the intricacies of the publisher's contractual obligations to the recently departed's estate. As well he had mentioned the "non-pecuniary" compensations Landsdowne might anticipate. Not the least, the future fusion in the reading public's collective mentality of the immature author of but a single slim edition of critically "auspicious" stories, with a *doyen* beloved of a universe of booksellers and possessing an *oeuvre* approaching that of Honore de Balzac: surely, DeHaven entreated, it was a welding powerfully beyond mere nummular value.

"The terms are...acceptable, but my temerity is rather of another order," Landsdowne managed to utter, the phrases long practiced during the longish Underground journey from Roland Gardens to Mayfair. "Rather it's of a discretionary nature. I'm to be honored by and then intimidated with diurnal matters of the distinguished one's personal, indeed private, doubtless singular nature. How am poor I to possibly determine what is to be withheld from more...comprehensive knowledge?"

She fluttered at him now, then gurgled throatily as her enormous eyes deigned to take him in, a speck in their vast, humid domain. "I understand your potential predicament," she at last allowed, utilizing that slightly guttural custom she had of late adopted, its precise grounds he might only imagine, perhaps as a pre-corrective to those who dreamed she would dare further presume upon the enormous honor of her dispirited predicament. "Save that it is not in any manner *to become* an issue. Neither yourself nor myself nor anyone *not* of my late husband's eminence would be capable, as you so prettily put it, *to determine*. You must present it *all*. All as it is written. Every glorious sanctified word of it, every bountiful phrase, every munificent paragraph, every resplendent page! His readers demand all," she went on to gently assert as though he'd dared attempt to practically challenge her. "Through decades of loyalty, they have after all merited their privilege to postulate it so. What can poor we, merely his providential caretakers, do but provide, provide what is so squarely desired?"

He started to pronounce how munificent she herself was, how compassionate and unselfconscious, when she rose and arranged the jet glitter of her just-shut fan upon that same spot of forearm she'd yesterday alit upon. "Then we are in covenant! Every last word is to be included, collated, and only if required notated and explicated—that the Van Pryor legacy be fulfilled!"

She flowed toward the parlor door and he pursued her sweeping course to a second floor along dim connecting corridors of the ample dwelling, to another, yet more restricted stair, rising in two increasingly precipitous landings that at long last terminated at a door. She prized it open to a small, crammed room, redolent of ink and blotting paper, tumbled about from every side and possible angle with open-leaved books and bookmarked journals, page-creased periodicals, and yet more volumes amidst a veritable frenzy of unassorted papers. The single mullioned window allowed a compressed and thus all the more perplexingly mutiplex vista of differently colored, jumbled rooftops, accented only by chimneypots of diversifying size and configuration.

This was unquestionably the site, the very altar of the Van Pryor aptitude. Landsdowne could barely collect his breath.

"Here, then, young scribe and devotee," she spoke with barely concealed vehemence, "shall be your new hearth and habitat! In this demesne shall your spirit guide Anthony Van Pryor's grand literary scheme to its foreordained conclusion!"

3.

The presence, because despite the gossamer impossibility no other designation could possibly explain what else it might entail, had bided its time, allowing itself to pass unnoticed for more than a month, indeed for that very same duration that had passed as though in the midst of the grandest possible romance, that same period that Landsdowne had been sanctified to labor, beetle-like if not more quiet, ordinarily nocturnal, as he still must labor for his living by daylight, only now and then interrupted by a lower-floors menial asking if he'd care for tea and cake, the which he so often refused, and so colored scarlet in doing so, that the indomitable borough-bred lass now simply carried it aloft unbidden upon an overflowing tray, insistent it would "go to thems scurrying in the wainscoting" if he didn't partake of it all. *She* came not at all, or if so, so seldom it was a marvel. Her approach would be signalized by an imperceptible distant fluttering as of poultry shivering off the remnants of a downpour, a nearly silent padded ascension, a shy tap on the ajar door, a murmur: dare she disturb?

Always he rose, paid reverence, osculated the beringed, dimpled fingers, averting whenever possible the overlarge, ever-moist, somewhat accusatory eyes, attempting to decipher within the tissue of civilities that drizzled through the laced intricacies of her omnipresent fan the content, should any be so bold as to represent itself, of her visit, her request. Never her remonstrance, though in fact certainly he'd sensed that too, hovering ambiguously at all times just beyond his grasp whenever she'd achieved one of her exceptional ascensions to the scene of his nocturnal communion.

No other word could presumably approach the sacerdotal, the hierophantic nature of what he so nightly labored upon than that which delimited the joining together of young acolyte and veteran host. All the more reason, then, to feel amidst the presence of those orphaned instruments of the trade, those excrescent volumes and sundry uncollected correspondent leave-takings of the master's art not only the sense of a time now vanished forever, but somehow also of an ongathering, onmoving, *en point*, a virtually present tense.

More than once Landsdowne had attempted to summarize these impressions, restricted as they must be to the Van Pryor workroom, and though his handsome usual companion had donated his fullest, his most cognizant attentions, somehow, each time, Landsdowne realized he had, after all, not at all truly accomplished his end. With the unfortunately crystalline result that the indefatigable DeHaven was all the more conscious of what he designated his younger's "extreme earnestness of intent."

What method, if method could be discovered then, to describe the sensations—for literally sensations they must be admitted to be, and not as his publisher would have it, some finer perception beyond the compass of the customary—that Landsdowne had begun to experience with increased frequency within the blessed chamber, especially those moments not strictly restricted to actual transcription but to rumination? Most recently he'd been ambivalently dumbfounded and yet simultaneously gratified to apperceive a sort of riffling, feather-light, yet indisputable, amidst the hair above one temple as he bent to his work, a riffling all the more incomprehensible, as it was non-attributable to any minutiae of a draught or other perceptible material causation. A riffling all the more explicit in that no other portion of his person was affected, as though naught but a pair of incorporeal fingertips had, in passing, extended a vaguely fond salutation. The titillation had continued, had in fact endured minutes beyond the sensation itself, endured and confirmed itself into a tingling of the epidermis as it were, that once initiated, must consummate itself in every nerve-ending, down to his lower portion.

Undoubtedly it compensated, this latest sensation, since reimbursement of a more remunerative nature was apparently to be unforthcoming. And along with reparation, another emotion gradually established itself within Landsdowne's breast: of unqualified approbation from, dare he consider it? *beyond*. Thus he labored on with incremented agreeableness, augmenting his tiny store of confidence that his selection had not been mere propinquity, nor the surety and ease of editorial manipulation, should such be required, but instead an authorization derived from the single, the only possibly authentic, origin.

4.

Indistinguishable was that evening, unextraordinary the circumstances, during which our young savant was to discern that all unawares he'd suddenly, lamentably discovered himself in a position most acutely felt and acutely deplorable. The literary-chronological mechanism upon which he'd long relied, which he'd for such a successful period plied, required that any uncollated paper, be it note, bill of sale, or missive, be paired to the naturally correspondent passage in the curiously irregular journal or record book Van Pryor had kept. Cognate thereby bred infallible. All the more inevitable therefore the communication Landsdowne now perused, unable to fully embrace its significance, except as it fit patchwork into the grander enigma of the diurnal events of this workroom's predecessor. Yet, once puzzled into place, once the fit was declared not inappropriate, the greater meaning became—all too inescapable. That the authoress of the epistle to his master was instantly recognizable to our acolyte, whose own matrimonial partner he'd tirelessly if only mentally accompanied as each new volume floated into the lending libraries, produced perhaps the most peerless of concussions. That Van Pryor had then actually notated another fellow helpmeet's initials into his ordinarily haphazard datebook with astonishing heedlessness, and later on compounded the egregiousness by commenting upon the encounter in his journal in a satisfied manner insouciantly approaching, well, it had to be admitted, approaching the vulgar, would thereafter be undeniable.

Ensuing passages, annotations, commentaries, in fact the entire ceaseless panoply amounted to several months' duration, resulting in the irrefutable: unfamiliar to any but themselves, and now alas to *his* abashed gaze, the aberrant twosome had continued to sully their matrimonial sacraments and earlier commitments, with, at various times, an almost unrestricted liberty of action, month after month after month.

Crestfallen, Landsdowne could do nothing but abscond from if not the setting, then at least the substantiation of the activity. But while he'd decamped from the stage, the performance all the more perpetuated itself in his imagination, so that even an unaccustomed double measure of fortified wine failed to generate that lethean surcease he required to fall asleep. Before the obliquitous dawn he resolved to relinquish a task no longer to be held as honorable. Resolution led to somnolence; with his artlessness restored, he at last slept.

The unexpected interview caught *her* not completely unawares. She bestowed, entered, allowed his anxiety its stammering moments, his resolution its exclamation, but nonetheless she continued to remain unswervingly in place, plumped among her ebony crinolines, fixing upon him a liquid gaze admixed as much with compassion as with more professional objectivity. Allowing his timorous vehemence its fullest extent, she then acceded immediately to his resignation, wholeheartedly so, if, if, if—*if only*—she begged she might be allowed to partake of and thus *comprehend* the source of this remarkable, this so precipitous turnabout.

Seldom had Landsdowne encountered such difficulty. At last, he intimated his discoveries, his trepidation, the understandable apprehension—for her reputation alone. Before he was done, she contrived to interrupt, her fan an instrument of regard and interaction upon his sleeve, as, almost inaudibly she reminded him of their earlier intercourse upon the subject of "determination," and how she'd understood them to have already abundantly agreed upon a course where any such selection would be utterly unnecessary. "You must present it *all*," she once more repeated. "*All* as it is written.

Every bountiful phrase. His readers demand all," she once more gently insisted. "Poor we are merely his providential caretakers," she reiterated.

Leaving her interlocutor at a temporary loss for further words. Was the personage then before him so extraordinarily charitable, so magnificent in her acceptance of the inadmissible? Without question he must now assume that his own recent detection must be a disclosure his hostess had somehow herself long before managed to arrive at herself, and further she had also managed to arrange it all to herself, processing the doubtless unwelcome information in a manner if not wholly acceptable than at the least bearable. It now came to Landsdowne, that without doubt his workroom's predecessor had himself selected his life's companion precisely for the possession of such a temperament, exactly such an ability at management, indeed for qualities beyond those at first glance apparent.

Grateful confusion led Landsdowne to bend his knee to her, but she soon elevated him to his feet, reminding him of their covenant and of the enormity of the task still left undone. He ascended to his exertions with a renewed stamina and sense of purpose, and once settled was again put in mind of that other, far less substantial Communicant, whose unquestioned presence consisted of a recapitulated riffling of his hair, as though overlooking in him the understandable, if surely not to be repeated, lapse of certitude.

5.

"But surely you can see how I've come around yet again?" Landsdowne moaned to his editorial contemporary, "From one bare credibility to another one, this time far more abominable."

DeHaven had been accosted at his office at the moment of leave-taking for his midday meal, and his customary high spirits decided for him the necessity of his young champion accompanying him to a dining establishment of the most arcane tenor, focusing as it did, upon a cuisine altogether unfamiliar, mid-Asiatic, and sapid in the extreme.

"Explicate, dear fellow." He attempted to calm his friend with a squeeze of the fleshier sector of one of his lower limbs. "For I'm afraid I'm somewhat at sea. Ah, and here is the tandoor dish I spoke of before with such tenderness!" he enthused as a be-turbanned attendant set down the savory vessel and uncovered it, releasing an amplitude of orientalia to ring their heads with its wreath of fragrances and to stimulate their gourmanderie.

"For days after, I'd persuaded myself she'd after all known all the while, the Widow Van Pryor that is, known perhaps with growing comprehension for months during the perpetration of the marital enormity and that she'd only *ultimately* forgiven, as who wouldn't. But that she was now willing to release all despite, if not given, the otherwise faultless origin of her understandable agony. Naturally, she could but rise in my estimation, as I labored on to corral the aberrant missives and nearly licentious journal passages... But then, and only yesterday it occurred to me, as I was frequenting a railroad tea-shop attached to Euston Station, a dreary yet at times fascinating situation from which to encompass the London universe, only then, as I said, late last night, awaiting an Underground to return me to Roland Gardens, did another, far more sinister interpretation all unassisted arrive. What if, by publication of it *all*, she seeks nothing less than a practically public vengeance upon the great man, a vengeance all the more distressing in that she alone is able to give voice, while her potential disputant is utterly unable to defend himself? Thus my torment and thus the newly understood falseness of my present position."

The carmine roast had been dissected, and unable not to resist, DeHaven had availed himself of the pleasures of the table. He ceased, however, now, elevating a fowl-filled fork aloft to declaim, "But my dear young marvel, it couldn't be any clearer! Should she become, as you say you fear, so publicly intemperate herself, then you are yourself to take up the cudgels in defense of your master! Who better to be his champion than one already so privileged?"

Landsdowne could do little but utter phrases of astonishment to his companion, who managed to "tuck" back into his luncheon with the sharpest of appetites. "But surely you give me too much credit. You presume to begin with, that I *would* challenge her and defend him, when in fact, I've not arrived at any such certainty. Surely she was wronged. Surely the world ought to know her blessed silent endurance of it all, equally along with *his* seemingly Olympian utter disregard."

"Then, my young starveling, for if you do not soon avail yourself, there will be none left and starveling surely you must become today, you must do *nothing*. And by all means follow the path your irksome conscience describes for you. This dish now is called a Korma. Experience, my love, to what a culinary pinnacle a mere kitchen garden marrow may aspire!"

Landsdowne did at last sample the feastling set before the two, and if he never quite rose to the occasion as did his editor, at least he contrived to taste sufficient of each platter before them to summarize for himself the varied buccal sensations that had been conjured. DeHaven was undoubtedly a boon friend and his advice worth heeding. Even so, he observed himself still unserene by luncheon's conclusion, and he stalked off to his labors with still-crimped brow and apprehensive mien.

Only to be greeted not a half hour after he'd settled into

the long-honored chair and desk by a new series of horrors which, if by no means as equal in number or manner to the great man's, were all the more intolerable for detailing as they so unswervingly did detail from the husband's perspective, the utter disregard of marital vows of the wife! The passages Van Pryor had penned in natural response partook of equal portions of jaded amusement and connubial irritation. His single remaining desire in the face of it all was merely that she and her unnamed companion become never quite so fatuous as to entitle the hoi polloi to deduce their clandestine alliance. In that at least, Landsdowne had to admit, they'd all succeeded very well, as he'd never heard the breath of a whisper against the woman.

Landsdowne's own stupefaction was quietly accompanied by a correspondent reanimation of the presence he'd so recently sensed, upon this occasion renewed by the long familiar hair riffling but newly accompanied by a soft respiration into the cup of his hearing organ, so subtle that at first he couldn't be utterly certain, until it was repeated, until the surety was undeniable. If earlier he'd been blessed, now surely he was doubly so.

Quitting the establishment somewhat earlier that night than others to attend upon DeHaven at the opera, he stumbled upon his hostess herself, in the house's foyer, preparing for the outdoors. He begged her pardon, asservating that he'd come upon yet more information of a particularly uncivil nature, and wondered did her command still stand, no matter the party involved in the potential damage? Or would perhaps she wish to know its details?

She was about to herself step out, apparently a second time for the night in company, all aflutter in jet and feathers, gemstones and furs, and at first she barely registered his presence, then did evince it with a graciousness he could only admire: "Every bountiful phrase," she reiterated. Then as she swept out to an awaiting carriage, she adumbrated: "His demanding readers must have it *all*."

"But… No matter the cost to him…or to yourself?"

"What is mere cost to such as he…or to I?" she in turn asked. And was gone.

6.

"Discretion means all in Service," a maternal-line relation had once intoned to him, then a barely comprehending child, "and discretion in Service is nothing more or less than a finely discriminating blindness in the matter of one's betters." The ancient and now munificently endowed old thing had unquestionably managed the artful practice of discretion, if one were to conclude only by external compensations. Her pension was unstinting, the very cottage in which she'd resided since the passing of her longtime mistress was charmingly situated; remarkably capacious; it even harbored its own service in the form of a slavy from the "big house," no longer required there, if gratifyingly essential to his aged relation's newly won gentility. Fresher generations of the great house unfailingly called upon the older person whenever they happened anywhere near the neighborhood, behaving when they did so with the openhanded, openhearted unconstraint, not of mere former employer's offspring, but indeed almost as though they themselves were but honored, respectful, younger relations.

As he advanced onward in his labors, Landsdowne couldn't help but recollect all that and himself attempt to apply some of these well-experienced lessons to his own more particularized circumstances. Nor had it escaped his apprehension that in the last few months of his nocturnal efforts among the Van Pryor papers, his own poor little pittance of repute had all unawares by himself become considerably elevated beyond what his slim volume of *contes* could genuinely warrant; among his own poor and scattered set of artists-in-training as would have been understandable; but also, dare one say it, among others less *en famille*, not excluding certain bellwethers gathered at the more established Athenaeums of erudition.

His late master's star continued its irrepressible ascent, undeterred by the vulgar fact of mortality, and as its rays more widely glimmered, casting further light over the house, the *oeuvre*, the uncollected papers, invariably the widow herself began to assume the unequivocal status of a personage among certain districts of society. It became at first intimated, then generally accepted, that perhaps one had been unjust toward the poor woman in the past, if only in one's conscious efforts to so set her husband so apart from the common run. Thankfully, reparation could only be more valuable in how utterly it must now be performed. These later months it was wholly in vain that our youth awaited her tentative footfalls upon the uncarpeted risers outside the chamber lintel. It seemed she now luncheoned, dined, even breakfasted abroad quite so systematically that were it not for themselves and his own meager little repasts, the kitchen staff would have found itself delightfully superfluous.

Even DeHaven's publishing establishment, by now so inextricably coupled with the great author's name, continued to batten and gorge upon the generalized radiance, as did DeHaven himself, spoken of as a noted "Clever Young Turk of the Arts." And, as did our simple scribe himself, granted the growing sincerity of regard evidently provoked, he was certain, at least partially by the aura of mystery that naturally surrounded his endeavors. One would have to be sightless, heedless, deaf, indiscreet, as well as indiscriminate in varied senses of those terms to not truly apprehend how very universal a sunset glow had come to suffuse all that lay within the ill-defined, ever-amplifying, Van Pryor penumbra.

In such a benevolently crepuscular ambiance, an accommodation with the less palatable specifics of his superiors did arrive, quite slowly at first given the galaxy of compunctions it must overcome—or illuminate—only to at long last fully scatter all contentions asunder, resulting one afternoon in our young man's completely uncharacteristic species of Gallically shoulder-shrugging insouciance.

Thus ensued the penultimate phase of Landsdowne's mission: the most recent year's journals, slipshod as they were, along with the accompanying, heretofore barely glanced at, aggregate of letters, notes, relevant and irrelevant paper effluvia. It went without needed having to be said that the previously eerie and by now more or less customary caresses from an unnamed source that had at first so alarmed our young savant whenever he sat in the master's chair at his labors were now redoubled in some hitherto unaccustomed manner, causing equal amounts of pleasure and consternation, and yet still he plunged onward.

The newest disclosure when ultimately it reached its destination—an undulating course dictated by unfolded note by scribbled note, twice-left visiting cards, multiple hansom cab receipts, not fully distinct journal entries, even once an invoice from a shared chamber at a less-than-estimable seaside resort—would sensibly enough be less effectively thunder-striking than had it come earlier and sans antecedent heralds, despite what its even more sensational content otherwise indicated.

Evidently, our collator was coerced to conclude that his very own editorial champion had felt the need only a few short months previously to ensure fertilization of the ground of his new ascension into the paternal position, by initiating what he, in a strikingly precipitate *billet-doux*, reminded the Master was a long-desired, long spoken of, and long postponed, joint intimacy. That it had been as corporeal as preceding amours concerning members of the house was wholly inevitable, Landsdowne supposed in retrospect, and thus equally unremarkable. After all, those above, as these three Demigods apparently so considered themselves, bestrode the world as Olympians; hence equally Olympian would be their inclinations and as well their transgressions. At times our poor scribe even pondered whether in the very heated moment of conception of the project, his *soi-disant* friend, the perversely public DeHaven, hadn't even fallen upon, nay relied upon, this very *denouement* being arrived at. He could today without a jot of difficulty envision the young publisher carefully deciding to do so, and simultaneously deciding exactly what tack to veer onto, once it were all broadcast. Indubitably only once he comprehended the prevailing westerlies of opinion, only then would DeHaven opt to deride it all as a simple, if all-too-graciously flattering, phantasy of his elder; or conversely to entertain it further, explaining it away as a conclusive, Hellenically developmental, stage in the life and art of a great author.

As for himself, Landsdowne recognized fully now that he was but an underling, instrument of them all, including, indeed especially, he who Landsdowne had for so long a duration and so intently admired from a distance, Van Pryor himself, and of late, from within his own private demesne, and who, it appeared, now so supernaturally reciprocated that admiration, so that all that could possibly matter given the extremity of the circumstances was to perform as capacious and discriminate a service as was humanly conceivable. Opportunity did not waver, so long as DeHaven existed in any proximity to his orbit, and soon enough one such sterling exemplar presented itself to our scholar with untypically equal portions of celerity and the possibility of expansiveness.

It appeared that a celebrated quarterly of more than ordinarily literate pretensions had perforce recently swept clear the accumulated cellars of elder statesmen of their more ephemeral scribblings and now sought, well, sought anything it might deem justifiably publishable. Insofar as Landsdowne was concerned, it sought his own slender pluckings among the incunabula of his more distinguished ally; if, that is, one might be assured of utter exclusivity. A distaff version of his handsome young publishing friend efficiently uncovered our young savant's comings and goings, and she daily waylaid him with unceasing application and absolute fortitude, virtually commanding his participation. The placement and position offered by her were to say in the least admirable, in fact they would be unquestionably conspicuous; the remuneration, although fiduciarily modest, would be of a binary nature: including not only whatever he might volunteer from the worktable where he had labored nightly—with its careful annotations naturally for comprehension—but also, it was desired, some piece not inconsiderably from his own poor personal stock of scribbling. Our scrivener's sole condition in turn, waved into reality the instant it was proposed, was that what would be delivered to her offices must become the final, the reading draft. The masculine young periodical she-wolf pondered and then pounced. Agreement was sealed with an athletic shake of her hands and a virile back clasp, and within a fortnight she had as good as her word already typeset and had printed up the material.

To describe the consequences of this publication as electrifying would be as much as ignoring it almost entirely. Landsdowne only began to understand the range of its fullest implications during the afternoon of the quarterly's debut issuance, when, during his diurnal labors, and from his semi-opaque view across a large chamber filled with clerks of equal or greater denomination than himself, he was able to briefly ascertain his immediate superior along with his own superior, communicating with a certain intensity and every once in a while, unable to keep themselves from turning to gaze in his, Landsdowne's, general direction; upon which perceiving themselves perceived, they rapidly gazed away again. When, upon exiting for the evening, our hero passed the administrative area, he was able to substantiate the presence of the latest number of the very periodical, partially hidden by overlying actuarial tables, yet indubitably already much thumbed through.

Upon arriving at his own chambers he found a quick note from some secretarial individual associated with DeHaven House, advising of the sudden cancellation of a previous engagement with her young employer; without in addition, he couldn't have failed but note, apology nor offer to reconstitute the appointment. He dined then alone in a neighboring tea-shop, upon bread soup and trifle, not unaware of the suddenly frequent, usually whispered stares of not familiar, oft-noted personages he had tended to think of as possessing some literary inclination, whenever he occasioned to look up from his evening paper or diminutive collation. His gaze was alas never in any danger of being in turn caught nor returned by any of them nor his physiology of being for a second glancingly skirted even within the most restricted of situations.

Nor was our savant, an hour afterward, in any way astonished to find the door to his nightly labors of recent and months-long duration adamantly shut against his ringing or knocking, while his erstwhile confederate from within the Van Pryor pantry appeared to shoot furious or alarmed glimpses at him from behind the poorly furled camouflage of an arras across an upper window.

He'd beforehand removed handmade copies of what he'd specifically required from the workroom, after all, and so he turned away in tranquil resignation from the house suddenly prohibited to him, its mistress doubtless in the most implacable dudgeon, as no doubt his earlier friend and benefactor was also now utterly enmitous. Landsdowne allowed himself the tiniest glimmer of a smile, before he revolved for a final moment within the once so beloved little court and then for the ultimate time bid farewell to its alabaster excrescences.

At home in his bed-sitter, later on, he allowed himself an indulgence, supping upon a treacle tea-cake salvaged from his earlier repast. With the two-penny coal grate filled, our hero basked in a solitude which he was cognizant would become far more customary, gathering for comfort around himself the remnants of his fine intelligence and his immense scruples.

7.

From one crystal-studded and holly-encrusted end of the vast celebratory groaning board to about midway up one side, some months further on, the Widow Van Pryor espied, among a brood of young female eligibles, the exceptionally distinct, candlelit fair hair and side whiskers of her publisher and business associate. Barely perceptible, beneath one glisteningly curved wing of his ashen crown, emerged a sprig of holly, which jiggled ever so slowly with every slight motion of his handsome young head, nearly requisitioning her fullest attention. For her own part, she recognized, the funereal materials that had virtually defined her physical presence within society for so long had been at last thrown asunder, replaced tonight by a sable and magenta conception arising from across the Channel, a study of fine fabrics and subtly woven gradations that if not yet merry still evinced the porcelain of her complexion and reflected the vast mystery of her eyes. It had been months, more than half an annum, since they'd last encountered, and she wondered if when they did more abundantly encounter, as seemed almost perilously probable this evening, they would actually deign to discuss what most persons of breeding in their midst considered to be utterly indiscussable.

A moment later she found herself distracted by a military gentleman of more than usual wit, and it wasn't until hours later, when she discovered herself in the house's great foyer, awaiting her brougham, that the widow again remarked DeHaven, himself just now fully cloaked and stepped into the festively decorated rotunda, a lackey sent out to his own driver.

They bowed and brushed fingertips, and even for a second, if not quite successfully, attempted to brush lips against cheeks. He flattered her, and she returned the insincerity with compliments upon his own not inconsiderable person. In the chill marble echoing antechamber they could discern as though from afar little calls and cries from guests in other chambers and halls still not ready to depart; even so at closer range silence frostily encased them, as they looked away from faces to gloves, nearby sculptures, the floor, anything it seemed but each other.

Only once the house's well-swaddled footman had stepped in to announce her car, then exited back out into the now totally white evening, did her companion in place step forward ever so slightly and utter in the most irresolved of voices, "Did he ever actually say *why* he did it?"

"How could he possibly?" she asked in turn. "As no further

communication from him was to be acceptable afterward. And not to you, either, I gather. No, of course not." Then she added, as she began gathering her mantilla more closely about her person, "The widespread presumption, if one is to even listen to it, is that he did it of course for the publicity."

"Ah, of course, for the publicity!" DeHaven replied. "The publicity, I must warrant was enormous, almost incalculable. Poor me, poor you, my dear lady, are as beggars to him these days in the size, the scope, the sheer intercontinental scandalousness of his all-abiding publicity."

Her driver had pulled up outside the sliver of doorway she held ajar and the courser's bells were subtly shaking as she turned a final time and said, "And then of course, there are those more sobering moments, when I wonder if after all, he wasn't merely, and yet so characteristically in his dim, chivalrous manner, attempting to protect us."

"Ah!" DeHaven uttered, "To protect us!" Then he groped. "To protect us from…our…not entirely…wholesome… pasts?"

"From that surely enough, but more crucially from our *instincts*!"

He once again groped. "Our instincts to admit…certain connections, you mean."

"He took them *all* upon himself, poor foolish doomed admirable young creature, declaring himself the perpetrator, the instrument, the receptor of any possible infidelity, thoughtless monstrosity, lubricity, or utter imbecility. We once, you and I, dreamed we might be able to cope. That was the very essence of our projected endeavor utilizing his services—that we *would* more than be able to cope: we'd as much as bask in it all. In retrospect, observing him, a veritable clod of solidity, barely able to retain his feet within the maelstrom of so much…self-admission, well, it's evident now we couldn't for a second have coped, not really, not at all, don't you see? Nor escaped without being ourselves mortally wounded."

"Yes, I see now," DeHaven admitted. "He did it all for us. Because he loved us."

"He did it because he loved us," she confirmed quietly. "But most of all, he did it because the fool acolyte adored his Master and wasn't it *he*, after all, who was *least* in need of protection, but *most* in need of perpetuation?"

It wasn't in truth a question, and the last thing she expected was a response, so they brushed gloved fingers once again, before allowing the footman to help her down the icy steps and into her brougham. A moment later, the footman was returned, her carriage driven off, and Samson icily fretting aperch the landau at the curb, whereupon DeHaven also descended.

They'd proceeded barely a furlong when he heard the first of morning's criers with his boy-sized chalkboard hawking the habitually salacious journalistic wares, and as usual, leading the dawn's sensations was yet another unimaginable revelation concerning the increasingly invidious juridical fortunes of his now infamous young acquaintance.

Within the carriage all was leather and wool, cashmere mufflers, fawn-skin gloves and shearling throws, toasty and warm; DeHaven had had such a long and tiring day of it; in seconds, without wishing it, he was dozing. All about him, if never ever quite touching him, the tempest intensified.

The Geology of Southern California at Black's Beach

Hang gliders dappled the sky as the T-Bird convertible ascended then flattened out onto the seashore plateau along Torrey Pines Road. Red and yellow, white and blue, purple and orange, the fragile little man/mechanisms seemed no bigger than dragonflies levitating upon the strong Pacific Ocean currents a hundred and eighty feet below, gliding in slightly askew formation as though out of a child's illustration.

"That's Jonas Salk's Institute," Craig said from the backseat, still playing tour guide. "He's supposed to be working on a new vaccine," he added. "Keep going to the end. The parking lot's a right turn." Craig's voice, normally strained, even raspy, was even more tense from him having to yell.

The turn-off led past where the hang gliders were taking off. I turned to face them, watching a gang of people gather around one glider just landing. Did they simply run off the cliff to get going? Or were they lifted by currents from the rock ledge? The latter, I supposed.

The geologist in me couldn't help but notice the cliffs. The rock here looked pretty undistinguished, but California's geologic history was complex. These Southern Peninsula Ranges were defined Quaternary laid over a basement of Mid-Mesozoic rock, all part of what was known as the Nevadan

Orogenic belt, the earliest lifting of this westernmost part of the continent when dinosaurs filled the land. Since then, under the influence of subducting plates and shifting masses, these coastlines had risen and dropped many times, picking up fragments of various plates that slowly drifted north to form Alaska.

"Now remember," Craig poked me from behind, "no shilly shallying! You must go directly down the cliff path! No matter how frightened you are!" He meant it to be a command, but the combination of Midwest twang and childish whine undercut his authority.

"Cliffs don't frighten me," I said.

"Nothing frightens Roger," Mark said as he lightly spun the steering wheel. He looked great behind the wheel of the T-Bird. For that matter, he looked great in any convertible in Southern California, his thick black hair riffling like a fine pelt in the maritime breeze, his skin quickly tanning, tiny tension lines resolving from around his eyes. We'd been talking about possibly moving out here, and this visit had been partly about him opening a San Diego office. Mark was staying with a law-school friend, Sue, a woman my age who'd returned to school after her children were grown. She worked in the attorney general's office but was still open to the idea of joining a commercial practice, especially one as successful as Mark's.

"Yeah! Well," Craig sputtered. "Maybe he's not frightened because he's never *seen* a cliff like this!" Craig insisted. "He'll be plenty frightened."

"I'm astigmatic," I explained. "All depths look shallower. That's why heights don't frighten me. I can't grasp how high they are."

Mark looked my way briefly, a smile hovering on his lips.

"We'll see! We'll see!" Craig warned darkly from behind

us, not getting the joke. That evoked another tiny smile from Mark.

What I really wanted was to get into one of those hang gliders and rise, rise, rise above the earth, the sea, into the sky, and just soar away. How much could that cost? A few hundred dollars? All I had to do was tell Mark to drive to where they were taking off.

"It'll be good to get more sun," Mark said. Although I'd just arrived in San Diego, he'd arrived five days earlier for the Bar Association Weekend. "The June Glooms," Diegans called the overcast, foggy weather, even though it was mid May, the city's thousands of jacaranda trees just reaching bloom, littering the lawns and streets with pale purple blossoms. Mark had caught a bit of sun the first few days around the pool at the Del Coronado Hotel where the conference was held, but since then the weather had been dismal. It was difficult to know how to adjust to it. We had formed today's plans just last night at dinner, with the four of us—Craig, Mark, Sue and I—down the Baja coast at that hacienda-turned-restaurant overlooking the channel islands near Enseñada. Craig had said he knew the most magnificent beach in this area. We'd go, he'd said, if the sun came out.

"...people have fallen from that cliff." Craig was now warning of dire consequences. "Miles Parker fell and almost died. He's got a metal plate in his head. His jaw was broken in three places and had to be rebuilt. A pacemaker had to be installed in his chest..."

Mark would have a conniption if I said I wanted to hang glide. He silently worried all those days in the Caribbean as I'd discovered, put on, and tested the snorkeling equipment. He grew more tense hourly as I taught myself how to use it all in the bayside house pool until I was certain I knew how to breathe right. I clumped along the deck in the big rubber fins down the ladder into that pale green baywater, where, from the first instant that I arranged the face-mask and breathing tube and put my head down and spread my arms and legs and floated, gently kicking, I knew this was what I wanted, what *I'd always wanted* to experience in the water. When I'd got back out, Mark was in the deck chair, right there on the quay—a first—wearing that worried face he couldn't shake. "You went so far! I could barely see you!" And even though I explained how safe it was, how easy, how I could see far off, every inch of water, enough to chivvy and chase a magenta-and-white octopus across the stark, barely vegetated, limestone sea floor, I saw how worried Mark continued to be whenever I snorkeled, afraid that I'd be sliced by a barracuda, stung by a ray. No: hang gliding was definitely out.

Mark pulled the T-Bird to the end of the macadam at the post and wire guardrail. Craig leapt out, grabbing bags out of the backseat.

"Ocean looks dirty," Mark said.

With less familiarity than I had of the West Coast, he was still surprised by how dark the sand was, how green steel rather than marine blue the Pacific usually looked.

"C'mon, Craig! Get off me!"

"You can't handle that! Let a real man carry it," Craig insisted. He'd grabbed me from behind and was trying to wrest the bag away, then shouldering it and tossing his own, smaller bag at my feet. "Once you get on the cliff's face, it'll drag you down."

Ever since I'd arrived at the airport, Craig had been doing things like this, designed to show Mark how tall, strong, virile and manly Craig was. In short, how desirable. Which he undoubtedly was. Why else would I be out here?

Not that anything Craig did would make a bit of difference to Mark, I knew. Except perhaps to the degree that it pleased or annoyed me. (Nothing should *ever* annoy me.) But Craig didn't know that. Despite how intelligent and well read he was, Craig wasn't very observant of others. Besides which he tended to act almost entirely out of a welter of instinct, exhibitionism, and petty revenge. All of which made him unpredictable and thus a lot more attractive.

We headed to the break in the guardrail and protective hedges to the path hewn into and down the cliff. It was very high. Even with my astigmatism, I could see that the beach lay quite far below. Suddenly across it ran the shadow of an insect. I looked up behind myself: another hang glider had taken off. It soared above us, off into the distance.

"I knew you'd be scared the second you got here," Craig was crowing. He'd already begun down the path, a makeshift steep decline around boulders and grass tussocks and through sand patches. I followed. Mark brought up the rear.

At most points in the descent, I was so busy trying to hold on and get around obstacles, that I seldom looked around. This portion of coast around La Jolla uplands is of the late Miocene Era, sedimentary rock on top of and cut through by striated metamorphic and plutonic rock, the whole business known as the San Onofre Breccia. I had lectured often about how these high cliffs were formed when the most recent part of this coast had risen, relatively late geologically speaking, long after the dinosaurs were fossils and the earth was undergoing repeated hard glaciations. And thus, all this was, for me, a source of great interest. All around I could make out a mass of indurated rock, gray wales, shales, bedded cherts, and an occasional limestone lens or two, and infrequently interbedded among it all, pillow basalt, indicating oceanic origin. It might have been a textbook diagram.

At one completely exposed turn-and-drop all-rock balcony about a quarter of the way down the cliff from the parking lot above we were suddenly facing north, along the beach, showing exactly how high up as well as how vulnerable we were. I found it thrilling, so I remained there while Craig went on, waiting for Mark to join me from behind so I could share the astonishing view with him.

He seemed upset: his normally cool demeanor jolted. I was about to say something about the rock, the stupendous view, when Mark reached a little shale shelf I was on and with a single glance realized where we were. His reaction was simply to turn away. "This the way?" he asked in a tight voice, gesturing down.

I went to where Mark was looking, where Craig had gone: a shallow sand slide between two outjuttings of rock, ending in a narrow sand pit. It looked like fun.

"Sure is! Follow me!" I started down, half-sliding, while grabbing at the worn smooth edges of rock on each side. When I landed with a thump in the little sand pit, Craig suddenly appeared from around the bend.

"What's taking you so long? At this rate, it'll take hours to climb down."

"Just go! Will you!" I gave him a little push. Then I looked up. Mark was where I'd just been, some ten feet above, sitting on the edge of the little shelf, his feet and bag hanging off to one side. He wasn't moving. "What's wrong?" I shouted up. Craig remained where he was. "Mark!" I shouted again.

"There's nothing to hold on to," Mark shouted back.

"Just slide down."

"I can't!"

"Sure you can. We both did it."

"I can't!" Mark repeated, and this time there was something else to the tone of his voice.

"I'm here. I'll catch you. You won't go anywhere."

"I can't!" he repeated and dragged himself up to his feet,

slipped, quickly grabbed at some grass that instantly gave way, so that he had to scrabble at nearby rock, where he held on as though for dear life. "I'm going back," he shouted.

"What's wrong?" Craig asked me, annoyed.

"Are you sure?" I called up at Mark.

"If we go back up," Craig was saying, "we'll have to go around to the other parking lot and walk to the beach. That'll take a half hour."

"You go down. We'll take the long way and join you later."

"I've got to show you where the other parking lot is. You'll never find it on your own."

"Do what you want, Craig. I'm going back up," I said. "Mark! Wait for me," I shouted and began scrambling up the sand slide.

Mark was hunkered down where he'd grabbed on, looking all-in, panting, his bag at his feet.

"Let me take that," I said, grabbing his bigger bag, "I can cope easier with it," I said, chatting away, trying to ignore the obvious, that Mark looked pale, out of it.

"I can't do it!" he repeated. Then, "When I was a kid I used to have this nightmare of going off the edge of a cliff. I'd be holding on to tufts of grass, then sharp rock, then I'd slide off."

In all our fifteen years together, I'd never heard of the dream before.

"It's my fault we're here in the first place." I tried changing the subject. "If I weren't so determined not to let Stupid have the last word. I mean this cliff *is* high, even to me, and it *is* scary and…"

I don't know how much of it Mark even heard.

"And all of a sudden," Mark went on, "there I was! In the nightmare! Right in it!"

"Nightmare's over," I said. "We're going back up."

"I don't know if I can," he said.

I couldn't ever remember seeing Mark, or hearing him, like this.

"I'll be right behind you," I said. "You know me, I'm like a mountain goat. You almost have to be on this cliff. You'll have to flatten me completely to fall, and that's not going to be so easy. C'mon, now! Up!"

He stood up a little shakily, but with both hands free now of the bag, he had more to grip with and so a bit more confidence. He began climbing again, at first inch by inch, then picking up speed. I remained less than a foot behind him as he ascended, crowding him at times, touching him at all times, and so letting him know I was there. When we finally got over the fence, he went straight to the car, while I looked around.

Mark all but collapsed on the hood of the T-Bird. And so he wouldn't look strange, I did the same.

Although he was clearly nonplussed by this turn of events, Craig must have been embarrassed by what happened, maybe by the fact that it was Mark who had been daunted by the cliff, and not me. Whatever the reason, Craig uncharacteristically didn't take advantage of the occasion with some comment, but instead decided to be sort of sweet.

"I'm sorry, guys," Mark said.

"The other way is a good path," Craig changed the subject brightly. "It's supposed to be one of the area's better nature trails."

A few minutes later, we all got into the T-Bird again. It wasn't a long drive along Torrey Pines Road to the cut-off that led to the other parking lot, and we would have easily found it without Craig, despite what he'd said. It was naturally less high than the previous parking lot, and while the ocean was visible, it was significantly farther away. Craig said it would be about a half-hour walk from here to the water.

The trail turned out even better than Craig had said. I was already familiar with Eastern shorelines, from the high sand cliffs of Truro on Cape Cod, to the flat marshy deltas of Rhode Island and Connecticut, from the low, white dunes of Long Island and New Jersey, to the even wider, flatter, if darker colored dunes of the Carolinas and the hardscrabble Florida islands further south. But this beach was high, solid, nothing at all like those nearly underwater fens and brakes I had trudged through as a teenager searching duckweed for amphibian life and its secrets. The dunes here were younger, of a coarser granulation and less regular hue. They lay heavily atop the questionable coastal soil they would eventually break down into, a first brush of icing on a crudely baked cake. The trail itself was cleverly constructed, mostly slatted wooden path or lightly fenced gravel, sometimes laid out between half-buried boards or semi-defining beach-drift, sometimes almost indistinguishable from its surroundings except that it was harder underfoot. You would think you'd gotten completely away from the path, only to suddenly arrive at a set of perfectly carpentered stairs rising to another set of wild-looking dunes.

"It's great!" I announced after a few minutes, and began pointing out the flora and fauna to Mark and Craig: the little habitats for tortoises and rabbits, the thin-leaved plants, thicker stemmed for better water collection, yet not quite succulents I'd never seen before, or the odd appearance of certain more familiar plants in disguise: a very slender sarsaparilla tree, a sort of wild raspberry bush. The bird life was smaller and faster than on comparable East Coast shores, more colorful, more flickering.

"That's not…" something or other, Craig would declare

suddenly, with irritating certainty. Then we'd reach an area with names tagged on the fences and they would prove to be exactly what I'd said they were. Which annoyed Craig, so he'd ask, "Well then, what's that?" pointing to some bush or reed, and before I could even suggest what it was, he'd declare, "Wrong!"

This game of egos-on-parade, which we'd gotten into since I'd arrived out here in San Diego, continued to draw us along the path, until we reached another set of stairs and a little deck that turned out to be the crest of the ridge as well as the halfway mark of the nature trail. Before us, the path swagged down widely, slalom-like, complete with angled side fences, apparently down to the water. It was beautifully done and I turned to point it out to Mark. But he wasn't just a little behind us as I'd assumed, but out of sight altogether.

Craig climbed onto the deck railing and from there quickly located Mark. He'd stopped and was seated on a bench in a little dale a few hundred feet behind us, or rather sprawled out, the way he'd been on the T-Bird's hood earlier, looking like an elderly pensioner stopping to catch his breath on one of those island benches in the middle of upper Broadway midway between Zabar's and home.

"Why didn't you tell me?" Craig demanded in that accusing tone of voice I'd come to know only since I'd arrived out here. In New York, a few months ago, Craig had been mellow, delightful; here he seemed angry all the time.

"Tell you what? What are you talking about?"

"Why didn't you tell me he…" Craig faltered. "You know! How bad he is!"

As Craig spoke, an electrical impulse raced up my spine and into my neck. Fear.

"What are you talking about? You heard Mark. He got

upset coming down the cliff because it reminded him of a recurring nightmare he had as a kid."

"There's no cliff here." Craig pointed out the obvious. "And this isn't that long a walk. It *isn't*!" he insisted.

That electrical thread of fear tingled again.

"He's just worn out from what happened before!" I sounded defensive even to myself. "I'd be too!"

Craig wanted to say something else, but he didn't or couldn't bring himself to do it. Instead he shook his head and jumped down the stairs.

"If you…" I began and ended my threat, having to yell, as he was now out of range.

At the bench with Mark, Craig and I hunkered down, and I pulled out fresh fruit I had bought that morning. Naturally when I threw away a plum pit, Craig questioned the environmental impact of my deed. I thought the soil too dry and too poor for peach or plum pits to take root. But Craig thought they might just take and he had dire predictions for the destruction they would doubtless wreak on the delicate biotic balance around us. As usual, Mark watched the two of us argue without saying anything. Craig and I already had disputed at last night's dinner and this morning at breakfast: it was clearly part of whatever we had together. Mark could see that and I could see amusement in his eyes. So at least we distracted him.

So much so, that when we started up again, he joined us in a chorus of "Follow the Yellow Brick Road," which the trail a little bit resembled at that point. By the time we'd gotten up to the little deck and slalom-like fence area, Craig was ahead. It was pretty much all downhill from here, easier going. Ten minutes later, we reached another stairway, which cut through cliffs to the beach.

"You must love this!" Mark often saw through my eyes.

As we descended, Craig was already rushing straight to the ocean, his shorts fluttering against muscled thighs, his red canvas backpack stretched over his shoulders glittering in the strong afternoon sun.

The lower cliffs that guarded the entire beach were low, only from twelve to fourteen feet high, and much older geologically than the high one, and they ran in a nearly unbroken line in either direction as far as I could see. As we walked along, more or less following Craig's lead much farther ahead of us and out in the shallows, we would pass occasional undulations in the cliff face, forming little vertical caves where sand had collected in spots now just large enough for one person to lay down a beach towel. At other spots, sudden breaks occurred, forming arches where sediment had eroded, leaving the more durable ultramafic rock threaded through with serpentinite and gleaming black basalt. At other points, even those had broken off aeons before and fallen forward in the sand where they lay glittering, their surfaces softly, inexorably abraded with every turn of the tide, making them ideally smooth now for basking mermen.

"Nice as it all is," I said, trying to tamp down my pleasure, "I still prefer that beach on Providenciales we found last time. And there wasn't a cliff in sight. Remember?"

"We'll go back," Mark said. "Around Thanksgiving."

"I hope so."

"This *is* what you wanted to see?"

"Sure is."

"Is it old enough?"

"Far older than the cliff we were on before. All this was laid down during the Middle Cretaceous. About a hundred and twenty million years ago. It was part of a primitive mountain range that didn't run north to south, like the Rockies or the present day Coastal Ranges, but horizontally, directly under what's now the Sonora Desert into Nevada and Arizona. A thousand miles away you can probably find this exact pattern of sedimentary striation in some spot in the Grand Canyon."

Mark always followed what I was saying so easily, so eagerly, I never felt I was lecturing. Maybe that's one of the things we'd discovered about each other first, that we could teach each other without fear of being bored, or worse, of unbalancing our equality. He made me blush once when he told friends that I was the most intelligent speaker he knew. But it was Mark's own way with words, rather than his glamorous good looks, that had won me over when we'd first met.

Walking along the streets of Provincetown and the beaches of Cape Cod in 1975, that first summer we knew each other, Mark would ignore all the other Speedo-clad beauties vying for his attention, and instead sing to me the complete score to some barely known Thirties or Forties musical, Porter's *Nymph Errant* or Gershwin's *Let 'Em Eat Cake*. The first few times it happened, I expressed amazement: how did he know all that? Mark laid a hand on my shoulder casually, looking like one of those Waspy studs in a Ralph Lauren ad, and said, "I know my musicals inside out." It was one of the few times he'd ever boasted, and I was thrilled. Of course someone coming upon us at that moment on Commercial Street in front of Spiritus Pizza might have easily assumed we were in love talk. And I guess in a way it was, since little else could have made me adore him as much as hearing what he loved.

"I found it! The spot!" Craig ran up to us. "There!" pointing down the beach.

"Where?" I asked.

"Just below those cliffs," Craig said, sparring at me so suddenly I almost dropped the bigger beach bag, before he rushed off again, his big feet splat splatting the wet sand.

"I hope it's not too much farther," Mark said, only half-joking.

❖

"Sto-op! Cra-ig! Don't!"

He'd just dumped a baseball capful of cold Pacific water over my bare midriff. I leapt up and chased him into the ocean. At the water's edge, he stopped and doubled back on me, using his superior stance and greater height and weight to throw me off balance into the swirling surf and there to grab handfuls of wet sand and thrust them deep into my Speedo. This proved to be incredibly annoying, and in addition, provided Craig with—if not the exact erotic stimulation he was looking for—then at least a substitute he could find gratifying.

"Cra-ig! Sto-op!"

I managed to pull away from his grip. But he wasn't to be stopped so easily. For the next ten minutes he was at me constantly, after me, up and down the beach until I heard myself squealing like a teenaged girl, and then I figured out a way to trip him up and we were both rolling around in the surf, him unexpectedly so, soaking his walking shorts.

Chastened, he only made faint stabs at harassing me while I edged back to our towels. Mark was ostentatiously ignoring us, reading an oversized Somerset Maugham biography and listening to his portable CD player.

"Now I'm going to have to take these off and dry them!" Craig complained.

I would be washing sand out of my genitals all night because of his shenanigans. "Too bad! You should have known better than to come after me," I said, searching through the beach bag for my own book.

"Well, I'm not going to sit around naked here in front of

everyone," he declared. He pointed behind us where the lower cliffs dropped into a half-natural, half-manmade stairway up, and where we had seen men dressed in only shorts and bathing suits standing about, striking poses: obviously the famous cruising area of Black's Beach. "I'll find a spot where I can be alone."

"Who's stopping you?" I let my disdain drip.

"Rat!" he said, without much heat.

"Dimwit!" I answered back, equally cool.

"I'd say more, except there's a third person here," Craig declared.

"He can't hear with those headphones on. And he doesn't care," I added. That, I knew would really irritate Craig: the fact that Mark was so completely ignoring him despite all of Craig's efforts to get his attention.

Craig grunted something under his breath, grabbed his backpack off the sand, and went muttering off.

I settled on the beach towel, covering myself with sunblock #30, then located my own paperback.

A few minutes later, Mark's CD ended. He dropped the book and looked around.

"Put some of this on my shoulder blades, will you?" I asked.

"Where did he go?"

"Up there." I gestured with my head.

"To cruise?"

"To dry off. And sulk."

"Why sulk?"

"Because you're ignoring him," I said.

"He's cute," Mark said, meaning that he thought Craig had a good body. Which was undeniably true.

"He's cute," I admitted.

"But that mouth!" Mark laughed. "Sue really hated it!

When I went to pick him up to come meet you at the airport, he wouldn't stop saying terrible things about straights. I thought I'd have to throw him out of the car."

"That's Craig's way of trying to impress you."

"Sure."

"No kidding. He's wondering what in hell he's doing sleeping with me now that he's seen you. He's wondering how to drop me and get in the sack with you."

"It's not going to happen."

"I know that. And Craig knows too. That's why he's sulking."

"You really pick 'em."

"What about you and the Christmas Child?"

Mark's own sometime boyfriend back in New York, nicknamed because of when and how he'd first appeared in Mark's life and because of his puerile temperament.

"He's no better," Mark admitted, then went into a long story involving the Child that ended with us both shaking our heads.

The sun was hot, the breeze off the water intermittent, all of it quite delicious. We lay on our towels enjoying.

"We have good luck with beaches," I said.

"I'll say! We seem to spend a lot of time together on them."

It was true. The long shorelines of Fire Island Pines, where we shared a house for a decade of summers, the more ragged, high-cliffed beaches of Truro where we'd take a house each September, the Hamptons, the nude beach at San Gregorio in the Bay Area, Las Tunas whenever we were in L.A., Jones Beach, Far Rockaway Beach, Gilgo. Our new favorites were on Turks and Caicos Islands. Mark's business partner owned a place and we'd begun going there a few weeks at a time in the winter: wide white beaches, five shades of green-water Atlantic on the north, with a western shore only ten minutes from the house by boat, a strand so untouched we'd see no one, not a boat, not a footprint, all afternoon, and fish so unused to humans they'd bite your toes, while birds with markings unlike any I'd ever seen perched on our sun hats and pecked at the designs on our T-shirts and towels, thinking them edible. The east side was limestone, rocky inlets, half harbors, dreary fishing dock areas. South was Sapodilla Bay with languorous pale turquoise waters where I snorkeled; beachless, although the house was built on coral shelf perfect for sunning under papaya trees. We took boat rides with a local named Hammerhead Joe (he'd lift his shirt to show you the long knotted black scar from a shark he'd fought off) to nearby Shell Cay, Pine Cay, or to unnamed islets favored by plumed egrets, or populated by iguanas the size of Dalmatians.

"At least I have beaches to remember," Mark said in that suddenly dark tone of voice he'd used earlier on the cliff: this time it was laced through with something else: irony? bitterness?

I wasn't thinking when I replied, "I, for one, plan to go to the beach when I'm so old I'm doddering."

"Not me," Mark said. "You saw. I've lost all my strength."

What was he saying. Surely he didn't mean…?

"It was your nightmare. You said…"

"At work I've got to take naps every afternoon," Mark interrupted. "I close the door and tell Cindy not to let calls through, and I put my feet upon the desk. Sometimes I curl up on the rug in front of my desk. Every afternoon. One, two hours."

"I didn't know that. Since when?"

"Every afternoon," he repeated. "It's started," he added in a smaller, less certain voice. "I know it. It's…started."

That electrical jolt rushed up my spine again.

"Sue noticed right away when I got out here," Mark went on. "And I don't mean she just noticed how much I'm sleeping since I got here. She…we always take photos of each other every time we see each other. This time she wanted to wait till today. After I'd gotten more color is the way she put it."

"Mark! You're not saying you're…?" Symptomatic was the word. Or sero-converted.

"I'm saying it's started," Mark said flatly. Then, "Do you like him?"

The change of subject was so odd that for a second I thought Mark was going to say that Craig was symptomatic too.

"We have good sex and all," I said. "But I don't think it will develop into anything or that he'll move East to be with me. In fact, I'd say my being here these past few days has pointed that out."

Not what Mark wanted to hear. I remembered how much he'd encouraged me to get the air tickets, to reserve the room in the Balboa Park Inn. I'd thought because he'd wanted my company here.

"I'm not that disappointed," I began.

"Because I'd like to know that you have…you know, someone…you like."

He'd encouraged me to come out here and go after Craig following our hot little affair in Manhattan two months ago, because Mark wanted someone to be around after Mark was gone. This was too much.

"Look, maybe this is all just stress?" I tried. "All the work at the firm? The paper you had to deliver at the convention?"

"Maybe." Mark didn't want to argue. We never argued.

"Soon it will be summer. You'll hang out more. And in the fall we'll go back to the Caribbean. That always restores you."

He let me go on, looking at me in that fond way that he had for no one else in the world, no one, so I felt calmed again. The subject had been breached and we'd shoved it back.

We went back to reading, listening to music, sipping soft drinks. Above us, hang gliders in loose formation, blotting out the sun, speckled the sands with shadows. I wished…

Craig chose then to return, his shorts already dry.

"I did not have sex!" he declared, unasked.

"No doubt you were asked by scores," I said.

"It was sug-ges-ted," Craig said, suggestively, looking at where Mark lay, gorgeous on his towel. "But I told them some nasty older guy down here had at me so voraciously I had nothing left to give."

"Poor you!"

"Had at me night and day," he insisted. "You're burning!" he said and used that as an excuse to turn me onto my stomach, straddle my hips, and seductively and thoroughly rub my entire back and legs with suntan lotion. When that had completely aroused me and failed to get Mark's attention, Craig climbed off, declared he had to wash the gook off, and headed for the water.

He decided to go for a walk. When he was too far to be seen, Mark sat up, put on a T-shirt. "Did you find what you were looking for?"

"The ammonite fossils? I haven't really looked."

"Let's look!" he said. I too put on a shirt and we aimed toward the nearest cliff face, the direction opposite where Craig had gone.

The cliff was layered like a wedding cake. Actually many more times than that, but the strata were all clearly delineated.

"Hard to believe each layer is hundreds of years," Mark mused.

"More like thousands of years."

"And this green streak?"

"Believe it or not that's aquatic life, algae and other early water plants. As they died, they dropped to the surface and were squashed. The streak represents a time when this was all covered with water. Given these sediments below and above, I'd hazard it was a huge shallow lake for a couple of thousand years. Then land rose, emptied the water, and covered it with soil."

"Your fossils would be there?"

"If it were a branch of the ocean they should be. They were so common then. Far more common than fish or shellfish today. The ocean was thick with ammonites during the Mesozoic. They comprised ninety percent of sea life. Eighty percent of all the animal life on the planet. They were wiped out during the great same extinction that killed off the dinosaurs. You can see the line where it happened on the big cliff. It's known as the K-T boundary."

"A giant lake," Mark mused. "With its shoreline where? Out there somewhere?" pointing to the Pacific.

"Pretty far out, I'd guess. Then it became desert. But of course during that time this exact chunk of land wasn't here at thirty-two degrees north of the equator. It was much farther south. Somewhere off what's now Peru."

"Continental drift," he said. "Big plates moving slowly. When was that, about sixty million years ago?"

"Scientists call it deep time. Remember back in 1987, on my birthday, when we read about that star that went nova in the

Southern Hemisphere, the one in the lesser Magellanic Cloud? That took place about the same time. Because it was so far away, it's taken all this time for the burst of light it caused to reach us. All this time for the light made in that huge explosion to stimulate our vision."

"Deep time." Mark was beginning to perspire. I moved us along a section of the cliff out of the sun. "Eighty percent of the animal life just vanished forever… There must be shallow time, too," he suddenly said. "The shallowest of all time." He laughed and turned and sat down on a little sand hill hidden by this bend of cliff. "That's *my* time."

"Mark."

"Go on looking. I want to think about eighty percent of all life vanishing forever and no one even noticing."

"They were noticed."

"You can't even find their fossils! And you're looking!"

There's a point in everyone who is interested in science's life when you are suddenly faced with having to specialize. It's a fearful moment, and the real fear is that you've missed something essential, some moment during that decade and a half of nature walks and difficult-to-explain-to-others experiments with planaria worms and dirt and matches and soot that all young scientists have experienced, some moment when—sitting in a shaft of sunlight, hidden in reeds, you watch an egg hatch, minuscule life emerge, kicking, clawing, scurrying—a moment that somehow you become aware of *must* happen. But in happening, forever will replace that other moment in which something else, somewhere else, equally directing in its potential, now *cannot* happen. There you are, however choosing: or having chosen for you: life—or once-life.

I'd decided on what had once lived over what was now alive. This, despite all indications that it was the wrong direction, that living nature, studying tadpoles and crickets and birds whose names you weren't sure of—soon to become known as Ecology—that was the real future! I chose the past, although my favorite children's books were *Min of the Mississippi* and *Nature for Everyone*. Dragged by something inevitable that told me some things were so old, immeasurably old, I chose, and instead of a botanist or ornithologist, I became a paleobiologist, a student of that paradox dead life, of life encased in stone and slate and if I'm very lucky, suspended in millions-of-years-old amber. In choosing, I found I'd also chosen to study the rock and shale and petrified tree resin wherein dead life might be located. Old rock. Dead wood.

I took it as a challenge, and on those few occasions when I felt compelled to explain my choice, I always said it meant that from now on I'd continually sharpen my senses, go through life opening my eyes ever wider, forced to see in the least hints of fossilized ferncombs and feathertracks the possibility of something greater. And by extension, that in life in general I'd always have the details. Never miss what was right in front of me. I'd prided myself on that.

But in the past few months, I'd missed something crucial. The man who above all I loved in this life, whose love I'd come to take for granted, even while I never once took him for granted, had become symptomatic, had sero-converted, and I had not seen it happen. Sue had seen it, although she'd told us last night she'd never met a person infected with HIV. Craig had seen it immediately though he was the most egocentric of human beings. And I'd *not* seen it.

I did now, walking away from Mark, ostensibly to look for fossils I didn't expect to find, and for the first time totally feeling Mark there behind me, knowing this consciousness of Mark would never go away again—until he himself did.

Stumbling forward, I thought I would cry. No, I'll wait

until I get out of his line of sight, I told myself, there, behind that escarpment, where he can't see me.

I'd just reached it and looked back to check that I wasn't seen, when something huge and catlike leapt down at me.

"Gotcha!" Craig yelled as he dragged me down into the sand. He roared and pawed at me and in general acted like an animal. I don't know what got into me, since we always fought as equals, but this time I cringed away from him, and when he half came at me, I cringed again, cowered, shaking.

Craig could see how upset I was as I stumbled trying to get away from him, but he caught me and slid me against the cliff and held me there, held me tight, his front to my back, his larger, stronger arms over mine, his beard burning against my neck, letting me shake myself out, silently sob myself out. It was the longest that we'd been this close since we'd awakened that morning in the hotel bed together. After a while, he let go.

Mark was coming past us, on the way to our towels.

"I think it's time to go," Mark said. "What do you think?"

Even with all the rest, the walk back was still too much for Mark and we waited with him on the same bench as before while he caught his breath. A few hours later, we drove him in the rented T-Bird to the airport to get his jet home. Much later, after dinner and more of our usual arguments at a diner in Hillcrest designed as though it were right out of the fifties, Craig and I went to bed together in my hotel room.

At first he was aloof. So I was too.

"He doesn't have long, you know," Craig said. He moved closer until he covered my body with his.

"I know."

Craig pinned me against the sheets.

"He's going to die soon."

He began to kiss me hard.

"Your beautiful lover is going to die."

He made love to me with complete wildness and total abandon and with the same unchecked ferality he'd displayed on the beach. And I responded in kind, both of us acting unforgivably, saying unforgivable things to each other as we did, as though knowing it would be the last time ever.

Everyone Has a Shazam!

He came in late, maybe twenty minutes after the reading had begun, certainly way past Roger's usual seventeen minutes of intro-with-vamping for the usual contingent of latecomers having trouble parking. He slid in the door, and so was easily visible from where Roger stood, addressing the two dozen or so people. He found a seat, nodded at Roger, some kind of apologetic smile on his face, and settled in to listen.

Because Roger didn't need glasses to read, he wasn't wearing his distance lenses at the time, and so when he first came in and for the first half hour or so, Roger thought he was that film producer Roger had known way back when, he hadn't seen in maybe fifteen years and who used to be a window designer working with Bob Curry and his partner, Candy what was her last name? How this producer had made it to Hollywood, Roger had never figured out, but he had, big-time, and if Roger remembered correctly the last time they'd had any kind of interaction it hadn't been in a chic Vermont Village bookstore and it hadn't been exactly pleasant either. In fact, Roger had called the guy a "consummate asshole" and had done so twice, first in front of about seventy people at

Sunday brunch at the Fire Island Pines Botel's Blue Whale restaurant.

The noisy table-full evidently being treated to lunch by the decorator-turned-producer had been annoying enough arriving loudly, confusedly seating themselves, boisterously ordering and reordering drinks, driving the waiter nuts with their lunch orders changes. The window designer/mogul was even more irritating, coming onto the nice, extremely humpy, waiter (Belmain a Swiss guy: he and Roger had done it once at the Burma Road) who made it clear he was not interested and definitely not amused. So when the waiter returned with their seven meals on a big tray, before he could even put it down on the table, the Hollywoodized window dresser had stood up, reached for the tray, and snatching it away from him, had hurled it over the metal railing, over the narrow strip of boardwalk and right into the Pines Harbor. He'd then said, "And that's what we think of your lousy service here."

To which the unconsternated Belmain had replied, "We've got your credit card number and I'm charging it all," while the producer's unfed guests bounced off the deck *en suite*, and down thirty feet away to where a water taxi had just sent spumes to wash the two-story stern of the yacht named *Barbara*, arriving in front of the Pines Pantry. The window dresser's party then boarded, headed, everyone assumed, to the Grove for lunch. "He's still paying for it," Belmain said aloud, then gussied up the table, turned to the next group waiting at the stairs near the Pines Bus Service window, and said, "It's all yours." Roger's comment had been repeated a month later at Nick and Enno's dinner party on Ocean Walk, when someone who knew the window dresser told the story, expecting us all to support him. No one did, as they all knew and liked Belmain, and that was when Roger spoke out a second time. "I was there, Bernardo, and you can tell Michael that everyone at the Botel that afternoon considered him a consummate asshole": words Roger was sure had been repeated back.

And here he was, doing what? Waiting two decades to get revenge? Who cared? Roger had a half-drunk, iced latte and he was fully prepared to throw it into the guy's face at the first hint of trouble.

He waited till last, until Roger was done talking with the last reader/buyer person, then came up, and Roger was amazed to see it wasn't the asshole producer, but instead someone he'd not seen for even longer, Cap Hartmann, his closest friend in college.

"So," Cap said, holding a copy of the new book open to the title page, "sign it to the head of the L.A. chapter of the Colgate Alumni Association."

"You're kidding."

"I'll hit you up for a donation later."

"Colgate doesn't know I exist," Roger said. "And I'd like to keep it that way."

"How? They're better at locating people than the C.I.A.," Cap said.

"After I made a big protest by not attending the graduation ceremony, they totally lost track of me. I was in Europe right after for close to a year, and when I returned to the States I moved to Alphabet City, where no one from Colgate would ever willingly step foot. Far as they know, I'm dead."

"Lucky you. I was sure no one ever eluded them."

The two men looked at each other and were once more delighted in each other's words and company. How nice.

Two clerks had come up to the makeshift table, each holding a stack of his hardcovers, and they were very definitely standing there waiting for him. Roger said, "I've got to John Hancock these or this event isn't kosher. Can you wait? Are you free at all?"

"Christ, yes," Cap said. "You think after this long I'm going to let you go? You know, when I saw you'd be here in the newspaper, I tried all the hotels I could think of. No go."

"I stay with friends in the hills," Roger explained. "Off Lookout Mountain."

"That's what Karina thought. I wanted to have dinner and catch up."

Karina: Cap's wife, woman, girlfriend, whatever. When you were Cap Hartmann, there would always be a Karina.

"Cool with me. Can Karina join us?"

"She's got business. A meeting with a client. She's an attorney. You want to do this, yes?"

"Hell, yes! I can't believe how great you look. How trim. How…young," Roger said. It was true. But of course Roger could say it because he knew he looked trim and young too.

"I lived with a dancer for five years. Eugenia," Cap explained, stepping away from the table so Roger could see how trim, how muscular his legs and torso were, how slender his hips. He looks like a 'mo, Roger thought. Full head of butterscotch hair with only a slight singeing of gray on the sides, only a few very shallow lines on his face, great skin, good tan: Cap was in as good shape as any homosexual of forty-five, Roger knew…And thank Christ for that!

"Give me ten minutes," Roger said.

❖

The large white elephant in the room during their hour-and-a-half long catch-up on the years over *steak frittes* at the glorified 1950s diner on Sunset was, of course, Trish Tanager. Cap and Trish had spent most of the three and a half years of college that Roger had known them in a famously passionate, famously difficult, and eventually famously broken relationship. Cap had ended it. Cap had graduated half a year early—or half a year late—Roger never knew which really, and before Cap had graduated, he'd joined the Peace Corps and broken up with Trish.

Leaving her utterly brokenhearted.

Roger knew to an iota exactly how brokenhearted, since Trish told him repeatedly for the next six or seven years. That's how long they'd hung out together in Manhattan before she'd taken off for San Francisco and a totally new life. Even after she was gone, he and Trish remained in contact: postcards, letters, phone calls, gifts, her visits to her folks in uptown Manhattan, Roger's less frequent visits out West, until he'd moved there, south not north. She told him about the breakup when she was drunk and when she was sober, occasionally when she was somber and almost in tears, and more often laughing over a joint of stuff they'd nicknamed Arthur it was so good, which they'd bought together, several kilos-full, and sold off slowly, cheaply, for good Karma's sake, earning just enough money to be able to always smoke it free.

Cap had vanished, first into Peace Corps training at Mayaguez, Puerto Rico, and then down to Namibia. There had been maybe four letters over two years to Roger, and then nothing, ever again. So Roger had inherited Trish Tanager. They'd gotten high together, gone to parties and Be-Ins and dance clubs and concerts together. They'd slept together once, not quite disastrously because it was so funny. But to the day they remained in contact. Roger had spoken to her by phone two nights before, as he was headed to the Bay Area and

Sacramento next on his little book tour, and he planned on renting a car and driving upstate to see her and her third, or was it fourth, husband? Roger knew he couldn't say a thing about Trish Tanager to Cap Hartmann, couldn't reveal any of their decades-long life together without Cap—unless Cap asked.

Cap didn't ask. Cap did, however, definitely want to hear about the others: the rest of their tight-knit, superior, overly literate "Hell Fire Club" in the English Department at Colgate. Roger had actually stumbled upon the three in a Russian Lit course, second term of his freshman year, when he arrived too late to sit anywhere but the back row of the room. It had taken him only that first class to realize that the three of them, Cap, Elliot, and Larry, already knew each other, and were already a group. He'd returned next class and sat in the back row with them, admiring Beatle-Paul-cute Larry Isaacson with his perfect complexion and almost blue-black helmet of hair. He'd slowly come to even more admire the masculinely handsome Cap Hartmann, And even, if non-sexually—he was definitely overweight, red-bearded, and dressed like a hippie—admire their leader, Elliot Dolgard, "the brains of the operation," as he'd once joked to Roger.

It was Elliot who'd told him that Roger had made an instant life-impression on all three of them when, in class number three of that course, he'd corrected the professor just loud enough that the last two rows in class could hear it, by naming Pushkin's true dueling assassin.

Leaving class that day, Elliot had turned to him and said in his flat Midwestern voice and with its insistent and always slightly offended edge, "How did you know who killed Pushkin?" as though this was utterly privileged information. To which Roger had admitted that he possessed an enormous fund of utterly useless, trivial knowledge: all the Indian tribes of North America, every eighteenth-century carriage built; insects of several classes and genera; all the constellations plus fixed stars of the first to third magnitude; and of course how every writer alive had ever died.

"Cool!" Elliot had responded, a bit less aggrieved. "You'll fill in some gaps of our own totally useless, trivial knowledge. Join us for coffee."

Roger had been two years younger than the youngest, Larry, almost four younger than Cap, certainly never as knowledgeable about film as Elliot, or about music and theater as Cap, or about poetry as Larry, one of whose ancestors was a noted seventeenth-century Yiddish poet. He'd always felt the baby among them: the one who spoke up least, who defended his point least well or aggressively in their discussions, and who followed their lead most often—usually Elliot's, but whenever Cap and Elliot disagreed, he'd always found himself taking Cap's side.

That was when Roger first met Trish Tanager. She'd been exceptionally pretty, physically voluptuous, seductive, flirty, sophisticated, and fun at what, seventeen? Very impressive. Meanwhile, Elliot's "women friends" came and went, albeit they were always surprisingly good looking and with great bodies. And then there was Larry's lifelong love, Loretta, encountered when they were high school juniors, and destined to be together 'til death did them part, by college already considered his "other half."

"Elliot is teaching high school in some outer borough in New York!" Roger reported to Cap over more *frittes* than he ought to be eating. "Did you ever meet Caroline? Well, they're still together. This I've heard from others." Not saying that the "others" was mostly Trish, who actually kept up with Caroline. "I last actually laid eyes on the two of them at the premiere of Albee's *Tiny Alice*."

"That's a while back," Cap admitted. "What about El and El?"

"Larry and Loretta? I last saw them ten years ago in the rain in the middle of Abdington Square, while coming home from Balducci's. They had a little sixteen millimeter set up on a tripod at the south corner and when I asked what they were doing, Loretta said they were quote filming yellow things, unquote. They got married and had a kid. I heard they'd moved out here to El Lay. El and El in El Lay… Haven't seen them."

Cap laughed and now was exactly when he should have asked about Trish Tanager but instead he said, "What a bunch! Just like bananas. But we had good times."

"Don't you think it's odd, how I turned out to be a novelist?" Roger asked. "Remember how all we'd talk about was how the novel was dead, dead, dead, and the rest of the twentieth century would be all about film? And I go and become a novelist! Closest any of us got to film was some messes I wrote that never got made a few years back and El and El's sixteen millimeters."

Cap startled him by saying, "I write screenplays," quickly adding, "got an option on one." Then deprecating, "Karina did the paperwork for it. Who knows? It still might be done. And sometimes…" here he got all little-boy-shy the way Roger remembered him being, when flirting, "sometimes I sub in for a cameraman pal on pictures. Both of those just kind of happened! You know, because of friends of Natalie's in the business."

Getting a summation of Cap's life since the Peace Corps in Namibia consisted, totally unsurprisingly to Roger, of women's names and their periods of time together with Cap: First there had been Aurora, a Venetian he'd met in Otopoho. That lasted four years and had moved Cap from Venice, Italia, to Venice, California, where he'd remained ever since. Then there had been Ursula, a Swiss interpreter for the French Legation; leggy, literate, and nebulous. Four and a half years for her, followed by six with Natalie, a drama-queen actress/writer into Indy Prod films and fidelity: the latter never Cap's long suit. Five more years with Eugenia, a Russian emigre jazz dancer who'd made a killing as one of the first Pilates instructors in the town. And now, going on four years, Karina, who despite her exotic name was actually a farm-bred American from Idaho, who reminded Cap of the girls he and Roger had gone to school with.

"Never got married. Never had kids. Actually don't think I can make kids," Cap added. "I haven't been all that careful over the years. If I could make them, something should have happened by now. So of course that ended me and Natalie and me and Ursula and even though she says we can always adopt, will probably end me and Karina too."

But before Roger could take advantage of that comment to ask him more personal questions, Cap said, "So tell me about this Mark you mentioned at the reading. He your guy?"

Roger looked into Cap's pale brown eyes and told him: the fifteen-year-long relationship, still going strong, the two of them more bonded than ever; even though the writing was on the wall as Mark was beginning to be symptomatic; so who knew, Roger didn't, how much longer they had.

"He's a dreamboat, a doll, a Rhodes Scholar genius and a Bourgeois Prince *par excellence.* His family owned a department store in New England! Do I know how to pick them, or what? He was never was a tenth the slut I was," Roger added, trying to keep it light, "so of course he's the one who gets sick while I did everything with everybody and can't get infected no matter how many times I try. The virus dies the minute it touches my body." He illustrated by making the sound water hisses on a hot stove top.

"That sucks. But still, Rog, *fifteen years*! And you actually found your soul mate! Wow! So you're three things none of us ever expected. A successful novelist. A total queer. And a solid husband."

"Go figure!"

They spoke a little more about Mark and all that implied, and that's when Cap looked at his watch, saying, "I promised a friend I'd tend bar for him while he's off doing an audition. It's a joint in Venice. Sort of beach shack. Kind of my hangout. Want to come by?…Free margaritas!"

Roger still felt their reunion was as annoyingly incomplete as a dangling participle. He had so many questions to ask Cap about the intervening years. And then he still had to say something about Trish, if he was going to be loyal to her, although that line about how lucky he was to have found a soul mate strongly suggested that Cap still hadn't found his and was still looking, no matter what Trish had thought and what she'd told Roger all these years.

"I'll go anywhere for free margaritas."

They got into two cars and he followed Cap, zigzagging through L.A.'s west side surface streets, which later on he'd realize were some of the best rush-hour shortcuts around.

"What I said before?" Cap commented an hour later, behind the bar, bar apron slung comfily low around his hips, a mixologist who did this a bit more often than subbing every once in a while, a bit more like in his element, actually. "You being those three things we never expected that I said before? That wasn't exactly true. Even though you were a lot younger than us, and even though you had to work your way through college and didn't have much time for anything else, we still thought that girls were a lot more interested in you than you were in girls!"

"Who said so? It was Loretta, wasn't it?"

Couldn't have been Trish, Roger wanted to add. She believed no man queer enough to resist her advances.

"It was Elliot, mostly."

"But you never thought it?"

"I did too…. Actually I thought you were too pretty to be totally straight."

Roger was stunned. *"What?"*

"You're a good-looking man now, Roger, very attractive. But you were a very, *very* pretty seventeen-, eighteen-year-old boy. Why did you think we went out to the Hamptons that weekend, just you and me together?"

"You had an invitation to a house there, no?"

"I had something. Not exactly an invitation. And we ended up sleeping on the beach. Don't you remember?"

Roger remembered, all right. One of the questions he'd always wanted to ask Cap was what had actually happened that weekend so long ago when he was too naïve or too tied up in himself or just plain too oblivious to understand.

"What are you telling me here, Cap?"

"I thought I could maybe seduce you?"

Roger laughed. "You're totally bullshitting me! It's revenge for having to attend my reading."

"Swear to God." Cap put his right hand on his heart. "I even told Elliot we were going out there that weekend so I could bust your cherry."

Roger laughed again, utterly amazed. Finally he commented, "If I had any idea, I would have agreed in a heartbeat. Close as we were. You being the handsomest guy I knew and all!"

"Yeah. Yeah. Yeah. Well, you weren't exactly *out* then,

I don't believe!" Cap said, swirling away to help a customer who'd just alit at the other end of the bar.

When he came back he added, "And also, by the time I got around to the attempt on your bod, too much had already happened. I was much too distracted…"

He made the guy a nice-looking Gibson—people still drank Gibsons?—handed it to him, got paid, and returned to add, "Don't you remember the couple who gave us a ride that we ended up hanging around with? The redhead who looked so much like Trish, whom you should recall I'd just a few weeks before stopped seeing? The humongous, crew-cut blond F.B.I. agent, with the fat roll of fifty-dollar bills?"

He remembered, all right. How could Roger forget?

❖

Mostly it was the light. And all that space.

The train stopped at Hampton Bays after hours of chugging along during which Roger stood—vibrating; then, once they'd gotten separate seats four rows apart, had attempted to read—a convoluted Borges story, and given his exhaustion from the past week of final exams and studying, instead slept. So when Cap awakened him, smiling, "We're here!" he'd could just about concentrate on getting his duffel and himself out and onto the platform.

Most of the other passengers disembarking knew where they were going and stepped unhesitating into waiting or weeklong parked cars or into a little jitney. Once the train left, he and Cap were in the middle of nothing: a small wooden station, couple of carved columns holding a schedule board, an overhung hip roof that would protect from a moderate but probably not from a thundering rain. Cauliflower fields stretched across the other side for miles to the horizon, already budding, glints of pearl amid the green, faintly reeking of *brassica.* On this side, the gravel turnabout and parking lot marked out by painted gray, ground level, two-by-eights led to a beat-up shack of a commuter diner, vintage mid-1950s given its adverts. Brown dirt rapidly changing to sand everywhere else Roger could see.

But there was also the light. At 7:03 of a Friday evening in late June it was an intensely soft sky, a vast blue velvet curtain powdered with talc. Everything else around was incredibly close to the earth compared to the city they'd left, the sparse buildings, the bird-bitten chokecherry bushes, even the single, wind-tormented tree he could make out over a rise of dune. It was very clean, as though scrubbed by sand-abrading breezes, and so fresh Roger could smell the ocean already. Spacious. He realized now that before it had been only an idea, them coming out here, but this was exactly what he needed: space, cleanliness, light. Needed it all badly.

The skinny old guy the same shade of the linoleum floor with a badly twisted right ear at the little railroad diner who fed them reheated coffee and hand glazed donuts for them said the town was another mile or so down that road, over there! The street Cap had mentioned wasn't far off, easy to find.

Once Roger was awake and they were ambling along the road, toward what even he could see was eventually and not that far away, the ocean, he suddenly felt invigorated.

Cap hadn't offered but vague information about where they were going: the summer place of a family of a friend of a friend, or something like that; and that there were certain to be some alcohol, grass, and girls there. His friend liked to party. They might have to double up, or sleep on the floor. That's why Cap had a roll of sleeping bags, one for each of them, bouncing against his own light, shoulder-strapped luggage.

The plan was they'd hang out there tonight, maybe go

into the "town," or what it consisted of, alone or with some of the folks from the house for dinner, and hit the bar scene. From what Cap recalled from a few summers before, that would mean crossing the bridge across the Shinnecock Bay onto a long sandbar where the nighttime commercial area had developed. Next day they'd do the beach. It was the best beach he'd ever seen, Cap enthused, as good as those in the Caribbean.

Roger almost didn't hear the rest. He wanted beach. He needed beach. For a Long Island–raised boy, its southern shore beaches already had spelled out long long hours, days, weeks, months of contentment, fun, and rest. Just get me to the beach, he thought: I'll take care of the rest.

They found the house after at least two miles and a half of walking, although admittedly on a sanded shoulder of a two-lane road, and slightly downhill all the way. At least Cap thought it was the house. It didn't fit the description. It looked shuttered up. Maybe the others hadn't come out yet? Were on later trains? No they'd been here all week, Cap recalled.

No one answered their knocking, and Cap finally tried and easily pushed open the front door. They looked around and asked if anyone was home. No one. The place looked both closed up and yet somehow lived in. They were heading across the entry again, past the steep stairway up, to look over in the other rooms they'd sighted before, when someone appeared at the top of the stairs above them; a good-looking, slim, naked young man, washing his erection with a small face cloth.

He wasn't Lowell, no, he told them. Lowell wasn't out this weekend. They'd switched. And no, Lowell hadn't at all told him they were coming. In fact, other people were invited. He kept washing his glans thoroughly at the top of the stairs, looking from it down to them all the while he spoke. He was expecting the others to arrive in an hour or so. That's when the next train came. Maybe they could get back to the station in time for it? No. Sorry, no room for them here. And no, it *wasn't* a good idea to put their sleeping bags around the back of the house, as Cap suggested, and come back later. People paid good money to come out to the Hamptons and they complained of anyone sand-squatting to the sheriff. Sorry."

Done, he tossed the face cloth into the bathroom sink nearby and said, "Lock the door as you leave, will you? As you can see," making his erection bounce up and down without touching it, "I'm kinda busy." And vanished.

Out on the street, Roger lighted a jay and thought, bummer! Though he didn't say it, he also wondered at the immense savoir faire of the guy, not only naked, but cute with a boner, and clearly in between bouts of sex. No doubt this was a party house. Too bad they couldn't stay.

Always the optimist, Cap said, "We're not going back to the city tonight. We'll find a place in town. One of us will rent the smallest, cheapest place—I will, since you're under aged—and you can sneak in later on." That became the new plan.

This walk was more difficult because either it was actually longer or because it had a less certain goal in sight. Past the score of aged wood houses, the road once more looped lazily and went downhill. But clearly ahead the bay water shimmered, and beyond that Roger could see a low glimmer on the horizon that was the beach itself.

The glimmer got brighter as the sun began to set.

They trudged on, reaching the bridge, which now that they were on it looked to be at least as long as the distance they'd already walked. Duckweed half as high as the pylons undulated as by some unseen force: possibly tidal.

Cap stopped for a cigarette. Roger wanted to ask what if they couldn't find a place. He wanted Cap to reassure him.

Cap meanwhile said nothing and looked down into the pristine water.

That was when the big white Eldorado convertible drove past, and Roger stuck out a thumb. To their surprise, it stopped twenty feet ahead.

At the wheel was a big crew cut blond in a business suit and hard-looking, two-finger-wide tie. In the passenger seat was a voluptuous redhead wearing a print sundress of big reddish and brown flowers against beige.

"You guys need a ride?" she asked.

"Do we ever," Roger said.

She opened her door and he slid into the backseat. She held Cap's hand long enough for Roger to realize her amazing resemblance to Trish Tanager. A few years older, her eyes bright blue rather than hazel, her hair twisted up with a pale yellow scarf and Irish red, but otherwise…

She was Diane, and the driver was Guy. Later on, Roger would wonder if the names, as well as the stories they told Cap, were totally fabricated. Her accent was local, New York; the driver's was Western-Midwestern.

Guy drove quickly and after Cap had leaned forward and told Diane their tale of woe, she tenderly yet firmly declared, "There's no available room here tonight for any kind of money. They sold out weeks in advance. But you can check if you want to."

Guy parked the Caddy in front of several restaurants and they tossed their bags into the vast trunk, which already held a folded-over winter coat, a small, dark gym bag, and three pieces of pink fabric matching luggage.

Diane went with Cap to look for rooms, and after a few minutes, Guy got out of the car, and without turning around, gestured for Roger to follow.

Wooden stairs led up to an empty deck bar around a pool. Guy sat at a table and ordered a martini. He pointed at Roger with his index finger stuck out shaping a revolver. Roger ordered a beer.

Guy drank the martini quickly and ordered another. Looked around at the dozen people at the bar and tables with a boredom all over his face, saying nothing. This gave Roger a chance to look him over more closely and confirm that he was perhaps the handsomest, most masculine man Roger had ever laid eyes on: six foot three, muscular even through the corporate suit, with huge, maybe forty-eight-inch shoulders, huge hands, a square-jawed, dimpled chin, almost blank green-blue eyes, your standard American-issue comic-book-hero gorgeous, especially topped as he was by an unvarying half inch of fresh corn-yellow hair sticking up in a perfect brush cut that sometimes swayed as he moved and sported a twist down peak in the center of his forehead. Roger couldn't believe Guy was real.

After what seemed forever, and was at least a half hour, Diane and Cap reappeared, very chatty and obviously newly friendly. Before they could say anything, Roger understood their quest had been fruitless. Guy downed his second martini and said to Diane, "This place is post-graduate. Let's go by the canal."

He got up and again gestured for Roger to follow. Diane and Cap dawdled, and this time they got into the backseat together, while he sat up front with America's most astounding male, and tried not to notice too much whenever Guy touched himself, dropping a big hand onto an obviously muscled-to-the-hilt thigh or teasing a chiseled upper lip.

Guy seemed oblivious to the others in the back, who truth to say seemed almost in another car as the wind was up, and they couldn't be heard. The few times Roger looked back, they acted as though they were alone. Even granting what a dish she was, and her resemblance to Trish, Roger was kind of resentful of Diane. This was supposed to be his and Cap's weekend together, the last time together before Cap flew away to P.R. At one point, Guy turned to Roger and he smiled weirdly, one side of his mouth dropped a half inch as though about to make some really snide comment. Instead he asked, "Okay?"

Roger hadn't a clue what he was being asked or why. He gestured okay and then said it, thinking screw it, screw the whole weekend. Guy went back to driving, the others in the backseat were now laughing.

They drove along the beach and back up another even longer bridge among weeds, ending up on a road that banked toward a white and gray wooden bar/restaurant at the Shinnecock Canal. They took a steep stairway onto a two-story-high roof-deck bar not fifty feet from the double locks of the canal. The ocean glittered on all sides and a very campy, unattractive waiter, with a slightly club foot, who knew both Guy and Diane, got them drinks and asked for their dinner order.

That's when the roll of fifties made its first appearance and Cap and Roger were informed, extremely offhandedly by Guy, that they were being treated to dinner. "On Uncle Sam," Guy added, "so eat, drink, and be…you know." He voice was tight. As though each piece of dialogue cost him one of those fifties.

Because of their elevation and the otherwise flat surrounding, the sun was just setting here and it made a glorious spectacle for a surprisingly long time. A little wind came up, and Cap and Diane went to another, even higher deck, to view it from there. Their heads together looked like a single lit match in the purple-orange final glow. Guy drank a fourth martini, heedless, and joked with the bartender nearby and gave the waiter complicated food orders.

"We're post-graduates too," Roger said, to break the silence. "At least he is. I graduate college next year."

"You're okay," Guy decreed. "Here's the food."

He ate fast, a big steak, and ordered another smaller steak dish, even before Cap and Diane returned. They remained at their table as the restaurant filled up and then got up and went to the bar, where they continued, eating dessert and drinking. Roger had maybe four beers, slowly nursing them, because despite the food, he wasn't that used to drinking. Diane and Cap were having mixed drinks like Guy and they danced a sort of lindy together at one point. They appeared to Roger as though they were out together on a date, which would make sense, given how good-looking and young Cap was, and how voluptuous, not to mention how amazingly similar to Trish Diane looked. How, exactly, this could be happening in front of Guy, Roger couldn't quite figure out. Wasn't she with Guy? Then they were slow-dancing, and the waiter from before was sitting next to Guy on the other side of Roger, speaking low into his ear, they were talking about someone Roger didn't know.

Guy had sort of loosened up meanwhile, Roger figured because he was among his friends, or at least people he knew. He let the waiter and some of the women flirt with him. Most of what they said went way over Roger's head, slang, argot, who knew, names and people he'd never heard of. Every once in a while, Guy would suddenly remember that Roger was still there and ask him if he wanted a drink or needed to use the john, or was okay. Like he was his big brother and he had to mind Roger.

Nothing was settled. In truth, everything was totally *unsettled.* Roger had never been in a situation before with so very many unknowns and so very many variables. Where would they go? Where would they sleep tonight? Were there rentals in one of those other beach towns that he knew ranged from here out to Montauk Point? Or would those be filled too? Of course they would be, he knew it already. And what was Guy doing here tonight? Was he a Fed? A G-man? As he looked to be? Was he on some case? Was Diane working with him? Or was she some kind of blind for him? And they too now, Cap and he, now that they joined, had they been picked up to make Guy even less suspicious? Was he going to arrest someone, here tonight?

At a certain point, Roger thought, it's like I'm in an Antonioni movie.

He loved Antonioni's movies more even than Bergman's; the Hellfire Club had taken part in multiple off-campus discussions of the great trio: *L'Avventura*, *La Notte*, and *L'Eclisse.* This whole thing today, Roger, thought, is exactly like one of those movies: not meeting who they were supposed to, wandering around without any goal, plotless, nothing explained, all sorts of odd happenings, strange people suddenly coming together with them while others didn't communicate at all, even though they were together hours on end. Sitting back in the bar chair, looking up at the stars, admittedly a little drunk, Roger thought, it's an adventure. I'm having a grown-up adventure and I have no idea where it's headed.

He must have laughed, because suddenly Guy said, "Now you're relaxed."

That's when his unbuttoned suit jacket opened enough for Roger to see he had a pistol holder and a pistol too: dark blue, tubular, glinting.

The waiter, whose name was revealed as Monte, was telling a story, about some people in a place called The Duchess, which ended with him saying, "At which point she went—*Shazam*!"

All of them but Roger laughed.

The waiter turned and out of the side of his mouth said. "A little before your time, kiddo. It's *Captain Marvel.* This regular guy, Billy Bates, becomes Captain Marvel whenever he says the word 'Shazam.'"

Roger had smiled politely. And that was when Guy said the phrase, "Everyone has a 'Shazam.'" He said it directly at Roger, as though informing him, or demanding a comment on what he'd said, or even a denial from him.

Roger didn't know what to say and was silent. Guy's statement, however, provoked both laughter and a great deal more discussion from those at the bar.

That was the moment that Cap and Diane left the dance floor and joined them.

Cap asked, "What's going on?" low voiced so only Roger could hear and Roger replied, "He's got a gun."

"I know. Diane says he works for the F.B.I. How are you doing?"

"Well, between the drinks and the past week, I think I'm completely blotto," Roger said.

❖

He didn't know how he made it to the beach. He probably passed out or fell asleep up there and some of the others dragged him.

Roger woke up about an hour later, wrapped in the sleeping bag. He was in the dunes, in a deep and wide decline. About ten feet away he could see a large dark figure that must be Guy, wrapped in some sort of outer coat. No sign of Cap and Diane, but suddenly he could hear their voices. They were out on the beach somewhere ahead, in that strong mist curtained over the water, talking low or perhaps they were far away. Then their voices were smeared by what must be kissing. Soon they were gone, or into it. But quieted somehow.

Roger was on the beach. He was drunk and exhausted. But he'd made it to the beach. He was within what looked like two sleeping bags zipped together.

So when he heard a sound like chattering, he listened more closely and decided it was Guy, cold with only the coat to cover him.

He dragged the bags over to the immense dark body.

"Get in!"

Guy had been sleeping. Chattering in his sleep.

"What are you doing here?" Guy awakened and asked. He sounded angry.

"There are two sleeping bags together here. Get in. You're cold. You're chattering. I could hear it over there."

"No!" Guy said and rolled over.

Roger lifted the zipped-together bags and threw one side of them over Guy. Guy squirmed around to look up at him. "Why are you doing this?"

"You'll freeze here."

He pulled the bag around Guy so his feet were in it. "C'mon, lift up your body. Get in."

"I can't sleep in this with you."

"Why not?" Roger asked.

"I just can't...You're a kid, right?"

"So what? Up you go, that's right! Pull it around! See, you fit into it fine! I'm getting in now."

"It's too small."

"I'll back up against you."

"Christ! You're kidding me."

Roger eased himself into the bag backward, then slid his feet in. "You don't need your coat. With the two of us like this, it'll heat up fine. Might be a good idea to take off your jacket."

"What about my pants too?" Guy whispered.

"Probably a good idea, otherwise you'll be overheated by morning. I'm in my shorts!"

"What?" Guy sat up. "I'm keeping my pants on."

"Suit yourself."

"No one will believe this," Guy said. "Gee, Officer, he forced me into the bag and then told me to strip too."

"Your body is nice and warm," Roger said, squiggling in deeper.

"You have no idea what a rocket I am tonight."

"How can that be?" he asked sleepily. "You drank so many martinis. Eight? Ten?"

"Go to sleep."

"I am. I'm now going to sleep."

Roger closed his eyes but when he opened them, the big blond head was inches away, and Guy was looking right at him.

"What's wrong?"

"Nothing's wrong," Guy said in the oddest tone of voice, strangely, hoarse. "It's just that suddenly…I remember why I do this. Why it's worth it. You know what I mean?"

"No idea at all," Roger admitted, mumbling very sleepily. Now that he was warm and comfortable, he was being rapidly overtaken again.

"Want me to…?" was the last thing Guy more or less

clearly said, and Roger mumbled back an unintelligible but he hoped positive reply as he sank deeper and deeper.

❖

"I don't know what happened," Cap admitted, decades later. "When I woke up, Diane was gone. Guy was gone. Their car was gone. You had a fifty dollar bill stuffed in your underwear. No! I'm kidding about the last part."

They were out on the beach again. Venice Beach, this time. It was sunset again, and the other bartender had come back, and they'd stepped out of the bar, across the very public promenade and onto the sand. headed to the water's edge. Cap said he would return and finish off a night shift as they were busy at the bar tonight.

"And you and Diane?" Roger found he had to ask.

"I couldn't! I just couldn't do it with her! Everything was too…weird! But I had a great time! I only got about two hours' sleep! We were up all night…In a sense, Diane was what I'd always hoped Trish would be. Grown-up, mostly. Not clingy. Not possessing. But it was all too late for me with…either of them."

"And the guy? The G-man?" I had to ask. "I'm *so* oblivious…Was he queer? Or what?"

Cap shrugged. "Their friends at that bar were. And the ones they talked about. But…who knows what either of them were. Or if they were anything definite at all… They *were* sensational-looking, weren't they?"

"He was a 'mo's dream come true! If only I'd known what to do with him then!" Roger laughed. "Or could stay awake."

That was when Cap said the sentence that would haunt Roger forever after. "You know, Rog, you turned out to be the lucky of the two of us in relationships."

"Some luck. Mark's dying," Roger reminded him.

"I know. I know. But at least you never had to feel that you were in sexual bondage to someone who was your inferior. You and Mark are equal, and strong together. Maybe that's what I was looking for back then, myself."

"You mean when you allegedly tried to seduce me. Which, by the way, I don't for a second believe or remember."

Roger did recall them lying side by side, later that morning, when he woke up, their sleeping bags half-opened next to each other, their shirts off, their shorts on, the morning sun radiating gently onto them, the mist rising off the surf, evaporating with this funny little noise, them talking quietly for maybe an hour, before they got up, got dressed, and walked back over a half bridge to the little town for breakfast, then spent the day at the beach, arriving back in Manhattan around midnight. He recalled nothing more.

"I guess I was a little too subtle," Cap admitted.

Or a little too hetero, Roger wanted to say.

Just then they heard someone shouting. It was the other bartender, holding up a phone, for Cap. Karina. It had to be Karina.

"This was great!" Cap said, "Great!" He hugged Roger and then turned and headed to the bar.

Roger remained where they'd stopped, watching the enormous sun drop into the burning red Pacific, guessing, without pain, or even wonder, that they'd probably never see each other again.

It was later, as he was crossing under the high, globed streetlights on the Venice Beach sidewalk that, among the crowds of nighttime strollers and men and women skateboarding, biking, jogging in wild and weirdly wonderful outfits, one roller skater, a middle-aged guy dressed in a silver and gold outfit of short skirt and tight bodice with puffy sleeves, a crown of a cap and a battery-lighted, sparkling wand, passed him, gracefully angling in and out of pedestrians, and ever so lightly but distinctly tapped him on the shoulder with the wand.

"Shaz-am!" called out the good fairy of the west. And was gone.

In the Fen Country

Going west beyond the Stockton, California, transport hub, all roads but rutted ones soon come to an end: what is still above water in the East-Bay has been completely Green for a century or more. There is a twice-a-day monorail that sweeps all the way along the increasingly ragged coastline, right over to the drowned remains of what used to be the city of Richmond, stopping at Berkeley Island. I know the route well, this being maybe the sixtieth and I hoped final visit to Cynara in the fen country around what had been the ancient container-port town of Martinez.

I'd grown familiar over the decades with how subtly the landscape alters as you head west, first little encroachments of water like tiny fingers, with here a cottage, there a mound-house surrounded in reeds, then water on both sides, until at last where it is land it's all threaded through with canals or drowned roads. Fields that once grazed cattle and horses are now marshes feeding waterfowl and dragonflies almost as large, while scarlet-throated sea eagles wheel overhead, screeching their dominion before settling to perch upon what remains of a column once belonging to a desalinization plant or upon the crumbling stanchion of a long-collapsed bay bridge.

Cynara has lived here among the bogs and meres forever, or so the Finnster had always told me, and from our very first crisis in a Centauri Outer-Cloud (a potential showdown with the Bella=Arths) he'd turned to me, half-serious for once, his fingers still dancing almost too fast to see over the touch-board for weapons and maneuvering, and he'd said, "Anything happens to this beautiful bod, promise to take it back home, even if I look to be ninety-nine percent not-there, Locke. Take me back to Cynara in the fen country, east of San Fran, and she'll take care of me. She'll make sure I come back, good as new, as amazingly gorgeous as I am at this moment."

Nothing happened that time, of course, and nothing happened for most of the following year real-time while we patrolled and explored and guarded Earth's stellar expansion and in general made pests of ourselves among the people actually doing the work and learning—mostly scientists.

We were stationed during the first part of that tour a few light-years out, in the so-called "New Territories." None of us expected that area to be anything other than a no-man's-land neutral zone for decades to come between the two cultures, so naturally we'd all then been astonished to see Beta C's system suddenly taken over by our own kind, leading to the eruption of the recent war.

A foreshadowing of that conflict *had* happened, the one time during that tour that I'd chanced to be away from the Finnster, off-ship at Charon station, undergoing my officer-upgrade Nanos.

My shipmates found themselves in a fracas and then quickly in a firefight with some trigger-happy Arth hauler that had wandered off course. The lower helm, where the Finnster and I always teamed up, had been badly hit and burned before a "diplomatic misunderstanding" was eventually sorted out between the Service and the hard-shells.

I'd always assumed Cynara had been the Finnster's childhood sweetheart or first university live-in girlfriend:

possibly even the love of his life who hadn't quite worked out for whatever reason—probably because he'd joined the Service. It's difficult for us to sustain relationships with folks at home when we are away six, eight, ten Earth years at a go, aging only ten or twelve weeks at a go, while they age normally.

Come to think of it, he never had explained exactly what Cynara was to him. But I'd promised him to do it. Notwithstanding the fact that in all the years we were actual mates in the Service, he'd never once mentioned her in any other context, never mind attempted to visit her, or even gotten her some weird gift from an exotic planet-fall. Given how free the Finnster usually was with his "beautiful bod" in those days, I almost would have been surprised to think he would be, *could* be, faithful to any one person.

I wasn't alone in the little monorail single car train during this latest visit to Cynara in the fens. An older, mixed race, but prevalently Af-Am fellow was in the car. He was Service, or once-Service, given his bulk and stature even now, not to mention his evident UV eye-op, how he still cut his hair, how he glared at you, and especially how he held himself erect, even though he had to have begun way earlier than us. Older too. Maybe two hundred, two-fifty by now. A good-looking man, of course, but then we all were, all of us nearly perfect physical specimens of whatever type or mix of types we were. This being the Service's unspoken motto, and I'd learned, also an actual requirement. "We want the best of the best in every possible way to represent us in front of some bug or fish or slime mold intelligence we encounter out there," the first Head of the Service had written in her memoirs by way of explanation. But the real giveaway was how he had all but ignored me when I got off first, at the platform raised above the dilapidated ruins of the old Amtrak station. As I hopped into a waiting two-seater solar Spinner, I was tempted to throw him a salute, just for the hell of it.

I always arrived at Cynara's at sundown, and the long light would glitter up the waters so intensely I could barely make out the hovering ellipse of green house, gravi-raised above the fen.

But there Cynara would be, on her wide bayfront deck, waving as I swept in for an air dock landing over the waters, one arm thrown up over her face to shield her eyes from the glare.

"I wasn't expecting you for another month," she said by way of greeting. Her long red hair would be always be newly tinted; just for me, I was sure, always a slightly differing shade, and she seemed to age nearly as slowly as we in the Service did, not having the same treatments we were guaranteed for life, naturally, but I believe receiving a fifth of the amount of Nanos because of her care of Finn; and those probably fortified by some witchy concoctions she herself brewed up.

"You look lovely as usual," was my response. Then, "You didn't read all of my comms.?" I opened my Service kit and removed the little mesh double-helmet that Service Medical Tech had prepped for this trip.

"I read it," she led me indoors out of the fen's maritime-tang air and into a more earthy indoor musk, "I guess I thought it was a joke."

"No joke. They want me to try it, using this new Delphinid-derived technique for neural synthesis. They figure he's sufficiently water-soluble by now that it might work."

During the prelude to the war, fleeing Arths had unwittingly led us to a Delphinid colony world. We'd known nothing of the Delphs. They were mammalian too, from out of the sea like us, and they hated the hard-shells. They had welcomed us and joined forces with us against the Arths.

"And you? You don't look very water-soluble to me," she commented.

"I'm supposed to take this!" I held up the vial they'd prepared—Delphinid and Human scientists together—"And wait an hour. Unless you think you two were closer and you'll do it yourself."

She laughed, pushing the vial away, sat me down, and there was tea at hand, one of her variations of Roibos and something off-world too. Even through the triple-pane-glass, I could hear the high scree-ing of the sea eagles performing their daring sunset acrobatics over the bay waters.

"It hurts me, Locke, to see you torture yourself like this," she said, sympathetically, and from this close up now I could see that she was heavily cosmetized and beneath it she had aged, was aging, even in the few months we'd been apart, and without the full Service-Nanos, she would continue to age quickly, far faster than myself, so that if I had to keep coming I would soon be a young man coming to visit an old woman.

"It's not torture!" I assured her. How could I explain?

"I keep thinking, I'll get a comm. from Locke and he'll say, 'I've found someone. A real keeper. And I'm not coming back, Cynara. Not now, not ever again.' And then you show up early, like this, with something new, always new that they give you to try, you with your undying hope."

"I promised him. We both did."

"Isn't it time you found someone you liked?" she asked.

"I have. She's the best friend of my grand-niece, who is always surprised by that fact, because we look the same age and sometimes go clubbing and hang out together. We're dating a few months. But I don't think it'll last…It never does."

"Because of him!" Cynara insisted. "Because you brought him back. Because he's here!"

"I'm taking this Med Tech," I said, holding up the vial

they'd prepped for me, "right now, as I told Vandenberg I would. In an hour we'll go down beneath the house and we'll try it." I drank it down.

"What is it?" she asked.

"It's supposed to neurologically link us and bring us to one key moment," I explained. "Hit one key moment and play it out for us. And after that he'll be okay."

"You dreamer!" she said. Then, "We have to go out to him, Locke. He's no longer under the house." Before I could ask, Cynara explained, "He's getting too strong to stay there, Locke. He invades my dreams, my musings, and my meditation. It's like he's feeding on me. Like he's trying to suck out my personality and replace it with his own. He's grown too strong for you too to do this neural synthesis business, if it's half of what I think it is. He's strong and he's persistent, Locke."

"Where is he?"

"Let's go. Dress warmly."

"Why bother? I've got to get right on top of him. I'll get wet if he's underwater."

"He's in the peat. He's lying in peat like he's been for the last twenty-seven years, Locke. So of course he's underwater. The things you do for him..." She shook her head.

She gave me the water shoes, tennis racquet things like fat openwork skis, required to cross the bog, and we finished our tea in a gulp or two and then set out. The sun was causing yellow-green lights to radiate from its position just under the horizon, some effect of the huge mirrors they'd placed in geosynchronous orbit for unlimited solar power. From our position walking atop the water, it was beautiful: not all Tech was bad or made things ugly.

One early visit Cynara had told me in great detail how she was keeping Finn alive and hopefully healing him with her concoctions and decoctions within the peat and slightly underwater. After her explanation I'd gone and looked it up under "Peat Conservation" "Below Surface Healing," and even the Service-pedia had entries on its alleged and potential abilities to retain and conserve human flesh and blood. Of course, it was a limited thing too, all of the texts said: after a certain period of time, chemical leakage would set in and it might happen quite suddenly that what was being kept barely alive would become petrified, or rather peat-rified. We'd not reached that date yet with my Service mate.

Cynara had gotten hold of a long-gone neighbor's long-abandoned concrete swimming pool and had it converted for her use. There he was, down there in a bed of six-feet-deep peat, flat on his back, face up, hands to his side, complexion only slightly green, within the shelter of a little tarpaulin, an inch or so of liquid covering him but otherwise looking just the same. As always, my heart jumped within my breast just looking at him: Finn: my buddy Finn.

I controlled it and said in as flat a voice as I could muster, "He's looking better even than the last time."

"He's fully healed, Locke. I did a thorough analysis and inspection when I had him moved here. They came from Vandenberg and confirmed it when they moved the monitors. He's physically healed."

She went to the side of the pool and opened up a rubberized wall unit that contained all of the I.C.U. gear that the Service Med Tech Support had provided when they first brought him here to her. All the machines looked to be humming along. I knew he was fully monitored every six minutes in some office computer link at Vandenberg.

"If he's all better, then this is exactly the right time to do this," I said.

"Tell me what you need me to do."

"I strip down and get flesh to flesh with him. I put the two helmets on us. I flip them on. The stuff I took makes a neural synthesis. After fifteen minutes, you switch it off and stand me up."

"Then what? He leaps out of the peat and does a dance?"

"There are a dozen possible scenarios for what happens next. Most of them are a great deal quieter than that. We don't expect an immediate effect."

"Then just do it," she said, sounding exhausted. Sounding like I'd taken her away from something, a Vid she was watching, a Pad she was engrossed in, something interrupted by me and my Service Med Tech foolishness.

He was cold, clammy, and of course wet to the touch. We were face-to-face. His eyes were closed. I waited until I had warmed up enough to be touching as much of his front as possible, then I reached up and switched the helmets on, as I'd been shown.

For maybe a minute nothing happened, and Cynara was about to say something, she had even begun to say, "Listen, Locke, I think you may have to…"

We were at the lower helm board and Scott Alan Finn, a.k.a. the Finnster, was there right next to me as he'd been for years on end, real-time, and he was unharmed, unburned, perfectly all right, laughing. "So she says to me, 'You're joking right? That's what you were bragging about to half the bar.' And I didn't let my ego be downed in any way and I said, 'There's a reason why it's called a surprise package, girlie-o!'

"'Great!' she said. 'I'll pretend to be surprised…wait! What the hell is *that*?'

"And it was the worm, Locke. Remember the Ice-worm from Titan we'd snuck onboard? I'd managed to keep it frozen-alive, and I just let it jump out at her from outta my pants and she ran screaming out of the room. I nearly fucking died, Locke. Died."

And he is more alive than he has been in years. He's alive. Right here twelve inches from me and I can't believe it. I simply can't. This neural synthesis thing is actually working and...

At that point I realized that we were back in real-time, Finn and me, back maybe twenty-eight years ago, not twenty-seven when the attack happened. So this must be our crux point, not later. Why this time?

"Don't look so surprised. Unless you want to see it too, Locke! Locke? What's going on, why are you staring? It's not like I never did an act like that before."

"You always surprise me, Finn," I managed to get out through my wonderment. He was so...alive! Then to cover myself I added, "But I know that someday you will actually grow up, and then where will we all be?"

"In some sleazebag retirement home on far side Pluto, I hope, zonked out of our gourds!" he added...typically.

But he sensed too that something was changed or wrong as he calmed down almost instantly, and when Drinibidian began teasing him a few minutes later about the worm, Finn was only halfhearted in his response to him, I could tell, and he even gave me a few looks as though asking, "Hey! What's up?"

Meanwhile I tried to remember what had gone down on this particular mission that would make it the key moment, the crisis we must return to, and for the life of me I couldn't, I really just could not remember or figure it out.

It had begun—now it was actually happening again as though in real-time—as a simple supply replenishment run to a Far-Oort Cloud world, I recalled, to that heap of dark slag they'd named Sedna in the early twenty-first century. There was a good sized paleo-archaeology station there for the past half century or so, with at least four score workers hired by Wally J. Liu, the Hypertronics trillionaire. He firmly believed just about every word of the Zechariah Stettin series, *The Twelfth Planet* et al. Therefore Liu was certain that Sedna was that planet filled with immortals that Stettin had written of, so lengthily, so academically, and at times even convincingly. According to Liu and his followers, Sedna's vast middle continent wasteland and its lack of any but radon-polluted waters were relatively new, the result of some huge internecine nuclear war. They were there searching for definitive proof of that civilization.

Besides that, all we knew was that the Service had decided that Sedna's elliptical orbit at aphelion kept it so far away from the center of our own solar system that at its farthest point, like now, the planetoid was the best outpost: a seeing and especially a listening post for any kind of movement the Bella=Arths might possibly make upon human-inhabited worlds and moons.

Never mind that every insect and human psychologist had agreed that the Arths would never leave their home space far enough to invade ours. And my bud Finn believed that Liu was somehow secretly channeling cash into the Service's Oort Cloud outposts and so the Service was engaging in what might have looked like cooperative, even humanitarian work, but was really payback.

Why should we care? For us, this mission and this particular run was totally recreational, right down to the five days we'd spend on the planet with its multiple canteens, full-service cinemas, and motels, which became more like orgy houses the minute we arrived. What had happened on this outbound run for it to be selected by the neural-synthesizer? I kept trying to recall.

In an eye-blink, we were no longer on the lower helm somehow and it must have been an hour, maybe two hours later. I was standing at the door to my little dorm unit, stepping in, when Finn turned the corridor corner and almost leapt at me.

"What's going on," he asked, with an intensity I didn't recall in him. No, this wasn't the memory I wanted. It wasn't even a memory I remembered. He put his face right up to mine.

"Nothing, Finn. Why?"

"The joke earlier. Come on, Locke. You know I like you best!" He shoved himself at me, grabbed my head, and began French kissing me.

To say I was surprised was putting it mildly. Naturally all Service members have to scan high-positive for bisexuality, given the time periods involved and the limited potential relationships on-ship, not to mention how our time leaps made any solid relationships back on Earth nearly impossible. Even so I'd never had a hint, not a clue before that Finn and I… This just wasn't the kind of friendship we'd actually had. What the hell was going on with this neural-synthesis doohickey?

He pulled back and looked at me, one eye cocked. "What? You don't want me anymore? You've got someone else?"

"No way!" I tried. And so he pushed me into the unit, lips and tongue glued to mine, and flipped the lock behind us and in the dimness of the cabin the guy took me totally, like I was a twelve-year streetwalker.

No. Worse: Like I was the love of his life.

I wasn't. Or at least I'd not been during our tour, or in real-time. So what was going on here? Finn was aggressive, assertive, and even though he was doing all the work and definitely ramping himself up to do all the work, still, when we climaxed, I was the one who felt drained, exhausted, and he was the one raring to go at it again, and I guess in that moment I recalled what Cynara had said, how she'd moved his body to a more distant spot because—how had she put it?—Finn was getting too strong for her: he was invading her dreams, her musings, even her meditation. Could that be what *this* was all about? Even so, what in hell was he *doing*?

"Satisfied?" I asked in the so-called afterglow of what had been for me a totally unexpected near-rape experience by my best friend.

"For the moment," he said. "But we're not done yet by any means," he added, and that wolfish look I'd first seen in the dorm corridor returned briefly to him.

"I'm ready for you any time, Finn," I said, playing out the script.

"I know Locke. I know. You're my guy. Always were. Always will be. Loyal to the end. And beyond that."

"Beyond?" I thought, wait, this has to be the *current* Finn speaking, the peat guy, not the Finnster that I last knew twenty-eight years ago. But if so, and we are now consciously relating together in some kind of real-time, me and this peat-preserved near-corpse, how do I test this? How can I be sure?

We were suddenly shifted again to another place, and now I was growing more certain this was Finn's doing, Finn writing and controlling the scenario.

We were in high orbit around another planet, not dim, ravaged Sedna, but one of Beta Centauri's six gas-giants' moons, Patroclus or Lakshmi, I couldn't recall which. We were outside the ship in fully automated suits, me, Finn, the woman named Lea, and a cyber that we all called Bernstein-Idaho, because of the seal on the bottom of one of his huge metal and plastic feet read that—name and place of its manufacture.

This was way after the delivery and after the R and R on Sedna. This happened when we were already into the second part of our tour, and what was going on then? Oh, right! Ship's brain had found some kind of anomaly out here on the hull and one after another we'd come out after Bernstein-Idaho to see what the hell to do about it: first Lea, then me and Finn.

Lea had just asked Bernstein-Idaho to check for the failure potential of this extremely minor part that we were all peering down at: some ion thingamajig that six people in the universe knew how to read. Bernstein-Idaho had done so and had come back with a reading of near zero for it to fail, and even then not for some months yet to come.

Finn made a "What the hell? Lea?" gesture with his heavily wrapped arms, then said the actual words. Adding, "I'm outta here." He turned, asking, "You coming, Locke?" I turned and we headed back in through the big hull-hatch. And *now* I recalled that incident and that nothing had happened then—*nothing at all!*

This time, however, Finn got into the hatch and Lea shoved right past me, arguing with Finn, and she gestured for me to remain out and go inside on the second rotation along with the big cyber. Now they were already inside the lock and cycling, and I saw the internal doors open for them, when from out of my peripheral vision I saw something or other zing past me and strike me glancingly on the side of the shoulder before sailing off.

I remember thinking what the hell, this never happened in real-time on this Beta C. mission! I felt myself shoved by the natural reaction of being hit, directly into the bulk of Bernstein-Idaho. The cyber lost balance for a second, then regained it, and it wrapped a big mechanical arm around me.

It was at that moment that Finn, already inside the ship, even with his helmet screwed off but his suit still on, glanced out through the transparent lock window and saw me half-lifted off the hull, but not yet fully in Bernstein's grip, and

I could see on Finn's face what I'd never in years ever seen there before as he went white with absolute panic.

He turned and furiously began to open the lock, and two people had to knock his hands away from it, and meanwhile, I was floating up and off the hull of the ship, held from floating off completely only by Bernstein-Idaho, the cyber making the oddest noises I'd ever heard come out of it. So I turned a bit and checked from my now-weird angle, and I saw that half of Bernstein's head was gone, taken off by whatever had ricocheted off me: probably the piece we'd all just agreed was perfectly safe.

This meant the cyber still had functionality, a brain—in his chest, but that its main eyes and speech center were gone.

It held me tightly, as, in a sort of continued slow-motion ballet, the others inside turned to watch us and their faces all paled or went taut.

Finn spoke into my helmet first.

"Don't let go! I'm coming out to get you, Locke." Then he said to someone inside, "How long can Bernstein hold on to both Locke and the ship hull?"

"We're trying to build a new communication link to Bernstein. No. Not yet," I heard one reply.

I spoke then and it came out all gargly and weird. I was trying to say I was okay. But clearly I was not. I'd been hit by flying debris and I was being held by a cyber that also had been hit and that had suffered worse damage than I had.

"Stay where you are, Locke!" Finn said in a low tight voice. "Don't move."

"Ship's brain has something new connecting them now," someone said and I saw and felt another cyber arm come up and imperfectly encircle me from the other end and hold me a bit tighter to prove it.

"That's a little better," Lea was saying.

"Why can't I open the airlock?" Finn demanded. He had his headpiece screwed back on.

I didn't hear the answer but I already knew the answer: ship's hull airlocks had all gone into a total automated lockdown as a result of flying debris damaging part of the ship—i.e. Bernstein-Idaho itself. They wouldn't reopen again until there was an accredited all-clear.

"Lea, get the goddamn all-clear!" Finn was already yelling.

"I'm not that hurt," I gargled and immediately regretted saying anything.

"Where's that all-clear?" Finn was repeating, his voice just this shade of hysteria.

"In a minute. Finn! Ship's got procedures."

"Screw procedures, Lea! Look at him!"

"Wait! We've got a verbal from Bernstein."

I could hear it too.

"Ship, this unit has slaved the punctured air tank to its own lower section, ensuring no more oxy loss, and a small supply from within the unit itself as backup. Please open the hatch."

That was when I realized my air supply had been compromised when I'd been struck. Great! Who was writing this script? None of this had happened before. None of it! We'd gone into the hatch together and we had de-helmeted and un-suited and that had been the full extent of it. Why was this happening?

Worst thing was it felt so *real*!

I tried saying something else, asking Finn something, then I went blank. Just blank. Then that time shift thing happened again and I was inside our ship, in an onboard i.c. unit, all but cocooned, and I could see Finn waiting outside the transparent wall and he kept peering at me and finally he saw some difference in me and he stopped talking to whoever it was, some Medic, and he charged in with the guy right after him, and he was at my bedside, at my head, blocking my view and saying, "Locke, Locke, Locke! Why do you do this to me? I thought I'd lost you for good, Locke! Then where in the fuck would I be, Locke? Huh?"

Just like that, the neural-synthesis was over. I was back in the watery, peat-stinking-pool-like-a-double-grave again, wondering what the hell had just happened inside my mind and why.

Cynara had switched the helmets off. Was it only fifteen minutes I'd been away? It felt like days, a week—and I was here almost wholly now and I was getting up and as a result the connection between my body and Finn's body was like some kind of gluey warm soup, not just water, so when Cynara finally managed to get me standing up, our bodies snapped apart with a loud wet plop, like our bubble had been burst. She removed the helmets and dropped them into my Service kit.

She wrapped a blanket around me, saying, "You went so deep. You went so deep, Locke. You never heard me shouting. You went too far. I warned you he was strong."

"What about him?" I asked as she tried to hustle me away. "What did his monitors read?"

"I was looking at you, Locke. You trembled so badly the entire time. I was concerned. Thinking any second you might convulse. He's grown so strong…"

"Cyn! Take a breath! Finn?"

"His monitors went nuts. I can print out a readout back at the house. C'mon, let's go there!"

We replaced the tarpaulin over Finn and she helped me water-glide back, weak as a baby as I was, as though I actually had undergone some life-threatening accident.

After I'd showered and dressed in dry clothes I'd brought and had coffee and brandy, we sat a long while and she stared at me, appearing even older, and she asked: "What the hell happened, Locke? Where were you? Tell me!"

I told her. And as I told her I myself slowly began piecing it together.

When I was done, she said, "But why would you go through all that insanity if that wasn't even a real moment between you? Why, Locke?"

And I was able to answer her, "I think because in the neural-synthesis events that we shared, Finn saved my life."

"He saved your life from something you told me *never really happened*, Locke. From something he manufactured you to experience. What if he'd made you die out there?"

"No. That wouldn't have happened. It was different, Cyn. *We* were different. Not like we were before."

"How, Locke?" She was wringing her hands and I had to hold them still to make her stop. I was still putting it all together myself. So I repeated, "We were closer. He saved me, Cyn." I added lamely, "Maybe that's what *he* needed—to save me."

To care for me the way he did this time, and then to save me, I might have told her. But while I was trying to figure out how to say it, she got a comm.-call and wandered into another room to take it. I knew who was calling: it was the people at Vandenberg. They'd been monitoring Finn's body there, had seen the spiking during the neural-synthesis, and were telling her what had happened.

"They say Finn is periodically quiescent now. He seemed

to come fully to life for the entire time you two were connected, but he's on-and-off quiescent at the moment," she reported.

And just so I wouldn't doubt it, "They say there's no way they can completely revive him, Locke. Not unless you're down there and attached to him all the time. They would never let that happen. Nor would I. Never! It would kill you. Or drive you mad."

So I commed Vandenberg myself and spoke to my contact there and she repeated Cynara's words pretty verbatim. "We came really close," she added. "I'm sorry, Locke."

Cynara didn't trust me yet on my own, and so after another while and a brandy and only after she was certain I was ready, we got back into the little Spinner and she flew it the short hop over to the old Amtrak platform at Martinez.

She waited with me the fifteen minutes or so before the monorail heading back to Stockton arrived, trying to revive our futile conversation. One comm. call came in then for her, again from Vandenberg. They'd lost contact with Finn's electronics; it was more than an hour now since a readout. They asked Cynara to go check in on him on her way home to see if some wires had come loose between his body and the monitors.

"Maybe it's better this way, Locke," Cynara said, I suppose trying to comfort me.

I shrugged off her final attempt at a hug. "Cyn, believe me. It's not over! Finn wants to live again. He knows he's healthy. He knows what he wants."

"Don't say that, Locke. You're scaring me. I'm locking my doors!"

I sent her home, and a few minutes later I boarded the single car train.

There were a half dozen teenagers at the end of the car as I got in and they all looked exhausted, arms and legs draped over each other as though they'd like to get sleep but wouldn't yet. They ignored me when I got on and they went back to their listless cuddling and halfhearted smooching.

Darkness had fallen, and there's little in the way of artificial floating lights this far west, but the moon had risen early; it was scudding through a lightly clouded sky and reflectively lighting the surface waters below.

I settled into some kind of inert, thoughtful trance in my seat, not caring when one of the kids somehow electronically shut down the interior lights of the car that we rode. Gloom was fine by me, I concluded.

I couldn't stop thinking about Finn, not the Finnster, the cut-up, the screw-up, but Scott Alan Finn, that other man newly revealed to me, who may have hidden so much, it now seemed—from me, even from himself. What if all that time he really had felt that strongly about me, and he had never been able to get it out in the open? Because why? Because it would dim his image? Change his image from the happy-go-lucky, care-nothing? And instead make him an ordinary guy? Not the wild and crazy Finnster?

I found myself recounting that scene between the two of us in my dorm unit on-ship during our neural-synthesis. Whatever happened, it had felt so casual, so…inevitable. Was that entirely his doing? Or something complicit we'd fabricated once we were so close together again, neurally linked, face-to-face in the peat? Would I ever know?

Suddenly one of the couples was standing up and pointing at my end of the car, two young women, and then all of them were standing and pointing.

I stood and stepped into the aisle and then I saw what had freaked them. This was a standard mono-train. Each car has a little platform on each end containing the mag-levs and mag-links to any next car. Those windows are smallish and nearly square and thick. But clear enough to all of us, especially in the moonlight, was a head, a wet head and a shining wet torso, and when I approached the window, I knew it for Finn, hanging on to the outside of the car for dear life.

I laughed. Sue me, but I laughed. Out of relief; out of disbelief. The Finnster was back. I didn't know how or why. And when I did, Finn grinned, whipped by the wind at eighty mph as he was. I mouthed the words, "You're crazy." And he kept grinning.

We stopped at the next stop of Antioch, and the kids charged out of the door and fled all the way down the platform, getting as far away as possible. I stuck my Service kit inside the door to keep it from closing and went to get Finn. He let go finally, and I got him inside the car and sat him down. He began shivering in the artificial chill, and I covered him with my jacket, and even found another bigger wrap one of the teens had abandoned in her haste to escape. That seemed to help. I moved us into the dimmest corner and I held him to warm him up. He seemed to go quiet. Maybe even sleep.

I all but carried him out at Stockton Hub and managed him into my skimmer to get him home. I put it on automatic and didn't warm it, not knowing what temperature he needed to be at.

Once home, he woke up. "Locke!" he said, and it was the most wonderful thing anyone had ever said to me, my name, in his voice once again.

"How long can this last?" I asked him, not unkindly. Then laughed again.

He wasn't offended. "Not long. We have. To go. Under. One more. Time. To finish. Now."

Following his instructions, I walked him into the bath area and stripped him down and then myself and got us side by side in my big tub there and let the water flow slowly. He controlled the temperature.

I put the mesh helmets on us again, wondering if it would work without me taking another dose. He didn't seem concerned. He relaxed in the water, becoming more himself. After a while, he was speaking in phrases and even short sentences again, although very quietly.

What he told me somehow only half-surprised me. "Locke, I planned this. I've been linked a very long time into the base at Vandenberg and I've been able to move around inside the brains there using my mind and I've learned a great deal, including how to influence a few people and some things too. Service Med Tech has no real idea how this Delph Tech works…but I do."

"We're directly mind-to-mind, no?" I asked.

"Yes. But it's beyond that, Locke. The Delphs explained it, but it's kind of beyond our way of understanding. Beyond our way of communicating what happens. This Tech derives from electro-chemicals that their savant-shamans discovered in their ocean hermitages. But as they developed it further, it went beyond even them. Their scientists grabbed it and perfected it."

I didn't understand and said so, and that was all right with Finn. The real question he said was, was I happy with what had happened when we were linked in the pool?

"You mean us together? Sure but… Well, you could have been gentler in the sack," I said.

"Sorry. I was so excited to see you, to touch you! to see anyone! to have anyone in touching range and so close again!…What about the rest of it?" he insisted.

"The accident wasn't a lot of fun."

"You live. It works out okay…If I'm linked with you, what we're doing can work, Locke. The question is can you go on with me totally, from that last point?"

I thought about it. We were face-to-face, inches apart,

covered in tepid water, and I thought how comfortable it felt, touching my friend who I'd missed so long, now healed and not even green anymore, and how maybe *he* might have been what I'd been missing for so long, searching for, going back to the fen country for.

"I can go with you from that point, Finn."

"Good. Then that will be our life, Locke."

"But...how?"

"The helmets and what you drank work with my altered chemistry. It exploits all of our molecular energy to...solidify the change. That's as much as I can explain without equations and formulas and shit like that."

"Who'll turn the helmets off?" I asked,

He smiled. "They won't have to be turned off. Anyway, after a while the battery would be drained...You don't get it, I see. But that's all right. You'll see eventually."

"You mean we'll live inside that altered past reality you created for us before?" I tried to understand.

"That *we* created!" he corrected.

"*We* created," I agreed.

"Yes, exactly. But it won't also happen that they'll find our bodies here in this tub. We won't end up being some App-net headline."

Now I really didn't understand. "It won't happen like that? Why not?"

He smiled. "You were always the smart one, Locke. But all I can say is that you'll see."

So I thought a little more and then said, "Fine, Finn. Any time!"

"I know Locke. I know. You're my guy. To the end and beyond that."

Without any fear at all, I switched on the helmets.

I was not there, chest-to-chest, facing him in the bath, but I was inside that last scene we had together, on the ship, on that mission to Beta C. and I was just inside the hull hatch, being carried into the internal air chamber by Finn, who had my air tube somehow shoved into a small breather and he was saying, "Any second. Any second. There we go!" We were inside the ship and they were ripping my helmet off and cutting my suit off me and I could see headless Bernstein-Idaho in the outer lock, being grappled by Lea to fit into the hatch. Next I was flat on my back on a levi-gurney with a mask over my mouth and we were charging down the corridor, the Med Tech guy and Finn and me, and then I was being shoved into a hyperbaric chamber and it was slammed shut. I faced the tiny window and there Finn was, on the other side, as they did a complete pressure readjustment, him saying things to me, his lips forming the words, "You're not going anywhere, Locke. You're not going anywhere!"

Then a buzzer went off and the chamber was opened and I was pulled out and he fell onto me, no hiding feelings anymore.

He slept next to me in i.c. that night, and when I got the go-ahead to leave the next day, he'd already requisitioned a double dorm unit for us and set up procedures for a public ship-union. I kept thinking, how can this be happening? How can twenty-seven years have just vanished? Am I totally electrochemically drugged?

It seemed to be actual. We were existing in real-time again, not living in sudden spurts and lapses, as in the beginning, but minute by minute, hour by hour. At last we completed our tour and we podded-up and took the Big Sleeper back to the Service H.Q. at Ganymede Station.

There we were checked out thoroughly, and debriefed. One night in our dorm unit, with bloated Jupiter filling the port windows, Finn told me that he had decided on no more dangerous tours for either of us. So it turned out just as the Delph and Human Techs had predicted. The accident, my near death, the crisis moment, had altered everything for us: for both of our lives.

That's when I told Finn of the past that I'd already experienced, and that now would never happen—him nearly dying in that flaming lower helm almost a year to come in the future. I also told him what I knew of the future decades too, including the Service's upcoming, long, eventually successful war against the Bella=Arths.

So we agreed that we would only half retire, remaining in the Service (remaining on full Nanos for decades more): teaching and training personnel; quietly but surely instilling fighting skills and attitudes in our young charges.

They would end up needing both, as it had been a century or more since any human had experienced war. But we two wouldn't stray from our solar system, not for a very long time. Meanwhile Finn wanted me to go meet his family and get what he termed "legally hitched" on Earth and spend real-time weeks of R and R after.

I told him yes, but that I'd need one day for some unfinished business; I'd join him later: I had somewhere to go to first. He never even asked where I was off to once we landed at the Stockton Hub—just hugged me good-bye.

I noticed once again how subtly the landscape alters as you head west toward Martinez, first little encroachments like tiny fingers of water, with here a cottage, there a mound-house in a field of reeds. Then it's all water, all around you in one form or another: nothing solid at all.

I got off at the platform built over the dilapidated ancient surface-train station. And there was a two-seat solar Spinner waiting for me. I knew my way, of course, and I was soon hovering over the familiar house in the marshes. I alit at the house's air-dock and a redheaded woman came to meet me, and she drew me indoors.

Cynara sat me down and offered me tea as I knew she would and she looked as young as she'd been when we first delivered Finn's body.

She knew nothing of who I was, or why I was there, or of what we'd experienced together for decades. She only just remembered Scott Alan Finn: a foolish, handsome boy she'd met long ago. She had no idea why he would have mentioned her name to me. I gently probed and probed and finally she said: "Come to think of it, one night, we talked for hours, after some concert event or other. I might have spoken of peat preservation or peat burial, I don't recall."

What she did recall was what a girlfriend who had dated him a bit and known him since they were children together had said about Finn because it had turned Cynara off him: "His greatest asset is his persistence. He always gets what he sets out for." She asked me, "Is that true?"

"He got me."

I repeated all that to Finn a few nights later, at his folks' house, on our wedding night, floating over Crater Lake: another of the "benefits" we in the Service receive. It was cold and cloudless out of doors, and looking into the black waters of that deepest natural lake in the country, we saw the sky reflected: an ocean of stars.

Finn didn't remember Cynara very well either. "It was always you, Locke," he told me. "Knew it the minute I met you. It just took me a while to realize it!"

We'll settle eventually at Crater Lake, me and Finn. If we manage to live out our Service we'll retire to that lake field of stars and probably, for a change of scenery, to one of those artificial isles west of Maui. We can afford both on our substantial pensions.

Or maybe not. Maybe we'll end our days in a levitating wooden cottage, ten feet above the snipe and fowl and those sea eagle–haunted marshes, beyond all polluting transportation or Tech-industry, in what's left above ground of the Bay Area's green and isolated fen country.

About the Author

Felice Picano is the author of over twenty books, including the literary memoirs *Ambidextrous*, *Men Who Loved Me*, and *A House on the Ocean, a House on the Bay* as well as the best-selling novels *Like People in History*, *Looking Glass Lives*, *The Lure*, and *Eyes*. He is the founder of Sea Horse Press, one of the first gay publishing houses, which later merged with two other publishing houses to become the Gay Presses of New York. With Andrew Holleran, Robert Ferro, Edmund White, and George Whitmore, he founded the Violet Quill Club to promote and increase the visibility of gay authors and their works. He has edited and written for *The Advocate*, *Blueboy*, *Mandate*, *GaysWeek*, and *Christopher Street,* and has been a culture reviewer for *The Los Angeles Examiner*, *San Francisco Examiner*, *New York Native*, *Harvard Lesbian & Gay Review*, and the *Lambda Book Report*. He has won the Ferro-Grumley Award for best gay novel (*Like People in History*) and the PEN Syndicated Fiction Award for short story. He was a finalist for the Ernest Hemingway Award and has been nominated for five Lambda Literary Awards and two American Library Association Awards. He was recently named a Lambda Literary Foundation Pioneer and one of OUT's GLBT People of the Year. A native of New York, Felice Picano now lives in Los Angeles.

Books Available From Bold Strokes Books

Three Days by L.T. Marie. In a town like Vegas where anything can happen, Shawn and Dakota find that the stakes are love at all costs, and it's a gamble neither can afford to lose. (978-1-60282-569-7)

Swimming to Chicago by David-Matthew Barnes. As the lives of the adults around them unravel, high school students Alex and Robby form an unbreakable bond, vowing to do anything to stay together—even if it means leaving everything behind.(978-1-60282-572-7)

Hostage Moon by AJ Quinn. Hunter Roswell thought she had left her past behind, until a serial killer begins stalking her. Can FBI profiler Sara Wilder help her find her connection to the killer before he strikes on blood moon? (978-1-60282-568-0)

Erotica Exotica: Tales of Magic, Sex, and the Supernatural, edited by Richard Labonté. Today's top gay erotica authors offer sexual thrills and perverse arousal, spooky chills, and magical orgasms in these stories exploring arcane mystery, supernatural seduction, and sex that haunts in a manner both weird and wondrous. (978-1-60282-570-3)

Blue by Russ Gregory. Matt and Thatcher find themselves in the crosshairs of a psychotic killer stalking gay men in the streets of Austin, and only a 103-year-old nursing home resident holds the key to solving the murders—but can she give up her secrets in time to save them? (978-1-60282-571-0)

Balance of Forces: Toujours Ici by Ali Vali. Immortal Kendal Richoux's life began during the reign of Egypt's only female pharaoh, and history has taught her the dangers of getting too close to anyone who hasn't harnessed the power of time, but as she prepares for the most important battle of her long life, can she resist her attraction to Piper Marmande? (978-1-60282-567-3)

Contemporary Gay Romances by Felice Picano. This collection of short fiction from legendary novelist and memoirist Felice Picano are as different from any standard "romances" as you can get, but they will linger in the mind and memory. (978-1-60282-639-7)**Nightrise** by Nell

Stark and Trinity Tam. In the third book in the everafter series, when Valentine Darrow loses her soul, Alexa must cross continents to find a way to save her. (978-1-60282-238-2)

Men of the Mean Streets, edited by Greg Herren and J.M. Redmann. Dark tales of amorality and criminality by some of the top authors of gay mysteries. (978-1-60282-240-5)

Women of the Mean Streets, edited by J.M. Redmann and Greg Herren. Murder, mayhem, sex, and danger—these are the stories of the women who dare to tackle the mean streets. (978-1-60282-241-2)

Firestorm by Radclyffe. Firefighter paramedic Mallory "Ice" James isn't happy when the undisciplined Jac Russo joins her command, but lust isn't something either can control—and they soon discover ice burns as fiercely as flame. (978-1-60282-232-0)

The Best Defense by Carsen Taite. When socialite Aimee Howard hires former homicide detective Skye Keaton to find her missing niece, she vows not to mix business with pleasure, but she soon finds Skye hard to resist. (978-1-60282-233-7)

After the Fall by Robin Summers. When the plague destroys most of humanity, Taylor Stone thinks there's nothing left to live for, until she meets Kate, a woman who makes her realize love is still alive and makes her dream of a future she thought was no longer possible. (978-1-60282-234-4)

Accidents Never Happen by David-Matthew Barnes. From the moment Albert and Joey meet by chance beneath a train track on a street in Chicago, a domino effect is triggered, setting off a chain reaction of murder and tragedy. (978-1-60282-235-1)

In Plain View, edited by Shane Allison. Best-selling gay erotica authors create the stories of sex and desire modern readers crave. (978-1-60282-236-8)